Someone to Watch Over Me

WILD WIDOWS SERIES
BOOK FOUR

MARIE FORCE

Someone to Watch Over Me
Wild Widows Series, Book 4
By: Marie Force

Published by HTJB, Inc.
Copyright 2024. HTJB, Inc.
Cover Design by Kristina Brinton
Print Layout: E-book Formatting Fairies
ISBN: 978-1958035702

"When it's over, I want to say:
All my life, I was a bride married to amazement.
I was a bridegroom taking the world into my arms."
"When Death Comes," Mary Oliver

"Bereavement is not the truncation of married love but one of its
regular phases."
"A Grief Observed," C.S. Lewis

"Behind the moonlight and the frost,
The excitement and the gratitude,
There stood how much our meeting owed
To other meetings, other loves.
The decades of a different life."
"When First We Faced, and Touching Showed,"
Philip Larkin

The Wild Widows Characters

UPDATED THROUGH SOMEONE TO LOVE

Adrian – lost wife Sadie after she gave birth to their son Xavier

Aurora – husband on trial for rape

Brielle – lost husband Mark in a skiing accident. Had their son Charlie after Mark died

Carter – son of Iris's late husband Mike and Eleanor

Christy – husband, Wes, suffered an aortic dissection; mother of teenagers Shawn and Josie

Darren Tabor – Roni's friend and former colleague at the Star

Darryl – Iris's biological father

Derek Kavanaugh – wife Victoria was murdered, daughter Maeve

Dylan – Roni's son

Eleanor – woman with whom Mike had Carter

Gage Collier – lost wife Natasha and eight-year-old twin daughters, Ivy and Hazel, in a drunk driving.

Gwen – Hallie's late wife who died by suicide.

Hallie – lost wife Gwen to suicide; seeing Robin, who has stage-four breast cancer

Iris – Mike was killed in a plane crash, children are Tyler, Sophia, Laney

Jim - Lexi's late husband who died of ALS

Joy – lost husband Craig to natural causes

Justine – Roni's mother

Kinsley – husband, Rory died from pancreatic cancer, kids are Christian and Maisy

Lexi Nelson – lost husband, Jim, to ALS after a four-year battle, lives with Tom Hammett, her old high school crush

Mimi and Stan – Gage's MIL and FIL, Nat's parents

Naomi – lost fiancé David to lymphoma

Nia – Adrian's sister, married to Mick, their kids are Chantelle and Malik

Patrick Connolly – Roni's husband killed by a stray bullet on 12th Street in the District

Robin – love interest of Hallie. Has two children.

Taylor – founded the group with Iris and Christy, has since moved on with second husband and is not part of the group anymore

Tom Hammett – Lexi's love interest/roommate

Trey – love interest of Christy

Veronica/Roni Connolly – husband Patrick was killed by stray bullet

Victoria – Derek's deceased wife

Wynter – husband, Jaden Hartley, died of bone cancer. Wynter's new daughter is named Willow Jaden Hartley.

Xavier Smith Parker – Adrian's son with Sadie

$\mathcal{O}$ne

Author's Note: A quick reminder that the timeline of this series is quite a bit ahead of the one in the First Family Series. Please don't try to make them line up because they do not. Thank you, and I hope you enjoy Lexi's story!
Marie

Lexi

Great tragedy comes with a line of demarcation—there's before the awful event, and then there's after. There's before your young, vibrant husband is diagnosed with a dreaded neurological disease that will trap him inside an immobilized body and kill him far too soon, and then there's after. There's before your husband dies, and then there's after. The line divides these things in a way that separates who you once were from who you've become and forces you to figure out a whole new life when you loved the one you already had.

And it makes you unable to cope when your new friend, the man who's sparked the first inkling of potential romantic interest in the years since your husband died, is unconscious on the floor of his living room. This is where I find myself as a new catastrophe confronts me, making my brain want to shut down and run away from what's happening right in front of me.

I can't do that. Tom needs me. He's been so good to me in the months since I took him up on his offer of a room at his place so I could leave my parents' home, where Jim and I lived during his ALS battle. I force myself out of the shock and reach for my phone to call 911.

"911, please state your emergency."

Those words in that official-sounding tone... They trigger trauma from the many times I had to call for help with Jim.

"Hello?"

"I, ah, my friend is unconscious."

"Was there an accident?"

"I don't know. I came home and found him this way."

"The address?"

My brain is so scrambled that I have to think about it for a second before I can recall the address.

After I provide it, the operator reads it back. "Is that correct?"

"Yes, it is."

"EMS is on the way. Can you check to see if he's breathing and has a pulse?"

I'm instantly terrified. What if he doesn't? "I, uh, yes, I can do that."

"Place your index and middle fingers against his neck and press lightly."

I know all too well how to check for a pulse, but I don't tell the dispatcher that she's dealing with an experienced caregiver.

I drop to my knees and lean over him, afraid to look at him or touch him or do anything to confirm my greatest fear—that *he's* left me, too. "Please, Tom. Don't do this to me." My hand shakes as I press my fingers to the spot. How many times did I check to see if Jim was still with me before he finally left forever? Too many to count.

I'm relieved to feel the light beat of his heart under my fingers.

"He has a faint pulse and seems to be breathing but not like usual."

"That's good news. EMS is less than five minutes out. Can the paramedics get into the house?"

"Y-yes, the door is unlocked." I force myself to look at his face, which is ghostly pale. His lips are, too. How can this be happening? He was fine this morning when we had coffee together and he sent me off to work with the lunch he'd packed for me, made from all my favorite things that he's taken the time to learn in our time together.

A sob wrenches from my chest. "Tom." I give him a gentle shake. "Tom, wake up. Please wake up."

He doesn't stir.

As tears spill from my eyes, I hear the siren in the distance. I start praying to a God I barely believe in anymore after what I saw Jim go through.

Please. Please save him. He's a good man who's been such a good friend to me when I needed one. He's so sweet and kind, and just when I've been thinking about giving him a chance to be more than a friend, this happens. We need that chance. I need that chance. Please.

The paramedics come storming through the door and up the stairs.

One of them draws me away from Tom so the others can go to work. "Are you injured, ma'am?"

I shake my head. I'm not injured. I'm terrified as I watch them work on him with the kind of frantic energy saved for the direst of emergencies.

This cannot be happening. What if he dies, too? What will I do then?

"Does he have any kind of cardiac history?"

"I, uh… I don't know."

"Is there anyone who would?"

His sister. They're close. She would know. I look around the room for his phone and spot it on the kitchen counter. As I go to grab it, I recall the night he rolled homemade meatballs and asked me to grab his phone to check to make sure he hadn't missed any of the ingredients. He'd rattled off his code then, but do you think I can remember it now?

Come on, Lexi. Think. His life might depend on you remembering that code.

"Ma'am?"

Oh my God. My mind is completely blank. My hands are shaking, and I feel like I'm going to be sick at any second.

His twin nieces. Their birthday. When is their birthday? Around Christmas, he said. They hated that. Too much all at once. Their mother holds a half-birthday party for them in June, so they can spread out the celebrating.

Twelve…

Twelve…

Ten days before Christmas, he said.

Twelve fifteen.

I punch in the number, and it works. Thank you, Jesus! But what's his sister's name again? I've met her a couple of times but haven't spent much time with her. She's always frantically busy and on the run when she comes by.

Come on, Lex. He needs you. Think!

I open his favorites and see my name first on the list. At any other time, I'd need a minute to process that I'm first on his list, but I don't have a minute.

Cora is number two.

Yes! His sister is Cora. I push the button to call her.

When she answers, there's music playing in the background. "Hey, shithead, what's up?"

"Cora, this is Tom's friend Lexi."

"Oh, hey. What's up?"

"Tom collapsed. I found him when I got home. The paramedics are asking if he has cardiac history."

"What? No! He's perfectly healthy. But our dad... He died of a heart attack at forty-two."

I convey information that adds to my own panic to the paramedics.

"Where're they taking him?"

"Where will you take him?" I ask them.

"Inova Fairfax."

"Did you hear that?"

"Yes. I'm on my way. Ask them what they think is wrong."

I ask the question for her.

"We aren't qualified to make a diagnosis."

Cora gasps. "Is he... He's not... I mean, he isn't dead, is he?"

"He had a pulse when I checked it. It was faint, but I felt it."

"Oh, good. I just talked to him an hour ago. He..." Her voice breaks. "He can't leave me. He just can't."

It occurs to me that if I hadn't accepted his offer of a place to live when I needed the change of scenery so badly, he might've died on that floor without anyone due home to find him there.

"I'll let you know if there're any updates."

"Thank you, Lexi. Thank you so much for calling."

As I grasp his phone, I watch the paramedics working frantically to save his life. I'm right back to that last night at home with Jim, when I had to tell the EMTs *not* to take any extraordinary measures to save him, when that was the last thing I wanted to say. I wasn't ready to let him go, even if his suffering had become unbearable.

I'd never have let him go if it'd been up to me.

Fortunately, he'd made the decision for both of us, and

when the time came, I respected his choice to end the battle that'd been lost before it ever started. Not that we'd known that at the beginning, when we'd been so determined to beat a foe that couldn't be defeated no matter what we did.

"Ma'am?"

I realize the paramedic has been speaking to me.

"Would you like to ride with him?"

No, no, I would not like that. I'm terrified of what I might witness. But I can't let him go alone, can I? No, you can't.

"Yes, I would. Thank you."

I grab my purse and jacket and tuck his phone into my purse after making sure mine is there, too.

The paramedics carry the stretcher down the stairs to the front door and out into the yard. As I close and lock the front door, I can't help but wonder if he'll ever come back to the home he built himself and loves so much.

When I glance at my watch, I'm surprised that only fifteen minutes have passed since I got home from another hospital. I went to see Wynter and Adrian's baby. Being in a hospital again was all but unbearable, even if it was one I hadn't been to before. The sights, the sounds, the smells make them all the same to me.

Wynter and Adrian are so thrilled with their baby girl, Willow, and I survived the trauma of walking into a hospital. I accepted a long time ago that it'll always be difficult for me to go anywhere medical, but showing up for the people I love is important enough to push aside my distress to be there for those who've been there for me.

Tom has been there for me.

More than some of the people I've known all my life.

As I climb into the back of the ambulance, I hope I can be there for him the same way he's been for me.

The speed with which the ambulance travels, the frantic way the paramedic continues to work on him... My anxiety spikes to levels reminiscent of Jim's final week. If I'd lived the whole rest of my life without ever again experiencing that kind of fear, that would have been fine with me.

I pull out my phone and draft a text to Iris, feeling as if I'm typing with fingers that belong to someone else.

Came home to find Tom collapsed on the floor. On the way now with him to Inova Fairfax.

After I send the message, I make the mistake of looking at him. His face has taken on a grayish tone, and if I hadn't felt his pulse with my own fingers, I'd assume he's dead.

"Is he…" I'm afraid to ask.

"Alive but critical."

I know from experience that even if the EMT is certain of what's wrong, he can't tell me. That's not his job. Memories of Jim in respiratory failure come rushing back along with emotions I haven't experienced since the final days with him —despair, fear, anxiety, overwhelming sadness, all mixed with a love so deep, it still touches every corner of my heart and soul.

Do I love Tom like that?

I think I might. I've known for a while now that my feelings for him have blossomed in our months together, but I've kept him firmly in the friendship zone because I'm not ready for more. I might never be ready. It's been almost three years since Jim died, and I'm still mired in the lingering anguish of his illness and death.

Loving someone else the way I loved Jim will take courage I'm not sure I possess anymore. I've learned the hard way not to risk more than I can safely afford to lose.

My phone vibrates with a reply from Iris. *Oh God, Lex. I'm so sorry. What can I do besides pray for your Tom?*

I want to tell her he's not my Tom. But isn't he? He wants to be. I've known that for a while, too. Iris and our Wild Widows friends were the ones who gently informed me that a man doesn't pack a lunch every day for a woman unless he has strong feelings for her.

Of course they're right, but I told them I'm not ready for all the things he could be to me.

They reminded me I'm not on anyone else's timetable but my own, which brought me comfort. The last thing I'd ever want to do is hurt him in the process of dealing with my own crap. I had the hugest crush on him in high school, but he never knew I was alive, or so I thought, until we met up a year ago in a local bar, and he definitely recognized me. That was interesting. We had a drink, and I shared my sorry tale of widowhood with him, including the strain of living with my parents out of economic necessity while Jim was sick and in the two years since he died.

I'll never forget the way he gave me his full attention that night, listened to my story of loving and losing Jim, and how we'd had no choice but to move into my parents' basement when his decline became more than I could handle on my own —and with both of us out of work and our medical insurance maxed out, we couldn't afford outside help.

Tom offered me a lifeline that very same night—a room in his huge, empty house, free of charge and no strings attached. After weeks of trying to decide if taking him up on his offer was the right thing to do, I moved in, insisting on paying some rent. He didn't want it, but I paid it anyway.

As I stare at him now on the stretcher, seemingly clinging to life, I'm suddenly in tears at the thought of losing this sweet, kind, amazing man who came back into my life at a time when I was certain my best years were behind me. Our relationship has evolved organically, one dinner, one conversation, one house project at a time. He's never pressured me for anything more than friendship.

Despite my initial concerns, there's never been any hint of a quid pro quo or anything like that. I love my parents dearly, but as their only child, I get their full focus and all their considerable love. That saved my life when Jim was sick and in the years since he passed away. But what had been so essential to me during a time of crisis became smothering as time went on, and my life remained stuck in the first gear of widowhood. With a go-nowhere job and medical debt that'll take the rest of my life to pay off, I had few options until Tom came along with his lifeline.

I reach over to take his hand and am immediately shocked by how cold he is.

"Tom, it's me, Lexi. I'm here. I'm right here."

The shaky sound of my voice reminds me of Jim's final days, when everything about me was shaky and rattled, despite having had plenty of time to prepare myself for what'd been coming for four years by then. I've learned through my widows that even with years to prepare, you're never ready to lose the person you love the most.

Thoughts of Jim and memories of my months living with Tom cycle through my mind during the rapid trip to the hospital with the siren screaming and the paramedic never losing his sense of urgency as he consults with the hospital. I'm sure it takes only minutes to get there, but every minute feels like an hour without a single indication that Tom is in any way aware of what's happening.

He commands every room he walks into, or at least that's how it seems to me. Seeing him like this is devastating.

We're met by a team of medical personnel wearing scrubs, masks and latex gloves. It's a scene straight out of *Grey's Anatomy* as they whisk him inside with the paramedics chasing after them. Their concerned expressions do nothing to soothe my battered nerves.

I'm like an afterthought as I follow them into the Emergency Department, where there's already no sign of Tom or the paramedics who brought him in. I stop at the reception desk. "I came with Tom Hammett in the ambulance."

"Please have a seat in the waiting room. I'll have the doctor check in with you when there's more information."

"I can't sit with him?"

"No, I'm sorry."

The empathetic look she gives me indicates it's probably in my best interest not to witness what's happening behind the scenes.

"Thank you."

I take a seat in a room full of people waiting to be seen. Their wait probably got much longer after Tom arrived in critical condition.

How can Tom be in critical condition when only this morning he told me to have a nice day at the office and that he planned to make the chicken dish that's become my favorite of all the things he cooks for dinner?

I'm trying so hard not to totally lose my shit in a room full of strangers who have their own problems, but as the events of the last hour overwhelm me, that's much easier said than done.

Two

Lexi

The Inova ER is frantically busy with ambulances arriving one right after the other. Is it always like this, I wonder, or did something big happen? Focusing on the activity around me keeps me from obsessing about what's happening to Tom. What will I do if they come out and tell me he's dead?

How do you come back from a second cataclysmic death when you're only thirty-five?

You don't. The death of someone close to you changes you forever.

I'll never again be the person I was before Jim was diagnosed. Sometimes I think about our life before he started experiencing odd symptoms, such as weakness in his right leg and a twitching thumb, both of which he chalked up to overuse in his work as a mechanical engineer supervising a machine shop and in his hobby as a triathlete. He spent long days on his feet, worked with his hands and was always training intensively for his next event, so of course we attributed his fatigue to the activity.

The weakness spread to his left leg, forcing him to seek medical attention that was an exercise in futility for more than two years. We learned that an ALS diagnosis is a process of elimination, which is like a hamster wheel that goes round and round without ever stopping on an answer.

Until it does, and the answer is a death sentence by slow degrees as the body fails while the mind remains sharp, which is the ultimate kind of purgatory for those who suffer and those who love them. It was especially hard on Jim, the most active person I knew until he lost the ability to do the most basic things, beginning with brushing his own teeth and progressing to breathing and swallowing.

Sitting in that emergency waiting room, waiting to learn Tom's fate, I fall into a rabbit hole of despair I haven't experienced in quite some time.

The hospital setting brings back memories I've worked hard to keep in the past where they belong. For instance, I haven't thought about the frustrating, frightening journey to Jim's diagnosis in quite some time. It's probably been six to eight months since those particular memories tormented me.

The smell of this place brings back the frantic search for answers, as if it happened recently, rather than more than seven years ago.

I fear I'm hallucinating when Iris and Gage walk in through the main doors.

She comes toward me with the determination to help that's so much a part of who she is. Her wild, curly dark hair is contained in a colorful headband, and her brown eyes are full of compassion and concern.

I stand and step into her outstretched arms, and that's when I lose the composure I've barely clung to since I arrived home to find Tom unconscious.

"Shhh. It's okay. He's in the best possible place for whatever he needs."

"Iris is right, Lex." Gage is tall and broad-shouldered, with wavy dark hair and an arrestingly handsome face. "They'll take good care of him and figure out what's going on."

I've never appreciated the two of them more than I do right now, the undisputed leaders of the Wild Widows, full of wisdom, compassion and advice that's always spot-on. Now is no different.

"Thank you so much for coming." I wipe away tears as I step back from them. "You didn't have to do that."

"Of course we did," Iris says. "What're you hearing?"

"Nothing yet, but there was a great deal of urgency when he arrived."

"Urgency is good," Gage says. "That's what you want."

I don't want any of this. "I need to get out of here," I whisper to Iris. "Please. Get me out of here."

She takes me by the arm and leads me to the main doors.

The second I step into fresh, cool air, I feel slightly better.

"Breathe," Iris says gently. "Just focus on breathing."

I do that for five full minutes before my heartbeat slows to a more normal rate. I no longer feel as if I'm about to hyperventilate, which is a huge relief.

"That's it." Iris rubs my arm as we lean against a concrete pillar.

"Why does something like this resurrect all the other stuff?"

"Because trauma is a bitch that way."

Leave it to Iris to make me laugh when I wouldn't have thought it possible.

Gage stands to my left, there in case I need him. His presence is always a comfort to me. I look to him as such an inspiration for surviving the loss of his wife and twin daughters in a drunk-driving accident. He's one of the wisest people I've met on this widow journey. Thinking about him and all the coping mechanisms I've learned from him through his daily Instagram posts is way better than wondering whether Tom is still alive.

What if he isn't?

I squeeze my eyes closed against a new flood of tears.

When I open them, I see Tom's sister running toward the entrance. She's petite with dark hair. The total opposite of her tall, muscular, light-haired, blue-eyed brother.

"That's Tom's sister."

I step away from Iris and Gage to greet her.

The fierce hug she gives me takes me by surprise as we only know each other in passing.

"How is he?"

"I don't know anything yet."

"I'll go find out."

Cora disappears through the doors.

"I... um... I suppose I could leave now that she's here."

"Is that what you want to do?" Iris asks.

I shake my head as tears slide down my cheeks. "It's not. I want to be here for him, but I can't go back in there. I just can't."

"You don't have to. Do you want us to take you home?"

"I can't go there either." It'll take years for me to get past the sight of him passed out on the floor.

"We'll bring you home with us, then."

"I've messed up your whole evening."

"No, you haven't." She squeezes my arm. "We're exactly where we need to be."

"I don't want to hear that he's..."

"We understand," Gage says. "Don't worry about anything."

"I should tell her I'm leaving."

"I'll do that."

"You should give her Tom's phone." I grab it from my purse and hand it to Gage. He goes inside while Iris leads me to his SUV.

"She won't understand why I'm leaving. She'll think I'm..."

"What she thinks doesn't matter right now."

Leave it to Iris to cut through the bullshit. That's one of the many special gifts she brings to the widow business, as we refer to it. Her husband, Mike, was killed in a plane crash, leaving her with three young kids to raise on her own. Long after he died, she found out he'd had a child with another woman. Despite that shock, which knocked her down for a minute, she's still the most supportive person I've ever met. Our other widow friends would agree.

Iris is our North Star.

She settles me into the back seat of Gage's fancy SUV. I think it's a Range Rover, but I'm not sure. Wondering about that keeps me from obsessing about what's happening to Tom.

Iris stands next to the open door, holding my hand, while we wait for Gage.

"If you'd asked me yesterday if I could handle something like this, I would've said of course I could. I'm an expert on all things medical and hospital... But I can't handle it. I can't handle what he looked like on the floor." I glance at Iris, blinking her into focus through more tears. "He looked dead."

"He's not dead."

"What if he is?"

"Let's not go there unless or until we have to."

"I'm preconditioned to go there."

"I know, honey," she says with a sigh. "We all are, but just because it's happened before doesn't mean it will again. Tom is robustly healthy. I'm sure whatever is wrong can be fixed."

I cling to the tiny burst of hope that comes with her reassurance.

Gage joins us a few minutes later. "They told his sister he had a heart attack, and they're taking him to the cath lab for a stent procedure on a blocked artery."

"That's good news," Iris says in a cheerful tone. "See? They're fixing the problem."

"Is that... Is it like open-heart surgery?"

"Not necessarily," Gage said. "I think they can do it robotically."

"Did his sister ask where I was?"

"I told her you were having a tough time, and we're taking you home with us. I gave her my number so she can let us know how he's doing."

"Oh, that's good." I'm so relieved at how he took care of everything for me. "Thank you for thinking of that."

"Of course. Let's get you home and settled."

As if I'm one of her kids, Iris leans across me to buckle my seat belt.

Her kindness has me in tears again. "Thank you."

She squeezes my arm. "Anything for you." After she closes my door, she gets into the passenger seat for the ride back to the house where she and Gage live with her three kids.

Since becoming a widow at thirty-two, my fellow widows have become some of the best friends I've ever had. They're the kindest, most compassionate, thoughtful people anyone could ever hope to have in their lives. We see each other through the good times, the bad times and the truly dreadful times in this new existence that none of us signed up for.

They say it's a club no one would willingly join, but it's also one I'm thankful for every day. I can't imagine what my widow life would be like without my fellow travelers, especially Iris and Gage, who set the gold standard for slaying widow life. Although I know for a fact they've had their share of setbacks as they build a new life together.

When we arrive at their spacious, two-story home, there's only one light on. I spend so much time there I can tell the light is coming from the family room.

Her home is our "clubhouse," or at least that's how it seems to me, and I'm sure to the others, as well. It's our gathering place, our safe space, our home away from home, all thanks to the welcoming vibe that comes directly from Iris. She and two of her friends founded the Wild Widows. Tracy has since remarried and moved on from the group. The other, Christy, has recently found new love with Trey, but is still active in our group.

Gage parks the SUV in the garage and leads the way inside through the door to the kitchen.

Iris's mother, Justine, is there with hugs for all of us. "How is he?"

"In the cath lab for stents on a blocked artery," Iris tells her.

"Remember how Uncle Bill had that last year?" Justine asks her daughter. "He's doing terrific."

"That's right," Iris says.

"I'm glad to hear that," I tell Justine.

"Try not to worry, honey. He's in very good hands."

"Thank you for babysitting so Iris and Gage could rescue me."

She hugs me tightly. "No problem at all. Try to get some rest so you can be there for your friend."

"I will."

What will being there for my friend entail? I've already spent years as a full-time caregiver to a desperately ill man. I'm not sure I have it in me to play that role again.

But then I think about everything Tom has done for me since I moved into his home nine months ago. I think about all the dinners he's made for me, the way he prepares my coffee each morning exactly the way I like it as he hands me a healthy lunch to take to work.

He's one of the best people I've ever known, and I already know that no matter what he needs, I'll never abandon him. But, God, this whole thing cuts me deeply in a place where I'm still far more tender than I would've thought all these years later.

While Iris and Gage see Justine out to her car, I bend at the waist in Iris's kitchen from the body blow that overtakes me at the thought of my kind, decent friend needing me when I don't have a single drop of gas in my tank to give him.

That's where Iris finds me when she comes back inside.

She puts her arm around me and guides me to the sofa.

We sit together, her arms around me as I sob. "I hate this. I hate that I'm m-making it about me when it's about him."

"Of course it's about you, too. It had to be so traumatic to find him in distress."

"It was awful." The image of him on the floor haunts me. "He... he was fine this morning. His usual self. He made me lunch, like he does every day."

"That's so sweet."

"He's the sweetest. Always taking care of me, and all I can think about is what if I need to take care of him and I can't do that? What kind of monster does it make me to recoil from the idea of it?"

"Don't do that to yourself, Lex. This entire episode has sparked all the latent trauma of Jim's illness. It's only natural to run from anything that reminds you of that difficult time."

"One whiff of that hospital, and it was all there, which is strange because I've been in hospitals since Jim died. I was in one earlier to see the baby, and as hard as it was, it didn't send me over the edge like this did."

"Tom's crisis was the trigger. The hospital only made it worse. You were visiting Adrian and Wynter at a happy time, so there's no trauma associated."

"Yes, I suppose that's true."

"Tom would want you to be kind to yourself, wouldn't he?"

"He's always telling me to quit being so hard on myself."

"That sounds like good advice."

"It's a hard habit to break."

"Yes, it is, but we all do the best we can. Nothing says you have to be the one to care for him. He has a sister and a family, friends and other people who can help. I'm sure his procedure will be a success, and he'll fully recover, which makes everything about this different from what you went through with Jim."

"That's also true." You see why we all love her so much? "How do you do that?"

"Do what?"

"Cut directly to the chase in any situation."

"It's her superpower," Gage says when he comes into the room carrying glasses of wine for both of us.

Iris takes both glasses from him and hands one to me. "Thanks, love."

"Thank you, Gage."

"You got it. Be right back."

The first sip of wine has the medicinal effect of taking some of the raw edge off my shattered nerves.

Gage returns with a cocktail glass containing the bourbon he loves.

"Thanks for this, you guys. I can't believe the way you came running for me tonight."

"We'll always come running for you, the way you have for us," Gage says.

We rallied around them when Iris had surgery and radiation for stage-zero breast cancer, but that felt like the least we could do for someone who does so much for everyone else.

I rest my head on her strong, capable shoulder, thankful every day for her continued good health. It never ceases to amaze me how important people I didn't know when Jim was alive have become to me in this new "afterward" since he passed. They're my best friends. I'm closer to them than people I've known since childhood. They get what I'm going through, and their support makes all the difference.

"You guys don't have to wait up with me. You can text my number to Cora."

"We'll wait," Iris says.

"I can't thank you enough for everything."

"You don't have to thank us," Gage says. "You're family."

The simple poignancy of his sweet words brings me to tears again. "I want to be there for Tom. I really do."

"We know that, honey," Iris says.

"He'd do it for me. He'd drop everything for me."

"That's an interesting observation."

I hear the smile in her words.

"It's true. He's been such a great friend to me, and he never asks for a thing in return, as if he knows I don't have it to give."

"I can't wait to get to know him better. From what I already know of him, he seems like a very special man."

"He is." I wipe away tears that refuse to quit. "He's the best."

"Just think," Gage says. "If he hadn't offered you a place to live, he might've died on that floor with no one due home to find him."

"I had that same thought. It's unbearable to think about what could've happened."

"You've already saved him, Lex," Iris says. "Whatever happens next, he has a fighting chance because of you."

That gives me tremendous comfort as I wait to hear whether I'll ever see him again.

Three

Tom

I have no idea where I am when I open my eyes to bright lights and my sister's face hovering above me. What's she doing here? Where the hell am I?

"Oh, thank God," Cora says as tears cascade down her cheeks.

I want to ask her what's wrong, but my throat hurts so bad, I can barely swallow.

"Don't try to talk. You had a procedure to put stents in a blocked artery to your heart."

What? What the actual...

"Lexi came home and found you collapsed on the floor. She saved your life."

Lexi... *Oh no.* That's the last thing I'd ever want her to have to deal with.

"She was here but left with her friends Iris and Gage. They're taking care of her."

That means she was upset, which I can't bear to hear. She's already been through so much.

I have so many questions but can't seem to muster the strength to ask any of them. I feel as if I've been run over by a truck.

The next time I open my eyes, the room is mostly dark. Cora is still there, as is our other sister, Lydia, and her husband, Rick.

Damn, if they flew in from Minneapolis, this must've been bad.

"Way to scare the shit out of us, brother," Lydia says as she leans over the bed rail to kiss my forehead. "Glad to see you awake."

"Sorry."

That one word makes my throat feel like it's been stabbed.

"Don't be sorry. We're just glad your friend Lexi got home in time." She brushes the hair back from my forehead the way she's done since I was a baby. With seven years between us, she's been like a second mother to me.

"Lexi."

Cora steps up to the bedside next to Lydia. "I texted her an update, and she said she'll be in to see you later."

I realize that I've somehow managed to miss an entire evening, and it's now the next day.

I'm glad to know Lexi plans to come see me. At least she's not running away from me, not that I would blame her. She's already done hard time in the caretaking trenches with her late husband. She'll take one look at me, feeble in a hospital bed, and run for her life away from me.

The thought of that is extremely depressing.

I've had a thing for her since I first saw her gorgeous face, all the way back in high school when she was two years behind me in school but three years younger than me. Too young to date back then.

I love to think about the night we ran into each other at a

local bar and restaurant and finally got the chance to talk to each other.

I felt guilty offering her a place to live when I already knew that I wanted much more than a roommate. But I've put any sort of romantic interest on the back burner while making her feel welcome in my home and giving her a soft place to land after her ordeal with Jim.

That's been my only focus in the nine months she's lived with me.

Do I wish it could be more? Hell yes. Have you seen her? Not only is she gorgeous, she's also sweet, smart, funny, snarky, fun and terribly wounded. So deeply wounded. I saw that the first night, when she told me about her late husband and the dreadful illness that led to his death.

My college roommate's mother had ALS. It's a fucking nightmare, and it pains me to think of what Lexi endured. I wish I could snap my fingers and make things all better for her, but that's not how grief works.

And yes, I've done the research. I've learned that every griever is on his or her own journey, that the so-called "five stages of grief" are mostly bullshit, as it never unfolds according to any kind of plan, and that the sort of grief Lexi feels for Jim will last the rest of her life. I've learned that many first relationships after big losses don't last and that a relationship with her would include a relationship with Jim and her grief.

I can handle that if it means I get to be with her.

But now that I've added to her already considerable trauma, I have reason to wonder if any of the things I've hoped for with her will ever come to pass.

Lexi

I WAKE in Iris and Gage's guest room after a surprisingly deep sleep. I'm wearing pajamas loaned to me by Iris and an oversized sweatshirt from Gage that makes me feel loved and cared for as I burrow deeper into the soft material to postpone dealing with reality for a few more minutes.

Last night before bed, I let work know I'm dealing with an emergency and will be out today and possibly tomorrow, too. I'm an incredibly reliable employee, so I hope it's no big deal to take a few unscheduled days off. If it is, I honestly don't care. I've learned what's important in life, and my stupid data-entry job doesn't matter in the least to me when Tom is lying in a hospital bed recovering from a heart attack and the procedure to stent his artery.

Not that I don't need the money from the stupid job, because I do. I've got hundreds of thousands in medical debt still hanging over my head from Jim's illness that I'll never be free of for as long as I live. I accepted that a while ago. I make the minimum payments every month to keep from having to declare bankruptcy, which an accountant friend told me not to do if I could avoid it because that, too, would stick to me forever.

It's one of many ways I'm bitter about what Jim's illness put us through. We were twenty-eight and twenty-nine when he was diagnosed, so no, we didn't have life insurance, and once you're handed a death sentence, you're uninsurable.

Luckily, Jim had good health insurance through his job, and his company kept him covered long after he could no longer work. That was one of the major blessings bestowed upon us during his lengthy illness. But insurance covers only so much, and we tapped it out long before all his needs were met.

Thus the staggering debt, which I try not to think about too often, lest my anxiety be triggered to the point of making me unable to function.

That's not an option.

Since not knowing what work had to say to my message is more stressful than knowing, I reach for my phone and find a kind text from my boss, Erika.

I hope everything is okay. Please let me know how you are if you get a chance. See you Monday.

I'm such an emotional mess that her words make me weep with relief. Four days off is just what I need to recover from last night's trauma, to make sure Tom is okay and to see to whatever he needs going forward.

Wait.

Stop.

That's not my job. I'm not his wife or even his girlfriend. I don't need to see to anything.

Ugh, I've been awake for fifteen minutes, and I'm already spinning.

I get up, shower in the adjoining bathroom and get dressed in yesterday's clothes, which bear the antiseptic scent of the hospital. Awesome.

Downstairs, Iris is seated at the table with her laptop and a cup of coffee.

"Morning. How'd you sleep?"

"Morning. Surprisingly well. Thank you again for taking me in. I'll be out of your hair soon."

"No rush. Have a cup of coffee and some breakfast."

"I'd love some coffee, thanks, but I don't think I can eat anything."

"Not even one of my famous homemade blueberry muffins fresh out of the oven?"

My mouth waters. "Um, yes, please."

"Coming right up!"

"Did you bake for me?"

"What if I did?"

"You're too much, Iris. What would we do without you?"

"Aw, thanks. Taking care of everyone is how I take care of myself."

"You're the absolute best friend any of us has ever had."

She brings a plate with muffins to the table. "You're going to make me cry."

"It's true."

"Thank you. That means a lot to me."

"I don't think you fully understand..." I shake my head when words escape me. "I don't know that I would've survived the loss of Jim without you and the group you founded and the love, support and understanding I've found with each of you. But you... You're the heart of the entire thing."

She fans her face as her eyes fill. "You guys give me back ten times what I give you."

"That's not true."

"Yes, it is!"

"Okay, whatever." I take a bite of muffin, and the flavors explode on my tongue. "Holy shit, that's good."

Gage comes into the kitchen and goes directly toward the plate of muffins.

Iris lunges for the plate. "You already had three!"

"One more. Come on... I'm a growing boy."

She snorts with laughter and hands him the smallest of the four muffins on the plate. "That's it. You're cut off."

"She's so mean to me, Lex."

The face he makes has me giggling. "Y'all are too cute."

Jim and I had what they have: lots of banter and good-natured teasing. So much love and laughter and hot sex that stopped far before either of us was ready for that. I miss him so much.

Iris's hand covers mine. "What can we do for you today?"

"Not a thing. You've gone above and beyond already. I'll grab an Uber back to Tom's to change, and then I guess I'll go see how he's doing."

"Don't be silly. I'll drive you home and go with you to the hospital if you'd like some company. Gage can pick up the kids from school."

"I'm sure you have other things to do. Both of you."

"We don't," Gage says.

"Now you're just lying to my face."

Goddamned tears! I'm so fucking sick of them!

Iris hands me a tissue that I use to angrily wipe them away.

Her offer has me almost sick with relief to know I won't have to face the hospital alone, which also makes me feel sort of feeble. Back in the day, I was a strong, fearless female who kicked ass and took names. Now I need a friend to go with me to visit another friend in the hospital because my trauma has been triggered by yesterday's events.

I hate that so much.

"Whatever you're thinking, knock it off," Iris says. "It's no big deal to want or need a friend to go with you to deal with something upsetting."

I stare at her. "How did you know that's what I was thinking?"

"It's all over your face, pal. You hate needing help. You hate feeling softer than you used to, before life kicked you in the teeth. I get that because I've lived it. One of the hardest parts of this journey is getting to know who we are now."

"Yes, that's so true. Just when I think I've got my new self all figured out, something happens to show me otherwise."

"You're figuring her out, and you're doing a fine job of it. Will there be setbacks along the way? Hell yes, but that doesn't mean you aren't winning the widow game. You got out of bed today. You're already winning."

"Thank you. I needed to hear that."

Gage squeezes my shoulder. "I agree with Iris. You're slaying it. Look at where you were when you first joined our group and look at where you are now. Give yourself some credit, Lex."

"Thank you both. Best friends any widow ever had."

"Right back at you," Iris says. "Now finish your breakfast, and then I'll take you home."

"Yes, Mom."

"That's a good girl."

We share a laugh that further raises my spirits. I can't imagine what last night would've been like for me if they hadn't swooped in to make everything better than it ever could've been without their love and support.

A short time later, we leave Iris's home in Gage's Range Rover, which smells as fancy as it looks. He'll take her minivan with the child seats to pick up the kids. "How sick is this ride?" I ask her.

"I know, right? It's as sexy as he is."

"TMI."

"What?" she asks, laughing. "It is."

"Have I told you how happy I am for you guys?"

"Aw, thanks. You have, but it's always nice to hear. We got lucky, and we know it."

"It wasn't luck so much as courage and determination and perseverance and a decision to live your best life after the worst thing happened."

"And a teeny, tiny bit of pixie dust on top."

"I'll give you that, but you two overcame a lot to get where you are now. So did Roni and Derek and Wynter and Adrian. I look at all of you and wonder where you get the courage to start over. Where does that come from?"

"I wish I knew. All I can say is that one night, I decided I didn't want to be just friends with him anymore, so I took matters into my own hands, and well..."

"Wait. What'd you do?"

"I told you that story."

"I don't think so."

"Oh, damn."

Her entire face turns bright red, which makes me laugh.

"This is gonna be good."

Laughing, she says, "That weekend at the beach?"

"Uh-huh. What about it?" I still feel guilty about how they all chipped in to pay for me to go because I couldn't afford my share.

"I might've crawled in bed with him and pretended like I mixed up the rooms."

"Iris!" She sputters with laughter. "*Oh my God!* What'd he say?"

"It was more about what he *did* than what he said."

"How did we not figure this out?"

"I don't know, because between us and Roni and Derek, there was enough sexual energy in that house to set the place on fire."

"What even is sex? I haven't had it in so long, I don't even remember what it's like." It's been more than five years since I had anything resembling sex.

"Yes, you do. You remember."

"I don't think about it very much. I feel like that part of my life is over."

"It's not over." While stopped at a red light, she looks over at me. "Two years ago, I would've said the same thing, and look at me now. Getting busy with my fiancé as much and as often as we can."

I put my hands over my ears as I scream.

The bitch just laughs her ass off. "Don't tell me that's done for you, because it's not."

"What if it is?"

"It's *not*. You're just not ready yet. When you are, it'll be game *on*, baby."

"How will I know if I'm ready?"

"You'll crawl into bed naked with a guy you already love

and respect—maybe you'll even do it on purpose like I did. But don't tell Gage that. He still thinks it was a big mix-up."

"Does he? Really?"

"Nah, he knows who he's dealing with. I never fooled him for a second, but let me tell you, I've never once admitted that to him."

"I love it. Such a great start to an epic couple."

"It was pretty great, but don't look at us now and think it was all sunshine and rainbows and wild sex. It was those things, but it was also a lot of compromise and risk-taking, especially for him. He was taking on a single mom with three young kids after losing his precious wife and daughters. He wasn't sure he could handle caring that much about people again. He didn't want to care that much."

"What made him change his mind?"

"He was faced with the choice of taking a chance on us or living the rest of his life without us. We're rather insidious. We get under your skin. By the time it came down to a decision, he was in love with all of us, so there really was no decision. At least that's what he says. I know he struggled with it, though, and understandably so. Out of all of us, I look at what he lost and just can't fathom how he's managed to go on as gracefully and courageously as he has."

"While giving so much to other widows through his incredible posts on Insta and his amazing friendship."

"That, too. He's the full package, if you know what I mean."

"Again, TMI. That's my *friend* you're talking about."

Her laughter has become the sound of joy to me, I realize as she loses her shit while trying not to crash Gage's Rover. "I'm sorry to be enjoying this so much, but do not tell me you're done with love and sex and all the rest of it. I refuse to believe that, unless, of course, you really want to be done with it. If so, I respect that choice, too."

"I don't know what I want."

She pulls into the driveway at Tom's. "Which is also fine."

At the sight of his house and yard, I'm immediately transported back to the horror of last night and the many other times I had to call EMS for Jim. I've never experienced an adrenaline rush that can rival that which comes from realizing emergency measures are required to save someone's life.

Iris's warm hand on top of mine makes me realize how cold I am.

I force a smile for her. "Come in while I change real quick."

She follows me to the door outside the garage, where I punch in the code. "Every time I do this, I think about how he turned over the code to his house, without hesitation, to someone he hadn't seen since high school—and didn't even know back then."

"He knew he could trust you. Remember how you asked around about him? I'm sure he did the same."

We step into the kitchen, which Tom has tricked out with gorgeous white countertops, a navy tile backsplash I would've chosen myself and high-end appliances. "He didn't, though. I asked my high school friends if any of them had heard from him, and they all said no, which means he took me at my word. That's such an enormous leap of faith, you know? To let someone you barely know into your home simply because she so badly needs a new place to be."

"I think it's marvelous that he stepped up for you that way."

"And in so many ways since then. Last night, when I thought he might be dead... I honestly didn't know what I would do."

Iris put an arm around me. "I'm so sorry that happened to both of you."

"I hate that I'm still making it about me when it's about him."

"It's about you, too, and I'm sure even he would understand that, knowing what you've been through."

"I hope so." I look around at the cozy kitchen that, along with the rest of Tom's comfortable home, has been such a refuge for me. "I've been so happy here."

"And you will be again. I know it."

I wipe my eyes with a tissue. "Thanks for propping me up. You're the best."

"It's no problem at all."

"I'll be quick."

"Take your time."

Four

Lexi

I go upstairs to the space above the garage that Tom made available to me, complete with an en suite bathroom, a sitting room and mini kitchen that smelled new when I first moved in. He denies he put it in for me, but I don't believe him. It's something we playfully bicker about once in a while.

Thinking about that makes me smile as I change my clothes and put on makeup to hide the ravages of the last twelve hours from him. He's got enough to think about without worrying about me, too.

When I'm as ready as I'll ever be to visit him in the hospital, I join Iris downstairs.

"You look great."

"You're too kind. I look like something the cat dragged in."

She sputters with laughter. "You're not capable of looking like that, so shush. You look fresh and pretty and put together. Tom will be very happy to see you."

"I hope so."

"I know so."

She's awfully good for a girl's ego, among many other things. I hope that one day, I can pay it forward to someone else who needs a fraction of what she and my other Wild Widows have given me on this journey.

At the hospital, I push aside all the fear and trauma to force myself to be there for Tom the way he's been there for me. I do my best to ignore the smells and other triggers and keep the focus on the task at hand. I follow the directions from Cora to the cardiac area of the hospital and ask for Tom's room at the nurses' station.

"Fourth door down on the left."

"Thank you so much."

I'm as nervous as I've been in a long time as I approach his room, filled with fear about what I might see in there.

Iris places a hand on my back. "Do you want me to come in with you?"

"That's okay. I think I can do it."

"I'll be in the waiting room at the end of the hallway. Take your time."

I give her a quick hug.

"And remember, whatever's happening in there, you saved his life and gave him a chance to fix the problem. He might look terrible, but he's better than he was yesterday."

I'm nodding as I soak up words that are an elixir to calm my wild heartbeat. "Thank you for everything."

"Love you."

"Love you, too."

After she walks toward the waiting room, I stare at the door for a full minute before I gather my fortitude and give a brisk knock before I step inside.

Tom is alone in the room, and his handsome face lights up at the sight of me. "Hey. There you are." His hair is a mess, he's paler than normal, and his voice is raspy. But he's alive, and that's what matters most.

"Here I am." I'm in full panic mode at the sight of tubes and machines and sounds that bring it all back in a rush of pure horror.

He holds out a hand to me. "Come here."

As I walk toward him, I feel disconnected from myself, as if my body is functioning outside my control. This entire thing feels like a massive setback for me. If you'd asked me yesterday, I might've foolishly said I've mostly recovered from what I endured with Jim. I would've been very wrong about that.

I take the hand he offers, which has an IV attached to it.

"Hey."

I force my gaze to meet his intense blue eyes.

"I'm okay. Thanks to you."

I'm overcome with tears and emotions that surge to the surface with the force of a tsunami. Before I know it, I'm sobbing as I stand next to his bed, frantically trying to get myself together.

"Aw, sweet Lexi." He gives my hand a squeeze. "I'm so sorry I did this to you."

When I look at his face, I'm stunned to see tears in his eyes, too. "Don't be sorry. You couldn't help it."

"Maybe not, but it was the very last thing you needed to come home to."

"It's not about me."

"Sure it is."

"No, it's about you and whatever you need to recover."

"I'm going to be just fine in a few weeks. I got very lucky. My dad died of a similar event when he was just forty-two."

"I didn't know that happened to your dad until Cora told me. I'm so sorry." I know his mother suffers from dementia and is in a nearby care home, but he doesn't say much about her situation. I sense it's painful for him to talk about, so I don't ask about it.

"It was a very tough loss for all of us. Both my older sisters have had extensive cardiac workups. Mine was next, scheduled for November." He gazes up at me. "If you hadn't moved in, I would've died on that floor, Lex. You saved my life. I'm so thankful to you."

"Oh God, stop. You've done more for me than I could ever do for you."

"Not true. You just paid me back in spades and put a down payment on fifty more years of me owing you everything."

"All I did was call for help."

"Which was the thing I most needed at the time."

"Are you in a lot of pain?"

"It's not terrible, but I'm told that's thanks to very good drugs."

"Yay for drugs."

"The worst is my throat. They said that's from being intubated."

"Ouch."

His smile goes a long way toward calming me. It's had that effect on me since the night we reconnected, almost twenty years after high school. Hell, who am I kidding? It's had that effect on me since I was fifteen and had a desperate crush on a boy who barely knew I existed.

He knows I exist now. In fact, he's holding my hand and looking at me as if I matter very much to him.

"Is Cora still here?"

"She did an all-nighter, so I sent her home to get some sleep. Our other sister, Lydia, and her husband are at a hotel."

"Where does Lydia live?"

"Outside of Minneapolis."

"I didn't know you had another sister."

"She's seven years older than me and has lived in Minnesota since she left for college. We aren't as close as I am with Cora."

"I see. Does Lydia have kids?"

"Two boys in college." When he shifts, looking for a more

comfortable position in the bed, he lets out a groan that puts me on alert. "Ugh. I hate this."

"Do you want me to get a nurse?"

"No, I'm okay. Just sore. They got to my heart through an artery in my leg, so that's not feeling too great today."

"Did they say what happens next?" I'm accustomed to coordinating with doctors, being one step ahead of whatever Jim would need after a hospitalization, figuring out home care and other details. I lived in a constant state of hyperawareness that depleted my reserves long before he died.

"Not yet, but probably cardiac rehab and a drastic lifestyle change. That's what my dad's brother had to do after he survived a similar event."

"Wow, the faulty cardiac gene runs hot in your family."

"So hot. Two of my dad's other brothers died young from widow-maker heart attacks, and one of his sisters had bypass surgery."

I process this new information with a growing sense of alarm and dread, which he immediately senses.

"Ah, shit. I never should've told you that."

No, you really shouldn't have.

"Lex, look at me."

I force myself to meet his gaze while telling myself how incredibly kind he's been to me. Don't I owe him the same in return?

"I'm fine. I'm going to be fine. I got very lucky, thanks to you, and I'm going to make some big changes to make sure I stay healthy. There's nothing to worry about."

I swallow the huge lump that's got my throat nearly blocked. I want to turn and run from him and his faulty heart, except he's holding my hand, so I can't go anywhere.

"Lexi."

"Yes?"

"I can see that you're panicking, and I totally get it. After everything you've been through, why would you want to hang out with someone who might drop dead at any second? All I can tell you is I'm going to do everything I can to live for a good long time, and I want to spend as much of that time with you as I possibly can."

That's the first time he's ever confirmed what I've long suspected—he has feelings for me that go beyond that of friendly roommates.

I know I should say something, but my brain has gone blank.

"This is a lot. I know it is, and it's not at all fair for me to tell you that when I'm lying in a hospital bed after getting a stent in a blocked artery. But it's the truth, and if this incident has shown me anything, it's that I need to tell the people I care about how I feel, and you're at the top of my list of those who need to hear the truth."

I recall how I discovered my name first on his list of favorites last night, which confirms what he's saying like nothing else ever could.

He pauses, seeming to gather the strength to continue. "This morning, when Cora told me everything that happened… All I could think about was you and that I could've died without you knowing…"

I need to ask him what he wants me to know, but that damned lump in my throat makes it impossible for me to say anything.

"I want you to know how much I care about you and how happy I've been since you moved in."

I clear my throat because a statement like that deserves some sort of reply. "Oh. Really?"

His smile lights up his tired eyes. "Yes, really. I love our dinners and our weekend coffee chats. I even enjoy doing yard work when you're there to help me and keep me entertained. I had no idea how lonely I was in that big old house until you showed up and helped to make it a home."

I'm so overwhelmed by his words and the emotion behind them that I can barely breathe. I knew he cared. Of course I knew, but I've sort of kept that information pushed off to the side for if or when I was ready to deal with it. Am I ready to deal with it now? I have no idea.

"I, um, I care about you, too."

"That means a lot to me, Lex. And listen, I'm not putting any pressure on you for anything more than what we already have. I respect what you've been through since you lost Jim, and I'd never want to take advantage of you in any way."

"You never would. I know that. It's just that I'm kind of still..." That damned lump again. My eyes fill, and I look away from him, wishing I could find a way to make it so I could control when tears decide to show up.

"I know, honey. I'm not telling you this because I expect anything from you. It's just that when you come close to dying and miraculously manage to survive, you want the people in your life to know what they mean to you. And you mean a lot to me."

Come close to dying...

Those words are on repeat in my mind. He came close to dying. He survived. This time. What if there's a next time?

I force myself to focus on the here and now, to give him a fraction of what he's given me. "You... you mean a lot to me, too. It's just that... last night was a lot..." I hate the way I sound like a stammering idiot as my emotions make a complete mess of me.

"I'm so sorry I put you through that."

"It's not your fault."

"Whose fault is it?" he asks, smiling.

"It's no one's fault. It happened, and we dealt with it, and thank God, you're going to be okay."

"Thank you for dealing with it, for calling for help, for coming with me to the hospital."

"Oh, you heard about that, huh?"

"I heard, and I appreciate everything you did. I owe you my life."

"No, you owe that to the EMTs and the doctors and nurses. I made a phone call while trying not to lose my shit."

He winces. "I'd give anything for this to have happened anywhere but at home where you had to be the one to find me. All morning, I've been thinking that you'll run as far from me as you can get after this, and I wouldn't blame you."

"I won't do that, and not just because I have nowhere else to go. Please don't think that."

"If you want to be somewhere else, Lexi, I'll help make that happen if it's what you feel is best for you. I'd totally understand."

"You would?"

"I would." He closes his eyes. "I'd hate it, but I'd understand."

"We don't need to talk about any of this today. The most important thing is for you to rest and recover."

He keeps his eyes closed when he says, "It's not the only important thing. You're important, too."

"Get some rest and try not to worry about anything but getting better."

"I'm worried about a lot of things."

"Don't be. I'm fine. I swear."

He opens his eyes to gaze at me with more affection than I've seen from him before. "You wouldn't lie to me, would you?"

"No, I wouldn't lie to you."

"Good." His eyes closed again. "That's good."

Cora comes into the room about ten minutes after Tom dozed off while still holding my hand.

"How is he?"

"He seems good. We were talking for a while before he fell asleep."

"I'm glad you're here. He was asking for you earlier."

"Oh, he was?"

She glances at me. "Why do you sound surprised? You have to know how much he cares for you by now."

Does she sound a bit testy, or am I imagining that?

"I, um... He's been an amazing friend to me at a time when I needed one very much."

"Yes, he has, and it's worried me on more than one occasion that he might end up hurt because you're not available for what he wants with you."

I'm struck dumb. Literally.

Cora sighs deeply. "I'm sorry. I shouldn't have said any of that. Blame the sleepless night." She glances at me. "I really am sorry. Disregard all that. Please. He'd have my head if he heard me say any of it."

"I, ah... I should go."

"Please don't go because of me, Lexi. Tom wants you here. He wants you here more than he wants me."

I need to get out of there. That's all I know. "I'll be back later. Please tell him..." I can't think of a single thing to say, so I leave it at that. In the hallway, I focus on breathing as I make my way to where Iris is waiting for me.

"Hey," she says, "how is he?"

"Good. He's good."

She takes a closer look at me. "And you?"

"Can we go? Please?"

"Yep." With her typical efficiency, Iris takes me by the arm and has me in an elevator in two seconds flat, or at least that's how it seems to me.

Five

Lexi

My entire body buzzes with tension and anxiety and... something else that I can't quite put a name to.

"What happened?" Iris asks when we're in the car.

"I..." I've never been such a stammering fool. "He was very thankful for what I did and apologetic for retraumatizing me. He... he said he was glad he didn't die without me knowing how much he cares or how happy he's been since I moved in."

"Oh. Wow. How do you feel about that?"

I give her what must be a wild look. "I don't know. And then his sister... She said..." That goddamned lump in my throat makes me choke.

Iris turns to face me. "What'd she say, Lex?"

"That she's been worried about me hurting him because I'm not available for what he wants from me."

"Oh damn. That's a lot for her to lay on you, especially right now."

"She said that when she apologized, blaming the sleepless night. She said he'd be mad at her for saying that to me."

"He should be. She had no right to dump that on you. Tell me you know that whatever he feels for you is not your responsibility."

Leave it to Iris to cut to the chase. "I know."

"Say it like you mean it."

"I know that whatever he feels for me isn't my responsibility, but... I really like him. Hell, I was more than halfway in love with him in high school when I'd never exchanged a single word with him."

"This isn't high school, and just because he did you a huge favor when you really needed it, you don't owe him anything but friendship and appreciation for his generosity."

I nod, grateful for her succinct summary.

"All the emotions are heightened after last night. A close call like he had would naturally make him grateful for the blessings in his life, including you. You're under no obligation to take what he said and run with it. You're on your own journey, your own timeline, not anyone else's, even someone who's stepped up for you the way he has."

It's a relief to fully exhale for the first time in an hour. "Thank you for the reminder."

"I won't let any of this be a setback for you, not when you've been doing so great lately."

I smile at her because how can I not? "I don't know what I ever did to get lucky enough to have a friend like you."

"You became a widow."

That sets us off into a laughing fit that I needed. "I love you so much, Iris. You're one of the best friends I've ever had."

"Likewise."

"That's not even remotely true."

"Shut up before I get mad at you."

We laugh again as she starts the SUV. "Where to?"

"I think I'd like to go home and maybe take a nap before I go back in to see Tom later."

"You don't have to go back today."

"I know, but I might go anyway."

"Stay away from his sister."

"She's been nice to me the few times I've met her before this and felt terrible after she said what she did."

"Good. She should. What a stupid thing to say to someone who's been through what you have."

"What is it we always say about how people can't possibly know what we've been through unless they've lost their person?"

"Still... In a case like this one, say nothing rather than word-vomiting things a widow doesn't need to hear."

"Don't be mad at her. She's traumatized. Their dad died of a massive heart attack at forty-two, two of their uncles also died of heart attacks, and an aunt had bypass surgery."

"Damn. That's a lot."

"Definitely, especially since she and Tom are super close."

"What happens next for Tom?"

"He said a drastic lifestyle change and cardiac rehab."

We're silent for several miles as Iris drives me back to Tom's.

"I really like him, Iris. If I were in the market for another man in my life, I'd totally pick him."

"But?"

"After what happened to him and then hearing his family's history with heart problems, I just don't know if I have it in me. I feel like being with him, going all in with him, would be like juggling dynamite or something equally dramatic."

"I get that. You've already done years of debilitating illness with your husband, and the possibility of another serious, chronic situation might be more than you can handle."

"Yes, that. Exactly that. Even if saying it out loud makes me feel like a wimp."

"You're the furthest thing from a wimp, Lexi. Look at what

you did for Jim. A wimp never could've handled years of caring for him the way you did."

"Well, I feel like a wimp at the thought of going through that again with Tom. They fixed the problem this time, but do I need to be worried about him dropping dead on me some other time?"

"That's a very good question that you're perfectly reasonable to ask."

"To him? 'Hey, Tom, I know you just went through this rough ordeal, but how worried do I need to be about it happening again? Are there some odds you could give me based on your family's hellacious history of people dropping dead in the prime of their lives?'"

Iris snorts out a laugh. "You might not want to put it quite like that, but it's info you deserve to have before you decide whether you're up for being more than friends and roommates with him."

"I should move out of his place."

"What? No, don't do that. Not yet, anyway. Remember when Jim first died, and people told you not to make any big decisions right away?"

"Yeah."

"This is kind of like that. You had a huge trauma last night. This is no time for big decisions."

I put my head back against the seat, as exhausted as I've been since Jim died. I hate feeling like this. It brings back so many memories I thought I'd left in the past. "Is it weird to be having a grief reaction to this when no one died?"

"Not weird at all. Grief colors everything that happens after a big loss. Every single fucking thing, even the good stuff."

"That doesn't feel fair."

"None of this is fair. Why is it that we had to lose our husbands while other people get to keep theirs for seventy years? Why did we have to rebuild lives we'd worked so hard to have in the first place? Why did we have to lose the one person we thought we couldn't live without? Why did any of this have to happen?"

As I listen to her list of questions, tears slide down my face. I brush them away. Why did any of this have to happen... I ask myself that question almost every day. How did we go from being blissfully happy newlyweds with big plans and dreams to one of us being terminally ill with the cruelest of diseases?

We arrive at Tom's a few minutes later.

Iris turns off the engine and turns toward me. "What can I do?"

I reply with a quick laugh. "You've already done so much, and I appreciate you more than you'll ever know."

"What else can I do?"

"I think I'm okay for now. I need to go sit with it all and figure out what's what."

"Please don't let him or his sister or anyone pressure you for something you're not ready for."

"I won't. I promise."

"Call me if you need me?"

"I will."

"If I don't hear from you, I'll check in later."

"Thank you for everything, Iris. Not just in the last two days, but always."

She reaches across the console to hug me. "Any time."

I love how she waits for me to wave from inside the door before she backs out of the driveway. What a friend.

Inside, I purposely avoid looking at the area of the upstairs living room where last night's nightmare unfolded. I go into the kitchen, pour a glass of the iced tea that Tom brews for me and then break down all over again at the many ways he takes care of me.

He's so incredibly good to me and has been since I first moved in. Somehow he always seems to beat me home and has dinner ready six nights out of seven. On the seventh night, he says, "Let's go out," and he casually takes me to dinner somewhere fun. Though these outings seem spontaneous, we're always taken right to a table, which means there's a reservation, which means he plans in advance.

The only exceptions to this routine are my Wednesday nights with the Wild Widows, as well as other outings with friends and my parents. Lately, I've started including Tom in dinner with my parents as if it was the most logical thing I could do. I have to give them credit for not asking me a million questions about him or what it all means.

They think he's great, and he's developed a nice, friendly rapport with both of them. Last week, my dad asked if Tom might like to go to a late-season DC Feds game with him. The question both lifted me up and broke my heart, because he used to share season tickets with Jim, and I know how much he misses his baseball buddy.

My parents considered Jim the son they never had. Witnessing his decline was as hard on them as it was on me as they helped to take tender care of him. We all put our lives on hold when he was so terribly ill, so I'm glad to see them beginning to travel again and going back to baseball games and picking up the lives they put aside to be there for us.

Speaking of them, I need to tell them what happened last night, even though the last thing I want to do is talk about it more than I already have. For them, though, I'll go through it one more time.

My mom answers on the third ring. "Hi, honey. I was just thinking about you. Why aren't you at work?" We never talk during the day, and I'm sorry I didn't consider the time when I called her.

"I took the day off after a bit of a rough night."

"What happened?"

I hate that she's immediately on alert for disaster, which is a byproduct of her grief over Jim. "I came home and found Tom unconscious on the living room floor."

"Oh, Lex. Oh no. Tell me he's all right."

"He is after a stent procedure to open a blocked artery."

"Oh Lord. And how are you? That must've been so triggering."

My mom learned about being triggered during Jim's illness. "It was indeed, but I'm hanging in there. As long as he's okay. That's what matters."

"I'm so sorry that happened, honey. I can't imagine how upsetting it had to be for you."

"It was rough, but I'm doing okay. Iris and Gage came to the hospital and took me home to their place."

"We would've come. I hope you know that."

I wince over having unintentionally hurt her feelings. "I do. Of course I know."

"I'm glad you were well supported, no matter who was doing it."

"I was."

"Have you seen Tom?"

"For a bit this morning. His sisters are with him, and I'll probably go back later."

"If it's too much for you, don't go."

"I'm okay. I want to be there for him the way he's been for me."

"Which is lovely, but you need to take care of yourself first and foremost. You've done a lifetime's worth of caregiving already."

"Yes, I have."

"If he's going to need a lot of care at home, make sure that's not being provided by you. I don't mean to sound harsh, but you can't take that on, Lex. Tell me you know that."

"I do but thank you for caring."

"Daddy and I were just saying that you seem to have gotten

some of your sparkle back lately. We'd hate to see that dimmed by a setback."

"I hear you. I'm being vigilant, but I want to also be a good friend to someone who's been one to me."

"He's a lovely guy. Please tell him how sorry we are that he's dealing with this."

"I will. I'll keep you posted, okay?"

"Please do. We love you."

"Love you, too."

I take my iced tea to my room on the second floor. In addition to the kitchenette he says he didn't put in for me, I suspect Tom took down a wall to give me the sitting room. All I know is it wasn't there when I first saw pictures of the bedroom and bathroom. It had magically appeared by the time I moved in. That was one of a thousand things he's done to make things easier, better, nicer for me.

After I stretch out on the bed, I check the new texts on my phone.

One is from Roni, another of my Wild Widows friends. *Hey, gang, does anyone want to go in on a gift for Adrian and Wynter? I checked her registry, and the super cool stroller she wanted is still up for grabs. Let me know who's in.*

One by one, the replies had come in: Brielle, Joy, Gage, Derek, Christy, Hallie, Iris, Kinsley and Naomi are all in.

I type my reply. *Count me in, too.*

While I have them, separate from the new parents who don't need to hear my drama on top of welcoming a new baby, I decide to update them on what's going on.

I was going to text you all today to tell you my friend (and roommate) Tom had a cardiac emergency last night. I came home to find him unconscious on the living room floor. Thankfully, we got him to Inova quickly. He had a stent procedure to open a blocked artery and is recovering. As am I after a tough night that was made easier by Iris and Gage, who came to my rescue.

The responses come flooding in.

From Brielle: *Oh no, Lex! What can we do for you?*

Joy: *So sorry, honey. Can't imagine how tough that must've been for you. Sending much love to you and your friend.*

Hallie: *So glad to hear he's on the mend. Sorry you went through that.*

Roni calls me.

"Hey, aren't you busy working at the White House?" She's the communications director for First Lady Samantha Cappuano.

"Never mind with that. How are you?"

"Better than I was last night. Still a little shaky, but I suppose that's leftover adrenaline."

"Damn, Lex. I can't believe you came home to find him that way."

"It was pretty terrifying."

"What can we do for you?"

"I'm good. Iris and Gage took great care of me last night, and I saw Tom this morning. He's doing well. His sisters are with him."

"Well, that must be a relief."

"It is. For sure. It's just that..."

"What, honey?"

"I also found out there's a significant history of early death by widow-maker heart attacks in his family. His dad and two of his uncles died in their forties, and one of his aunts had bypass surgery."

"This is a lot after what you've already been through," she says, seeming to choose her words carefully.

"Sure is. He... he said some stuff this morning, about how much he cares about me and how sorry he is to have done this to me."

"That's very sweet."

"He's so sweet and kind and thoughtful. He's wonderful."

"I love that for you. Do you?"

"I don't know. A big part of me feels nowhere near ready for what he seems to want."

"Which is also fine."

"Yeah, I know, but now there's this heart thing, and I don't know if *my* heart could withstand losing someone else I might love."

"That's a fair concern."

"None of this feels fair."

"It's not. It's extremely unfair that this happened to a young man in seemingly good health and that you were the one who found him."

"Thank goodness I was living here, or he might've died on that floor."

"Oh, Lex, I wish I could hug you right now."

"Thanks for that and for calling. I'm all right. I promise."

"Check in later to let me know how it's going?"

"I will. Thanks again."

"Any time."

After ending the call with Roni, I read more texts of support from Derek, Naomi, Christy and Hallie. Their kindness brings me to tears, but that doesn't take much at the moment.

Tom's name pops up in another text: *Have I scared you away? Are you moving out as we speak? Running for your life from the guy with the bad ticker? Please don't. I promise I won't drop dead on you.*

I'm laughing even as I continue to cry. He makes me laugh a lot. That's one of the things I love best about living with him. People say laughter is the best medicine, and he's certainly proven that to be true.

I'm not moving out. Not yet anyway...

Ouch. Nurse, more pain meds, please.

I respond with laughter emojis. *Quit being funny. You're supposed to be recovering.*

My heart will never recover if you run away from me. Don't do that, okay?

Tom...

Lexi... Please don't go.

I close my eyes, as if that will stop the flood of tears. It seems that nothing can stop them, especially when I'm standing on the precipice of a much bigger deal with him—and I know it. There's no denying that's what he's asking for from his hospital bed after having a freaking heart attack.

I summon all the courage I have left after the grueling battle I endured with Jim before I respond to Tom.

I'm not going anywhere.

Six

Tom

My sisters are driving me batshit crazy with their hovering, their unsolicited advice about all aspects of my life and their bickering with each other. I wish they'd leave so Lexi could come visit and we could pick up where we left off by text earlier.

When she said she wasn't going anywhere, my fragile heart soared with hope, excitement and anticipation. I'm surprised the nurses didn't come running due to a spike in my heart rate.

My sisters are talking over me as if I'm not here. "Ladies." They continue as if I didn't say anything as my throat continues to protest any form of speaking or swallowing. "*Ladies!*"

This time, they hear me.

"What?" Cora asks.

"Enough with the arguing. I've already spoken to the hospital social worker, and she's arranging for at-home nursing care for when I'm released. I don't need to go home with either of you, and frankly, I don't wish to."

"Be serious, Tom," Lydia says. "You can't go home alone after nearly dying."

Tall with dark hair and eyes, Lydia and Cora look like our late father, while I favor our blonde mother.

"I'm being dead serious, and that's what's going to happen. I won't be alone at home. Lexi is there."

"Oh, right," Cora says, "Lexi, who crumpled like a house of cards under pressure last night."

"Watch it, Cora. You have no idea what you're talking about." Hearing Lexi's reaction described that way breaks my heart.

"I know you like her—"

"I more than like her. I think I could be in love with her, so watch what you say."

"It's just that she didn't seem very strong in the face of an emergency."

"Because a couple of years ago, she lost her husband after a four-year battle with ALS, during which she was his primary caregiver. Needless to say, what happened last night was extremely triggering for her, and as far as I'm concerned, she held up well enough to save my life. So you'll have to pardon me if I'm uninterested in your critiques of her emergency performance."

Cora has the good sense to look a bit guilty. "I'm sorry. I didn't know that about her husband."

"There's a lot you don't know about her, so keep the judgment to yourself. I like her. I want her around, and I've already set up care for when I go home, so this entire argument is a moot point."

"So you and Lexi have been, like, seeing each other since she moved in?" Lydia asks.

"Nope. We're just friends and roommates for now."

"But you want it to be more than that?" Cora asks.

"We'll see."

Cora's brows furrow. "What does that mean?"

"It means that she's been through a lot, and I'm not looking to pressure her for anything she's not ready for. I like being her friend, and I like having her living with me. That's all there is to say about it."

"I, um... I might've screwed up," Cora says.

"What did you do?"

"I, ah, I said something about how I've been worried she might hurt you."

"For fuck's sake, Cora. Stay out of my business, will you?"

"I'm sorry. I know you like her, and I haven't been able to get a read on her, and..."

"You don't need a read on her. I'm the only one who needs to know what she's about, and I love everything about her. I swear to God, if you scared her off, I'll never forgive you."

"I don't think I scared her off. I'm sorry. I didn't know about the husband with ALS or any of that."

"Which is why you should keep your opinions to yourself."

"I'll apologize to her again when I see her."

"That'd be good."

"So she might be the one, huh?" Lydia asks.

"She *is* the one, but I'm not in any rush. If anything happens between us, it'll be on her timetable, not mine."

"What if she never comes around?" Cora asks.

"I'd rather be just friends with her than be with anyone else."

"Wow," Lydia says. "That's awesome, Tom. I hope it works out for you guys."

"I do, too, but again... The last thing either of us needs is any kind of drama with my sisters. Please. The health scare is enough without adding that to it."

"Understood," Cora says as Lydia nods. "I'll fix it with her."

They've worn me out with their emotional energy, but I don't fault them for that. I'd be the same way if one of them were in this bed. None of us will ever forget the day our dad went to play golf and never came home. We've lived with the specter of sudden death hanging over us since we were kids.

What happened to me is our worst nightmare come to life. Luckily, my incident didn't play out like my dad's did, on the fifteenth fairway, long before cell phones and far enough from help that he was dead before EMTs arrived.

I have no idea how long I was on the floor before Lexi found me, but thankfully, she got there in time. I don't remember anything about yesterday.

I cringe every time I think about her coming into the house and finding me that way. She doesn't talk a lot about what it was like to care for a husband with ALS. Rather, she uses words like *dreadful* and *excruciating* to describe that time in her life. My college friend documented his mother's journey on Facebook, and *dreadful* is an apt way to describe it.

With every new update, it seemed like she lost some other essential function.

What would it be like to watch the person you love the most decline that way while their mental faculties remained as sharp as ever? It would be torturous.

I can't keep my eyes open, even though I'm worried if I close them, my sisters might take over my whole life. They've always thought they were the bosses of me, even Cora, who's only two years older. Lydia was often put in charge of us after our dad died and Mom had to go back to work to keep a roof over our heads, as she put it.

The strain on her was enormous since my dad didn't have life insurance.

On the night we first connected, Lexi told me her husband didn't have life insurance either. Why would he? Most people don't think about stuff like that in their twenties.

I did. Even though I've checked out fine at my annual cardiac workups, due to how my dad died, I've had life insurance since I was twenty-five. I don't want my family burdened by funeral expenses if history repeats itself.

Cora is my beneficiary, not that she knows that. I was sort of hoping she'd never need to find that out.

It must be the medication that's making me so tired that I'm sucked under before I can say another word to my sisters.

The next time I open my eyes, it's much darker in the room, and Lexi is there.

I'm unreasonably happy to see her. I wouldn't have blamed her if she never came back despite her promises to stick around.

"Hey."

"Hey, yourself. How're you feeling?"

"Like I got run over by a bus or an eighteen-wheeler."

She grimaces. "That bad, huh?"

"It could be much worse."

"What's the doctor saying?"

"That I'm doing great and already bouncing back quickly." The doctor didn't say that last part, but she doesn't need to know that.

I can't help but notice she looks fragile, which is new. I hate knowing I'm most likely the reason for that.

"Hey." I extend a hand to her. "I'm okay. I swear."

She takes my hand and gives it a squeeze but doesn't hang on the way I wish she would. I want her to take my hand and never let go. We were making progress toward that before this happened, or at least I think we were.

Now? Who knows? Are we back to square one, or have we regressed into negative numbers? Before this happened, I wasn't sure where I stood with her. Does she see me as only a good friend and roommate who stepped up for her when she needed a favor? Or does she see the potential for more with me the way I do with her?

I saw that potential from the first night we connected, when she told me her husband had died after a long illness.

"How're you feeling?" I ask her.

She seems surprised by the question. "I'm fine. You're the one we're worried about."

"I'm worried about you."

"Why?"

"I know this was rough on you, Lex. Don't try to pretend otherwise. I feel terrible about it. I don't want it to be a setback for you."

"I, ah... Huh. That's rather insightful of you to realize it could be."

"Of course I realize that. I can't begin to imagine what you went through before. I'd never want to be the cause of reopening an old wound for you."

"It's nice of you to be worried about me."

"I care about you, Lexi. I hope you know that by now."

"I... I do. I care about you, too."

Frustration overwhelms me. The last place I want to be having this conversation is from a hospital bed after I recently scared the living shit out of her and disclosed a family propensity for sudden death. If she has an ounce of sense, she'll run for her life away from me.

"The timing is terrible," I say softly.

"For what?"

"For me to tell you how *much* I care about you."

"Oh." She looks down at the floor or her shoes or something other than me.

"Lex?"

Her dark, expressive eyes flip up and connect with mine.

The impact takes my breath away. "I want you to know how much you've come to mean to me." Fuck if I don't have to take a second to fight back another wave of unrelenting exhaustion. I want to cut back on whatever med is causing that. "I wouldn't blame you if you wanted nothing further to do with me."

"Don't say that."

"Or if you're not ready for us to be more than friends, or if you're not into me that way at all..." I feel like such a tool for bringing this up now, but I can't bear to wait another minute to put it out there. Almost dying makes you take stock of what's really important, and she's what matters most to me in the aftermath of near disaster.

"Tom... We should talk about this when you're feeling stronger."

"I feel fine."

"I... uh... I'm not sure of anything anymore. I used to make decisions without much consideration, but now?" She shrugs. "I don't know whether I'm coming or going half the time. You're such a good and decent man. You deserve someone who can give you everything you deserve. I'm not sure if I'll ever be capable of that again."

Good and decent isn't exactly an insult, but it lands oddly with me. I want her to see me as exciting, sexy, fun, engaging, intelligent, witty.

Healthy would be good, too.

It becomes clear to me that I'm going to have to start all over with her, which is fine. As long as I'm still in the game, I can work with that.

"I don't mean to pressure you for things you're not ready for."

"You never have, and I appreciate that more than you know. You've been so good to me." She covers my hand with hers. "We talk a lot in my widow group about the new friends who step up for us when old friends are nowhere to be found in the aftermath of disaster. Out of everyone who's been there for me, and that's a lot of people, you've been..." Her eyes fill. "You've been such an incredible blessing."

I'm deeply moved by her words, but they don't tell me anything new about whether we're stuck forever in the friend zone or if this might be something more. But I can't push her, or I'll lose her. That much I'm sure of.

"That's nice to hear, Lex. I'm so glad I could be there for you when you needed a friend."

"I want to do the same for you. When you come home, I'll be there for you."

"I don't expect you to take care of me."

"Why not? You've been taking care of me since the day I moved in."

"You've already been a caretaker."

"This is very different from that. Trust me. I can handle it."

"But do you want to?"

"I'll do whatever I can to help you get back to full health. Knowing that's possible makes this different as night and day from what I went through before."

"I'll have visiting nurses coming in when I get home."

"Then I'll provide company and anything else you want or need for as long as you need it."

"It's important to me that you know I don't expect that of you."

"I know." She smiles, and for the first time since disaster struck, the smile lights up her gorgeous eyes.

I turn my hand over and curl it around hers. "I can't wait to be back at home with you."

"I can't wait for that either."

Seven

Lexi

For the first time in a while, I've been counting the days until the regular Wednesday night meeting of the Wild Widows. I'm usually more of a listener than a talker at the meetings, but this week... This week, I've got stuff to say. My emotions have been all over the place, the way they were when Jim was first diagnosed and then later as I saw him through hospice and the final days of his life.

I hardly welcome the return of wild emotions, even if almost everything about this situation is different than it was then.

I've come to vastly prefer a calm, quiet, peaceful life where my emotions are more of a straight line rather than the ragged ups and downs they've been this week.

Tom is due to be released from the hospital on Friday. He'll be partaking in cardiac rehab and will be closely monitored by his new cardiologist, but otherwise, he's on the road to a complete recovery, which is a huge relief.

Even with nothing but good news coming from his doctors,

I can't seem to shake the overwhelming dread that comes over me any time I recall the scene that greeted me the night I found him in distress. I see him on the floor and break into a cold sweat every time. I try not to think about it, but the memory comes to me whether I want it to or not.

I can't stop thinking about how close he came to dying without feeling as if I'm going to be sick.

It's been three days since that night in the hospital when he told me he has feelings for me that go beyond friendship. And it's not lost on me that the wild emotional outbreak indicates that I probably have similar feelings for him.

Feelings.

I hate that word.

It's so stupid, and so is the song of the same name that my mother used to listen to on repeat when I was a kid.

By the time I get to Iris's house, I'm in a pisser of a mood and ready to let loose about the bullshit that comes with having *feelings* for someone who almost died.

"Hey," Iris says when I come in carrying the buffalo chicken dip I brought to share. "I tried to call you earlier to see how you're doing."

"I got your message, but work was crazy today, and I had to run home before I came here."

"No worries." She takes a measuring look at me. "How are you holding up?"

"Just great."

"Uh-oh."

Brielle, Joy, Roni and Derek arrive, full of chatter, laughter and energy that take some of the piss out of my bad mood. It's hard to be cranky around the most positive, upbeat group of people you'll ever meet. Even after life kicked them in the teeth, they're such an inspiration to me and to one another.

Gage comes downstairs and gives me a one-armed hug. "How goes it?"

"Better now." I take a sip of the wine Iris poured for me. "Much better now."

"Glad to hear it. How's Tom?"

"Good. He's coming home on Friday."

"That's great news."

I nod because it's the best news, but do I dare tell him or anyone how afraid I am of him having another incident when it's just the two of us in the house?

If I say that out loud, I'll give it oxygen, which is the last thing I want to do.

We fill plates, get drinks, catch up, laugh and tease one another. It's a typical gathering of the Wild Widows, who have come to feel in many ways like the siblings I've never had. One thing is for certain—they're among the best friends I've ever had. Don't get me wrong. My longtime friends— most of them, anyway—have been amazing since Jim got sick and died. But several of them disappointed me a long time before I lost him, and they've made themselves scarce since he died.

These people... They're the ones I'd run to in a crisis because I know for certain they'd have my back and know what to do. They always know what to do, which is an amazing resource to have available as a widow.

When we're seated in a circle in Iris's living room, she takes the lead. "Wynter texted new baby pictures to the group chat."

That has all of us reaching for our phones to ooh and aah over baby Willow.

"My God," Roni says. "That is a pretty baby."

Wynter used sperm her late husband banked before his cancer treatment to have his child, and Adrian has stood by her every step of the way despite his fears about something happening to her in childbirth like it did to his wife, Sadie.

"Would you expect anything else with Wynter and Jaden as her parents?" Gage asks, smiling.

"Nope," Roni replies. "She's destined to be a stunner. How's Wynter feeling today?"

"Still sore but elated. The baby is doing really well and sleeping a lot, which is helpful to the exhausted parents. And, of course, Xavier is smitten with his baby sister."

Adrian and Wynter plan to raise their children as siblings, and their little family has made them all so happy.

"I'm so thrilled for them," Brielle says wistfully.

I understand the wistfulness. Adrian and Wynter have been through their own hell losing their young spouses to childbirth and cancer. They've worked hard for what they have now with their children, and I'm thrilled for them. Even still, it can be hard to watch widow friends moving into new happily ever afters, especially when everything is still upside down for some of us.

"Who wants to start?"

Joy raises her hand before I can raise mine, which is fine. I need more wine before I take the floor. "Mama had a second date with *the guy*."

Brielle pumps her fist. "Yes!"

"Easy does it," Joy says with a quelling look that makes Brielle giggle.

"How was it?" Derek asks.

"It was... surprisingly enjoyable. I took y'all's advice and stopped trying to find Craig in him."

Her late husband died in his sleep of natural causes, whatever that means. I don't like thinking about that or knowing things like that can happen, especially considering recent events.

"I'm so happy to hear that, Joy." Hallie takes a seat in the circle, holding a plate and a glass of wine. "Sorry I'm late."

"You haven't missed anything," Iris tells her. "We just started. Tell us more, Joy. What's his name?"

"Bernie."

"What's he do?" Gage asks.

"He's an OB-GYN, of all things." She makes a face that has the rest of us laughing. "Not sure how I feel about him being all up in lady parts all day."

"Eh, you've seen one, you've seen them all," Derek says with a smirk, knowing we're all going to jump on him, which we do. He just laughs and holds up his hands to fend us off.

"As you well know," Roni tells him, "some are way better than others."

He gives her a dopey grin. "You're *so* right about that, love."

The rest of us laugh while they make eyes at each other.

They're so damned cute and happy and in love.

"How do you guys do it?" The words are out of my mouth before I even decide to say them.

"Do what?" Roni asks, brows furrowed in confusion.

"Make it look so easy. You two, Iris and Gage, Wynter and Adrian... Where do you find the courage to try again?"

Derek and Roni exchange glances.

"May I?" he asks her.

"By all means." Roni crosses her arms and smiles as she settles in to hear what her fiancé has to say. They, too, plan to raise each other's children as siblings.

"If I'm being entirely honest," Derek says, "you'd have to be crazy to let yourself fall in love again after what we've been through."

Roni sputters while the rest of us laugh. Clearly, she wasn't expecting him to say that.

"I'm serious. You'd have to be certifiably insane to risk that kind of hurt a second time. But... It's a matter of asking yourself which is worse... The thought of losing this new person you care so much about or living without them for the rest of your life. When you look at it that way, the equation starts to feel a little less bonkers."

Roni stares at him. "How is it possible that makes total sense?"

His smile lights up his handsome face. "Because you get it. You had to make that same decision." He shifts his gaze my way. "We all have to make that decision at some point, and there's nothing wrong with deciding you'd rather not risk it all again. If that's what's best for you, then so be it."

"How do you know what's best?" I ask him.

"All I know is that by the time I met Roni, I was ready for something more than what I had being Maeve's dad and the deputy chief of staff to the president. While those things are wonderful and fulfilling, being with Roni and now Dylan, too, helps to fill the gaping wound that Victoria's death left inside me. I'll always miss her and wish she could see Maeve growing up, but the raw ache of that loss isn't as intense as it used to be."

"Just to add to what Derek is saying," Roni says, "I wasn't in any way ready for him when he came along." They met shortly after she lost her young husband to a stray bullet on a DC street. "That he was willing to wait for me to be ready told me everything I needed to know about who he is and what he's about."

"Thank you both for sharing that." I hesitate before I add, "This has been a tough week with Tom in the hospital and trying to deal with the PTSD his emergency resurrected. It's been a while since I've been in this screwed-up place, and I have to say I don't miss it."

"How is Tom?" Joy asks.

"He's doing much better. Due to come home Friday with cardiac rehab in his future."

"And how are *you*?" Brielle asks.

"I can't stop seeing him unconscious on the floor."

"Those memories will lose some of their sharpness in time," Hallie says.

Her late wife, Gwen, died by suicide, and she was the one who found her, so she knows of what she speaks. She's been seeing Robin, who has stage-four breast cancer. Hallie has been struggling with whether she can cope with being in a relationship with someone who has been given a terminal diagnosis.

"You're right. They will." Memories of things that happened when Jim was ill, things I thought I'd never forget, don't haunt me the way they used to. Likewise, Tom's emergency will fade in time. Intellectually, I know that to be true. In the meantime, however... "I've also learned that faulty hearts are prevalent in his family. His dad and two uncles died prematurely, and his aunt had bypass surgery."

"Oh shit," Derek says.

"That about sums it up. He... he finally came right out and told me he wants more than just friendship between us."

"How do you feel about that?" Iris asks.

"I don't know. I like him. I mean... I was crazy in love with him in high school."

"No, you weren't," Gage says. "You had a mad crush on a guy you hardly knew and who hardly knew you. That's not the same as being in love."

"You couldn't tell that to my desperately-in-love teenage heart. I thought I'd *die* if he didn't notice me."

With a wave of his hand, Gage says, "Teenage drama isn't the same as real life. What does current-day Lexi think about having more with current-day Tom?"

"She doesn't know what to think. On the one hand, he's been an amazing friend to me, and the low-level high school crush never really went away. Years ago, when one of my friends mentioned him, my heart did a crazy little skip at the thought of him, and I was married at the time."

"It's so sweet that you've reconnected with your high school crush," Brielle says, "and that he's stepped up for you the way he has."

"Don't forget, he barely knew I was alive back then. He was older than me and way out of reach. I crushed from afar."

"I've always thought it was tremendously meaningful that

he offered you a place to live with no questions asked," Gage says. "He certainly didn't have to do that for someone he allegedly barely knew back in the day."

"That's true," Derek says. "It was a big deal for him to do that, and I've suspected it had as much to do with him wanting you around as it did with doing a favor for someone who needed it."

"How much do you guys charge for this male perspective?" Joy asks.

"It's free to you guys," Gage says with a wink.

"I appreciate that male perspective very much," I tell them as I process what they said.

"Do you feel better after talking about it, Lex?" Brielle asks.

"I do, thank you. Feel free to move on to someone else's problems."

"But yours are so interesting," Christy says.

"Not as interesting as your barnburner of a new romance," Iris retorts.

"It is indeed a barnburner," Christy says with a goofy smile.

"Tell us everything," Joy says. "Leave out none of the dirty details."

Christy laughs. "The details are very dirty, but I'll just say that I wish I hadn't held out so long with Trey because, as it turns out, I was only denying myself something amazing." Her husband, Wes, died suddenly of an aortic dissection that severely traumatized Christy and her children, who witnessed it. "I still feel guilty sometimes, like I'm cheating on Wes or something, but I'm working through that. He'd want me to be happy, and Trey makes me happy."

"That's fantastic, Christy," Roni says. "How are the kids adjusting?"

"They're becoming more comfortable around him. Shawn teased him the other night about how he uses a spoon to twirl his pasta like he's a fancy pants, or something like that. While they laughed, I had to fight off tears because it felt like a big deal that Shawn said that to him and knew it would be well received. If that makes sense."

"It makes all the sense," Iris says. "That's how strangers become a family—one teasing joke at a time."

"Just ask me," Gage says. "I'm the favorite victim around here. The kids are ruthless."

Iris laughs. "They don't miss much, and you do give them plenty to work with."

Listening to them, witnessing their happy second chapters, and that of Adrian and Wynter, too, fills me with a new *feeling* that might be called hope. If they could find the courage to move forward, especially with children to consider, then surely I can find it in me to at least try with Tom.

"When do we get to meet Trey?" Iris asks.

"I was going to suggest another Mexican night and invite him to come, if that's okay."

"We'd love it," Iris says. "Let's bring the kids, too. Laney has been asking for Maeve and Dylan. They haven't seen each other in a couple of weeks."

"What's everyone doing next Friday night?" Joy asks.

While they make plans, I fully exhale for the first time since I came home to find Tom on the floor. Being with them is always a reminder of how important things like resilience and courage are in the aftermath of loss. I'm at a crossroads with a big decision to make. Who do I want to be in this widow life? Do I want to be someone who hides from anything that can ever hurt me again? Or do I want to risk it all on a second chance at love?

I'm not sure yet which path is best for me, but I'm comforted in knowing that whatever I choose, these special friends will be by my side to make the journey less lonely than it would've been without them.

Eight

Lexi

Tom is released from the hospital on Friday afternoon. I offered to take the day off to drive him home, but he'd already lined up Cora to do the honors. He said he'd see me when I got home from work. I stop at the grocery store and get what I need to make a big salad for dinner with grilled chicken.

That's heart healthy, right?

I need to do some more research to help him adjust to his new lifestyle without some of his favorite things, such as steak.

For now, I hope the salad will be okay.

I'm excited to have him home, as it's been so quiet in the house without him and his music and amusing commentary to entertain me. The quiet reminds me too much of what it was like to continue living in my parents' basement after Jim was no longer there with me. I didn't like it then, and I don't like it now.

Cora's car is still in the driveway when I get there.

I gather the groceries and my work bag and head inside, excited to see him back where he belongs.

Upstairs in the living room, he's in a recliner that must be new or rented since it wasn't there before. He's still paler than usual, and his face is leaner than it was, but he looks a whole lot better than he did the last time I came home to find him in that same room.

His face lights up with a smile when he sees me, and the sense of homecoming is profound. At some point in the last few months, this house has truly begun to seem like home to me, but only when he's there. He's the one who makes it a home, which is an interesting thing to realize when you're expected to say something.

"How was your day, dear?" he asks.

"Boring as usual, but it just got much better. Welcome home."

"Thanks. It's good to be out of that zoo called a hospital. I might actually get more than an hour of sleep at a time."

Cora comes in from the kitchen carrying a steaming mug that she hands to Tom. "Hi, Lexi."

"Hi."

Tom takes a sip from the mug and grimaces. "What's in that?"

"It's herbal tea. It's good for you."

He makes another face that only I can see.

I bite my lip to keep from laughing. "I got stuff to make a salad for dinner."

"Oh joy."

"Welcome to your new life, my friend." Cora checks her watch. "I've got to run to pick up the kids, but I'll check on you later?"

"I'll be here."

Cora leans over to kiss his forehead. "You'd better be."

"Thanks for everything this week."

"No problem. Lydia will be here tomorrow but call if you need anything in the meantime."

He glances at me. "I think we'll be okay on our own this weekend. The doctors said I was doing so well I don't need the visiting nurses."

I swallow hard at the thought of being responsible for him, but I nod for his sake and Cora's. "We've got this."

Do we, though? I mean, he's fine, or they wouldn't have released him, right? A wave of panic threatens to drag me out of the good mood I was in when I arrived. Thanks to tons of therapy during Jim's illness and since he died, I recognize the PTSD reactions, but that doesn't make them any easier to handle when they arise.

Especially with Tom and his sister looking at me as if I've suddenly grown a second head.

"You okay, Lex?" Tom asks.

"I'm good. I'll get that salad going."

In the kitchen, I'm cutting lettuce when my phone buzzes with a text from Iris. *Did Tom make it home ok?*

Yep. He's all settled in, and his sister is about to leave.

Are you ok being there alone with him?

I think so?

Lex! Do you need help? I can come over.

No, no, no. I'm fine. He's fine. It's all fine. Thank you tho. You're the best.

Call us if you need ANYTHING. I mean it.

I will, and thanks for checking on us.

You didn't ask my advice on this... But I think you like him, and I hope you're giving yourself permission to figure out if there might be something to it. I know the living situation makes it more complicated, but don't let that stop you from following your heart, ok?

I'm blinking back tears by the time I finish reading her text. *I won't. Thank you for saying that.*

I'm butting in where I don't belong, but I so so so want to see you find your happily ever after. But only if that's what you want.

You can never butt in or not belong with me, and I wasn't sure I wanted that, but seeing all of you living that happy second act has me wondering what might be possible. We'll see how it goes.

Hang in there and let me know if you need me. I'm right here.

You'll never know what comfort that gives me.

Love you.

Love you too.

As I wipe away a stray tear and put down my phone, Cora comes into the kitchen. "I feel like it's a lot to ask you to be here with him when we can't be. I was planning to stay, but he told me not to bother because you'd be here."

"It's no problem. I'm glad to be able to help."

"Tom told me you lost your husband to ALS. I'm very sorry for what I said the other day. I was way out of line."

"It's okay. You didn't know."

"A neighbor of ours had that. It's a terrible disease."

"It truly is."

She picks up a pen from the counter and writes something on the pad Tom keeps there for when he gets work calls after hours. "I'm leaving you my number. If anything comes up, please call me. I can be here in twenty minutes."

"I will. Try not to worry."

"That's easier said than done. This has brought up a lot of memories from when it happened to our dad."

"I'm sure. PTSD is a bitch that way."

"Definitely."

"The good news is that Tom is on the road to recovery, and history didn't repeat itself." She takes a tentative glance toward him in the living room. "This time."

"What do you mean?"

"It's hard not to be worried about what the future holds for him after this."

Great. Something else to worry about. "The doctors said he should make a full recovery, right?"

"Yes, but they said that about our aunt after her first incident. She dropped dead two years later from the same thing."

This must be how Alice felt when the trapdoor to Wonderland opened under her.

"Lexi?"

It takes half a minute for me to realize she's still talking to me. "I'm sorry. What did you say?"

"I asked if Tom told you about what happened to our aunt after she had the bypass surgery."

"N-no, he didn't."

"It's got to be a lot for you to hear after everything."

All at once, I begin to wonder why she's saying these things. Does she want me out of his life? Is that her goal? Because I'm not sure how to respond, I don't say anything. I simply stare at her without blinking until she looks away.

"I should get going. Call if you need anything."

"We'll be fine."

"Okay, sounds good." She retrieves her purse and keys from the counter and goes to say goodbye to Tom while I remain riveted in place, still processing the information she so casually imparted.

I hear her leave and force myself to get it together, to push the anxiety aside to do what needs to be done for him, the way he'd do for me. I have no doubt about that. He's always doing something for me, even though I've told him he doesn't have to. He says he does things like make my lunch because he wants to, not because he feels he has to.

As much as I loved Jim, and I loved him with my whole heart and soul, he wasn't one for making lunches or cooking meals.

"Lex? Are you still here?"

I take a deep breath, force a smile and return to the living room while the chicken finishes cooking.

The first thing I notice is that the blanket over him has shifted, revealing a pair of tan hospital socks with the grippy bottoms like the ones Jim wore every day of the last two years of his life. I grew to hate those socks and everything they represented. On the table next to him, the collection of prescription bottles is another triggering reminder of days gone by, even if the number is half the quantity of Jim's.

"Hey."

I glance at him.

"Everything okay with Cora?"

"Yeah. All good."

"I hope she apologized for what she said to you the other day."

"You heard about that, huh?"

"Yes, and I hit the roof. I filled her in on a few things she didn't know."

"She was very nice just now. I appreciated the apology."

"I think she was surprised I hadn't told her about Jim's illness before now, but your business isn't mine to share."

"I wouldn't have minded if you told her or anyone else in your life who should know."

"Good to know." He gives me a look that has my skin pebbling with goose bumps. "I missed you when I was in the hospital."

"You saw me every day."

"Never enough."

Post-near-death Tom is much more forthcoming about how he feels. "Why do you look so spooked?" he asks.

"I'm trying not to equate all this," I say, using my hand to encompass the chair, the meds, the goddamned socks, "with the past, but it's hard."

"I hate that I've resurrected painful memories for you. I'd never want to be responsible for that happening. I hope you know that."

"I do. Of course I do." I take a seat on one of the upholstered chairs. "Can I get you anything?"

"Nah, I'm good. And I'm able to get whatever I need."

"I don't mind doing it for you."

"I'm perfectly capable of taking care of myself."

"I know you are, but I'm offering to help you the same way you've helped me when I needed it. That's what friends do for each other."

"Friends don't ask friends who've been traumatized in the past to reopen a wound for them."

"I'm okay. I promise. Have there been some things that bring back upsetting memories? Yes, but I'm coping with that. I want to help you if you'll let me."

"This whole thing just pisses me off. It seemed like you were doing so much better lately, and then this had to happen to screw up everything."

It amazes me that he has had those thoughts about me and my grief journey. But of course he has. That's who he is. He pays attention. "I've been doing better, which means I'm much stronger than I was and able to face things that would've been impossible only a few months ago. I have you to thank for a lot of the healing I've been able to do since I moved in here."

"How so?"

"For one thing, getting me out of my parents' basement where we spent the last few years of Jim's life was huge. Nothing good happened there, you know? We moved in there when it became impossible for me to care for him on my own anymore. I needed their help. Everywhere I looked in that space was a memory of something horrible. You'll never know how much of a lifeline you extended to me with the offer of a place to live."

"That was a somewhat selfish offer, you know."

That shocks me. "What? No, it wasn't."

"Yes, it was. I'm ashamed to admit that I was—and am—quite smitten with you, and the thought of seeing you every day was a huge incentive."

I have no idea what to say to that.

"Something about almost dying has filled me with truth serum or something. I hope that doesn't offend you."

"Not at all." He's never been anything other than a total gentleman with me. "You've been such an amazing friend when I really needed one."

He gives me a playfully stricken look. "Am I stuck forever in the friend zone, then?"

"No, not at all." I stifle my embarrassment to speak my truth. "Do you have any idea what level of crush I had on you back in the day?"

His eyes go wide with shock. "What? For real?"

"God yes. It was pathetic. You didn't even know I was alive."

"That is absolutely not true! I most definitely knew you were alive."

Nothing has ever surprised me more than that does. "You did?"

"Hell yes, but you were so much younger than me. My parents held me back for an extra year going into kindergarten, so I was an almost-nineteen-year-old senior. You were fifteen, so my mom told me I was absolutely *not* going to date someone so much younger than me. But I certainly knew you were there."

"I had no idea. I thought it was the most tragic unrequited crush in history."

"Definitely not."

"Wow," I say with a laugh. "Who knew?"

"I did. I knew. And that night when we met up again for the first time since high school, it was rather amazing to realize I still had a massive crush on you all these years later. You were even lovelier than I remembered."

"As I recall, I looked ridiculous, as I'd just come from the gym to have a drink before going home, and there you were."

"You looked gorgeous."

"Stop it."

"I'm serious."

Finding out he'd been aware of me in high school is a huge shock. I felt like I walked around with a sign taped to my back that said I LOVE TOM HAMMETT in those days.

"What are you smiling about?"

"I'm thinking about how silly I was over you back then. I felt like the whole world had to know I was crazy about one of the most popular guys in the school and how ridiculous I was."

"You weren't ridiculous. I remember you as a very serious student who played the flute and was the cutest member of the marching band."

I cringe. "Said no one ever. Those uniforms were hideous."

"Not on you."

"Stop it."

"I won't stop it. You were adorable. I used to watch for you when the band took the field during halftime when I was supposed to be listening to what the coach was telling us."

"If I'd known that then, I would've literally died on the spot to know you were watching me in that ridiculous uniform."

"You rocked the uniform."

"Now you're just lying to my face."

He laughs—hard—and then winces. "Don't make me laugh."

"Then don't say ridiculous things!"

"Every word is the truth. I swear. I was this close to asking you to the senior prom, but my mother told me I absolutely could not ask a fifteen-year-old."

His confessions have left me breathless. "I was almost sixteen."

"Still. My mom wasn't having it. She reminded me that I was a legal adult, and you were, technically, still a child, and I wasn't taking you to a dance or going to be alone with you in a car. So I didn't go, which made her really mad."

"You're making this up."

"I am not! I swear to God."

"You skipped your senior prom because you couldn't take me?"

"I did."

"Do you have any idea how much time I spent trying to figure out who you went with?"

He laughs again and then groans. "What'd I say about making me laugh?"

"Stop saying crazy stuff, then."

"All true."

"I can't believe any of this. Wait until I tell my high school friends about this. They'll die! They already can't believe we're roommates after the way I carried on about you back in the day. When I first moved in, one of them asked if they should arrange security for you."

That makes him laugh again.

"Whoops. Sorry."

He holds out a hand to me.

I stare at it for a long moment before I reach out to take what he's offering.

"I think that for all this time, I've been secretly waiting and hoping I might run into you again sometime."

"Really?"

He nods. "I've had a lot of girlfriends, but I never got seriously involved with anyone because none of them was you."

"Tom." I release a nervous laugh. "You're medicated. Clearly, you've lost what's left of your mind or something."

Grinning, he shakes his head. "When I heard you'd gotten married, I was heartbroken."

What in the hell am I supposed to say to that?

"People said he was a good guy, and you were happy, which mattered to me. But I was still heartbroken to know I'd missed out on knowing you."

"I have no idea what to say to any of this."

"You don't have to say anything. I'm sorry if I lured you to my house under false pretenses."

"You didn't. I never would've guessed any of this, so you've done a good job of keeping the rest of the story under wraps."

"You weren't ready to hear this when you first moved in, or even a few months ago. I'm not sure when or if I would've told you if I hadn't nearly bought the farm. Now, it just seems silly to keep that kind of secret from you any longer. But," he quickly adds, "I'm certainly not expecting anything to change between us."

Everything will change after this. How can he not know that?

"You've been through a lot. I'd never want to put pressure on you for something you're not ready for, and after what happened this week, I'd totally understand if this is all too much for you."

It is. It's way too much. Didn't I suspect that underneath all the lunches and the dinners and the sweet gestures to make me feel comfortable in my new home that something much deeper than friendship was lurking between us?

Now that I know for sure, I have no idea what to do with the information. High school Lexi would've been doing cartwheels in the front yard at hearing Tom Hammett liked her as much as she liked him. And we didn't even know each other then. Not really. Not like we do now.

Everything I've learned about him in the months I've lived

with him has only reinforced the fact that high school Lexi had excellent taste in men.

"Are you freaking out?" he asks after several minutes of charged silence. "Tell me the truth."

"Not entirely."

"But kind of?"

"Maybe a little? I've been in such a strange place since Jim died. Well, honestly, I've been in that strange place for much longer than that. Probably since he first started experiencing baffling symptoms that didn't make sense until they added up to the worst possible thing."

"I can't begin to know how hard that must've been for you or what you've been through since he died. I know that what happened this week was super traumatic for you. But I promise I'm going to do everything the doctors have told me to do and take super good care of myself because Lexi Nelson is finally holding my hand, and that gives me everything to live for."

"What's in those meds you're taking, anyway?"

He gave a careful chuckle. "It's a relief to finally tell you the truth."

"Does that mean I have to tell you the truth, too?"

"Only if you want to."

I do. I want to. "I sort of knew you were hoping for more."

His eyes widen in surprise. "Since when?"

"Basically since you offered me a room in your house. I mean, who does that out of the goodness of their heart?"

"I did! I swear."

Now I laugh. "I know, but in light of all these confessions, you have to admit you had a tiny bit of ulterior motive."

"Maybe this much." He pinches his fingers together. "But after you told me about having to live in the place where your husband was so ill and where he died, I wanted to get you out of there. That was my top priority in offering you the room."

"It's made such a huge difference in my ability to move on

with my life to get out of that house. Not that I don't love my parents with my whole heart."

"I know you do—and they do, too. What the three of you did for Jim was heroic, but it took a toll on all of you. Remember the first time I met your folks, when your dad and I walked down to the river while you and your mom had dessert?"

I nod. "What about it?"

"He thanked me for what I'd done by asking you to be my roommate. He said it was a badly needed change and that he and your mom really appreciate knowing you're with someone who'll look out for you. Not that you need looking out for, he quickly added. But I knew what he meant. He was glad to see you were with a friend who cared."

I can't believe my normally taciturn dad said all that. "Wow. That's amazing. Thank you for telling me that. Part of me has felt like I abandoned them or something when I moved out."

"They don't see it that way. It's probably a relief for them to see you moving on."

"Yeah, I'm sure it is."

"I want you to know something else that I've already told you once, but I want to be sure you know I mean it."

"What's that?"

"Since you moved in, I've tried very hard to be respectful of what you've been through and what you're continuing to deal with. I'd never want you to think that you owe me anything other than your friendship. If we were never anything more than good friends, that would be fine with me."

"Is that right?"

"Uh-huh."

"You wouldn't be bummed if we were only friends?"

"I'd be super bummed, but you'd never see that."

I'm still holding his hand—or I should say he's still holding mine. "You've been nothing but respectful and incredibly thoughtful and such a great friend. The lunches, the dinners, the coffee... Hell, you even took my car for gas before that snowstorm. That was way above and beyond the call of roommate duty."

"I like doing stuff for you, and I appreciate you doing the laundry and cleaning way more than this house has ever been cleaned before you moved in."

"That's the least I can do in exchange for the room."

"Not sure if you've noticed or not, but we make a pretty good team."

"I've noticed."

"Again, no pressure, no expectations, no need to bite your bottom lip."

I didn't realize I was doing that until he drew my attention to it.

"Nothing has to change, but I feel better that you know how much I care about you."

"I care about you. Just as much. When I saw you on the floor that night..." I shake my head.

He winces.

"I was so scared I'd lost you before I ever got the chance to tell you how much you mean to me."

"I knew."

"How did you know?"

His smile makes his tired eyes twinkle. "Guys know these things."

I give him a skeptical look. "Guys do, huh?"

"Yep." He gives my hand a squeeze. "Seriously, though, sometimes you look at me as if there's something else you want to say, but you always think better of it."

Wow, and not only is he observant, but he's also insightful. "You're not wrong."

"I hope you know you can say whatever you want to me, and I'll always be glad to hear what's on your mind."

"Are you sure about that?"

"I am."

"The mind of a grieving widow isn't always a fun place to hang out."

"I'm interested in anything you want to talk about, even the hard stuff."

"You've got enough on your plate right now without taking on my grief, too."

"I'd like to think I took on your grief months ago. I'm well aware that Jim and the grief over his illness and death are part of who you are now, and I thought I just told you how much I like who you are."

"You've given me a lot to think about."

"Have I scared the crap out of you? Are you already thinking about how fast you can move out of here?"

I love that he makes me laugh. It's been such a long time since I laughed as much as I do with him. "The only thing that scared the crap out of me was when you were unresponsive. Don't do that again."

"I won't."

"How do you feel about salad with grilled chicken for dinner?"

"That sounds good. And healthy."

"We're all about healthy around here."

"That's right."

"You've got to let go of my hand so I can get it."

"What if I don't wanna let go? It took me a long, long time to be able to hold your hand."

"What if I let you hold it again later?"

"Is that a promise?"

"It could be." I'm not sure where this flirty girl is coming from. I haven't seen her in years.

"All right, since you promised, I'll let you go."

Smiling, I get up and go into the kitchen to finish dinner,

thinking about all the things he said and trying to figure out how I feel about them. I'm astonished to know he had a crush on *me* in high school. I can't wait to tell my friends that. They won't believe it. I wonder how my life might've been different if I'd known that then.

But if I had known, I might never have met and fallen for Jim in college. The thought of missing out on him and us is heartbreaking. We had a wonderful five years before disaster struck. They were the best years of my life so far, and I'll never regret them, even knowing what was coming.

Life is so freaking weird. Just when you think you have it figured out...

As I cut up the chicken and toss the salad, I'm not thinking about Jim. I'm thinking about Tom and the things he said and the sincerity I heard in every word. I believe him when he tells me he's cared about me for a long time, even though I didn't know that. *He didn't go to his senior prom because he couldn't ask me!*

Now that I do know how he felt, however, I'm filled with a kind of giddy excitement that I haven't felt in ages. I've been so dead inside, slogging through years of terminal illness as well as Jim's tragic, premature death and the devastating aftermath.

It's such a relief to feel something other than awful. Not even what Cora said about their aunt dying two years after her bypass can bring me down tonight.

I have no idea if anything will come of this new stage of my relationship with Tom, and I'm still seriously unsettled about his health situation, but for right now, today, it feels damn good to feel good again.

Nine

Tom

I hope I didn't make a mistake by laying it all on the line with Lexi. I've had a big wake-up call that time is precious and all that matters is the people we care about.

I care about her. I want to be with her, but only if that's what she wants, too.

It's such a relief that she knows how I feel. Keeping it secret from her all these months has been torturous, but she was extremely fragile when she first moved in. I didn't want to do anything to add to her grief, so I played it cool. I gave her friend-ship, because that's what she needed most.

I don't want anyone to think that I'm a jerk, or that I invited her to live with me with ulterior motives. I knew from the beginning it was possible nothing would come of it because she was in such a difficult place in her life. I offered her the place to live before I even gave it half a thought. I had something she needed, so I made it available to her. I wasn't thinking, *Oh, maybe someday Lexi will be more to me than a roommate.* First and foremost, I was thinking I could make her life easier, so I did.

I'll never regret offering her a place to live. If she moved out tomorrow and said, *Let's just be friends*, I'd be fine with that, even if it would be disappointing. At some point during these last few months of living under the same roof, Lexi's happiness has become more important to me than my own. After hearing more about what she endured during Jim's illness, I know no one deserves happiness and peace of mind more than she does.

I'll never do anything to mess with either of those things, especially in light of recent events. She's probably thinking she'd be crazy to get involved with a guy with a faulty ticker, especially after spending years as a caregiver to her terminally ill husband. She'll probably give it some thought and decide to cut her losses before things get any more intense.

I wouldn't blame her for that. When I think about her coming home to find me laid out on the floor, I cringe. I have no memory of that entire day. I haven't told anyone that, lest they think I'm nuts, but my brain is a total blank. I went through my phone to see what I was doing that day, read texts from customers and employees and was able to unpack most of what went on, but I don't remember any of it.

Doctors, family and friends have asked if I had any symptoms.

I didn't have a single ache or pain, no shortness of breath or any indication that I was primed for a massive heart attack, except maybe being more fatigued than usual. I'd chalked that up to the hectic schedule I keep while running my own business. The lack of a real warning is seriously unsettling. I never got the chance to ask my dad if he had signs that his number was coming due, because he died almost instantly. None of us recalled him saying anything about not feeling well or any changes in his overall demeanor before that day.

It's scary as shit to know that something like this can strike like lightning and end the whole ballgame in the early innings.

Why in the world would someone like Lexi want to risk that when she's already been through so much?

She might want to, but when she has time to consider it, she'd be wise to bail out before it's too late.

That thought depresses me as much as anything has in longer than I can remember. Even nearly dying wasn't as much of a bummer as surviving would be if my future doesn't include her.

I sound overly dramatic, even to myself, but in the years since I fell for her in high school, I've dated a lot of women. I had more first dates than any guy I know. Cora tells me I'm too picky, that I don't give people a chance, and she's right on both counts. I can tell in the first five minutes of a date whether I'm going to want to get to know the person.

Is that fair? Absolutely not, but I can't change how I'm wired. If I could, I'd do something about my cardiac wiring first and foremost.

What my sister will never know is that every one of those first dates was measured against a girl I knew years ago, and they were all found to be lacking in comparison. She's my one. She always has been, and how funny is it that she achieved that status before we ever even had a meaningful conversation?

Some things can't be explained. They just *are*. She's that for me. The night I saw her sitting alone at the bar of a local restaurant will go down in my personal history as one of the best nights of my life. As I took the seat next to her, I told myself to breathe and relax and not be weird.

Easier said than done when the crush of all crushes is sitting next to you for the first time ever.

She did a double take when she recognized me, which was a relief. I didn't have to say, *Hey, I'm Tom Hammett, and I remember you from high school.* Thank God for small mercies.

"Lexi, right?"

"Uh-huh, and you're Tom."

"I am."

"You come here often?" she asked with a small smile.

"First time in years."

"Same."

The coincidence of us being there for the first time in years —at the same time—is something I've thought a lot about since that night. Was it the universe finally getting involved to give me something I'd wanted for a long time?

The bartender came over to ask for my order. "I'll have a Sam Summer and another for the lady."

She put her hand over the top of her glass. "Thank you, but I'm one and done. I have to drive."

"I owe you one, then."

The bartender returned with my beer. I held it up to her.

She touched her glass of wine to my beer bottle. "Cheers."

"Cheers. So, what've you been up to since high school?" I knew she went to college at UVA in Charlottesville and got married shortly after, but it's been a while since I heard anything about her. I'm not on social media, so I'm clueless about people I don't see frequently. After I heard she got married, I pushed my crush into a closet in my mind and closed the door.

"College, marriage, work and now widowhood."

"Oh damn, Lexi. I'm so sorry. I hadn't heard your husband passed."

"Yeah, it was about three years ago now. He had ALS. Four years of hell."

The words were like a punch to my gut. "I have a friend from college whose mother has that. I'm very sorry. It's a cruel disease."

"It truly is."

I had no earthly idea what to say next. "Are you... I mean... You're doing okay?"

She shrugged. "Good days. Bad days. Today was the latter, so I took myself out for a drink after the gym to get a change of scenery. A couple of years after my husband got sick, we moved into my parents' basement because we needed their help so badly. I still live there since neither of us thought life insurance was a priority in our twenties, so... I'm kinda stuck."

I'd had the idea right then and there.

"It's okay, though. My parents have been amazing. They helped us with everything, and I never would've survived it without them—and his family, too, of course."

"I'm glad you were well supported."

"Enough of all that. What've you been up to? Did you get married?"

"Nope. Never even came close." Because I was still thinking about a girl I'd never even talked to back in the day, who looked positively adorable in her marching band uniform. "I own a construction company. We build houses and do some commercial stuff all over NOVA." That's the local abbreviation for Northern Virginia.

"Wait. Hammett Homes. That's you?"

"Yep."

"Wow. Impressive."

That made me laugh. "If you say so."

"I see your signs everywhere. I say so."

"It's mostly a gigantic pain in my ass, but hey, it's a living."

"How is it a pain?"

"How much time do you have?"

"I've got nowhere to be."

"In that case... It's always something going sideways. Materials on backorder, customers in a red-hot rush, employees who don't show up for work or flunk a drug test, permitting offices that take forever, building inspectors who nitpick, people who don't pay their bills... To start with."

"Yikes. Sounds like fun."

"The fun never ends."

"The houses you build are gorgeous. Two of my friends from college who married each other saved for five years to buy in one of your neighborhoods."

"Who was it?"

When she told me their names, I smiled, because they were among my favorite customers. "They're a great couple. I loved working with them."

"They loved working with you, too. They told me about it long after the house was done. It never occurred to me to ask what their contractor's first name was."

What would it have mattered? She was married then.

Hearing she was no longer married had me spun up in a way I didn't often get. I wanted to ask her to dinner. I wanted to ask her to marry me. Haha, just kidding. Sort of.

"So, what's your plan for this next part of your journey?"

She gave me an odd look.

"Is it okay to ask that?"

"Of course, it's just that most people don't ask me things like that. They ask if I miss Jim, or if I'm angry with him for getting sick and dying, or if I'm dating, or if I wish we'd had kids, or a lot of other things that are none of their business."

"I can't believe anyone would ask you those things."

"They do. They *love* to say, 'Thank goodness you didn't have kids.'"

"Stop it."

"True story."

"Oh my God. What the hell is wrong with people?"

"Is that a rhetorical question? I'm especially thankful for my Wild Widows, who keep me from losing it."

"Wild Widows?"

"A group of young widows focused on figuring out what we plan to do with our one wild and precious life, per Mary Oliver."

"So it's like a support group?"

She nods. "That's become a family."

"I love that. Not the reason for it, but that you have each other."

"They've saved my life—and my sanity. Anything that's happening to me has also happened to one of them. It makes you feel less alone with the grief. Young widowhood is very different from the usual white-haired-widow stereotype. We often have most of our lives ahead of us rather than behind us, so it's a unique experience that way."

I was ashamed to admit I'd never once considered how young widowhood would be much different from the older version.

"But to answer your question about what's next in my journey, I'm still trying to figure that out. It took forever to find a job after being out of the workforce for years. If you can call basic data entry for twenty bucks an hour a job, but it's helping me to pay down some of the massive debt we incurred during Jim's illness." She glanced at me. "Do you have life insurance?"

"I do."

"Good. I tell everyone to get it, no matter how young and bulletproof they think they are."

"It's excellent advice."

"It would've made all the difference for me, especially after his illness all but bankrupted us. I'll be paying off medical debt for the rest of my life."

"Our system is so messed up. In what world should an illness like what Jim had financially ruin his family?"

"The world we live in, unfortunately."

"Ready to eat?" Lexi's voice pulls me out of my memories from the night we reconnected. Or I should say *connected*, since we'd never spoken to each other before that night despite our mutual awareness of each other in high school.

I open my eyes and look up at her. "I'm ready."

"Did I wake you?" she asks as she puts a tray on my lap that has a bowl of salad and a glass of ice water.

My days of steak and well-done burgers on the grill are over. "No, I wasn't sleeping. I was thinking about the night we first met up."

She sits across from me on the sofa to eat her salad. "What about it?"

"Just how great it was to see you."

"That night changed my life in so many ways. You changed my life in so many ways."

"Likewise."

She gives me a puzzled look. "How did I change yours?"

"You have no idea how nice it is to have your company around here, do you?"

"Um, well... I guess I hadn't really considered that."

"I thought I liked living alone until you moved in."

"Is that right?"

"Yep. I never wanted a roommate until you said you needed to get out of your parents' basement, and then suddenly, having a roommate was the best idea I'd ever had."

A smile blooms slowly, lighting up her entire face. "You're pouring on the charm tonight, Mr. Hammett."

"No time to waste." The stricken expression on her face has me immediately regretting that I reminded her of my near miss. "Hey, I'm fine, and I'm going to *be* fine. I promise."

As her brows furrow, she pokes at the salad with her fork.

"Lex."

When her gaze shifts my way, I see the torment she's trying so hard to keep hidden from me.

"I'll follow every order from every doctor to the letter. I'll do whatever it takes to stick around for many, many years so I can spend as much time with you as humanly possible."

Ten

Lexi

Long after I'm tucked into bed with the door open in case Tom needs me during the night, I'm still thinking about him following doctors' orders so he can spend as much time with me as "humanly possible."

High school Lexi would've been writing *Lexi + Tom* in her notebooks with hearts all around it if Tom Hammett had said such a thing to her. Hell, she'd done that without having exchanged a single word with him.

Widowed Lexi had learned to be guarded and cautious about allowing people to become too important, especially people with a potentially faulty heart. I simply couldn't bear to lose another person I love. And yes, I love Tom. While being an amazing friend, he's also given me an up close and personal view of what a relationship with him might be like.

I appreciate that he hasn't put an ounce of pressure on me for more than friendship. It took a health crisis for his true feelings to emerge, and now that I know how he feels, I can't un-hear it or un-know it. Not that I'd want to.

Being with him gives me a warm, cozy vibe. He's begun to feel like home to me, and not just because we live under the same roof.

Once upon a time, Jim was home to me, so I know what it's like to find that in another person.

Allowing my relationship with Tom to turn romantic would take a massive amount of courage, especially after his heart attack. What if he has another one? What if I wake up one day and he's dead in bed next to me? That happened to Joy. Her perfectly healthy husband died in his sleep. Tom isn't perfectly healthy—not anymore. He intends to be again, but is that a realistic goal?

I understand that if I allow myself to fall in love again, one day—hopefully when we're old and gray—I may find myself in a caretaking role again. What I can't fathom is doing it again any time soon.

My stomach aches when I think about losing Tom, which is when I realize it's already far too late to protect myself from grief where he's concerned. If anything happens to him, I'll be as devastated as I was to lose Jim.

"Goddamn it," I whisper into the darkness. "When the hell did that happen?"

Slowly. One pot of coffee, one lunch, one dinner, one animated conversation after another. He's worked his way into my heart with his kindness, generosity, thoughtfulness and companionship. He's made me feel less alone with my grief, even if we rarely speak of Jim, his illness, our marriage or any of the hard stuff.

Is it too late to text Iris?

Probably not. She's a night owl.

What do you do when you find out a guy wants more with you than friendship and you think by saying no you're protecting yourself from more grief, but then you realize it's already too late for that kind of protection where he's concerned? Or when you find out he had such a crush on you in HS and that he DIDN'T GO TO HIS SR PROM bc he couldn't go with you bc you were too young (according to his mother)??!?

If anyone will understand this dilemma, it's Iris, who's been through it herself with Gage.

I see the bubbles that indicate she's typing and wait breathlessly for what she has to say.

First, holy SHIT on the prom and the mutual crush. That makes me feel like you two were fated or something. The rest of it is a conundrum for certain. If you walked away before anything more happened, you'd wonder "what if" for the rest of your life. If you stay, you'll worry about lightning striking twice—and not in a good way. There's no easy way out of loving someone.

God, if she didn't sum up my quandary in one simple paragraph.

I'm mad at myself for not realizing it was too late to run for my life until it was too late to run for my life.

She responds with laughter emojis.

It's not funny!

It's kinda funny. The rest of us could see that you were falling for him, but you didn't see it yourself?

Not really. I had him firmly in the friend zone because that's all I was capable of at the time.

And now?

I DO NOT KNOW!

Yes, you do—and that's the problem.

I hate you right now.

HAHAHAHAHA.

I don't really hate you (said out of fear of ever losing my Iris).

I know you don't—and no need for fear. I'm right here where I'll always be.

Widows know better than to make promises like that, but she also knows what I need to hear.

It's okay to care about Tom, Lex. He seems like a fantastic guy, and he's been so good to you as a friend. That's a nice place to start.

What about his faulty ticker?

What about my breast cancer? What keeps Gage here after that?

I don't like to think about her cancer scare.

Hint—he decided he'd rather be with me for whatever time we have together than to be without me. Look at what Adrian just endured during Wynter's pregnancy, having to dread every day that the same thing would happen to her as happened to Sadie.

Adrian's wife died hours after delivering their son, Xavier.

When you put it like that...

Everything is a risk. Allowing all of you into my life after losing Mike was a risk. Not only did I fall in love with the best group of friends I've ever had, but I also took on your grief and you took on mine. But I wouldn't trade my Wild Widows for anything.

Neither would I. I have no idea where I'd be if it weren't for you guys.

Same. I like your Tom. I like how he stepped up for you without wanting anything in return other than your friendship.

After he told me about his HS crush on me... What I would've done for that info back in the day!

If you'd known that, you might've missed out on loving Jim.

I thought of that, and I wouldn't have wanted to miss him.

Things happen the way they're meant to, or so I'd like to believe.

I guess so. Everything just feels so BIG when I think about an actual relationship with Tom.

Forgive me for saying this, but you've been in a relationship with Tom almost a year already. You're just thinking about making it official at this point.

Why do you have to be such a smarty-pants?

LOL. My curse in life.

More like your gift. Thanks for chatting so late.

No problem. Gage is sound asleep, and I was reading.

You two give me courage...

Aw, that's sweet of you to say. It hasn't always been easy, but it's worth it. I promise. Jim would want you to be happy, right?

Yes, that was his most pressing concern after he was diagnosed.

Then you need to give yourself permission...

Trying.

Sending you love and hugs.

Thank you for always knowing what I need most.

You've got this, Lex. I have faith in you!

Sleep well.

You, too.

Not sure how I'll ever sleep with all these thoughts running around in my head. My heart is beating so fast, I worry that I might be having my own cardiac incident.

Now that I know how he feels about me, it's harder to deny that underneath the friendship, something else has been simmering, waiting for me to be ready for it.

I think about Roni falling for Derek not that long after her husband was killed. She was nowhere near ready for him and held him off until she was, while he stood by her side as she prepared to welcome her late husband's baby. They're another example of two people who've been through the worst and found a new life with each other.

Iris and Gage, Adrian and Wynter... All around me are examples of people who had every good reason to stay hidden behind the cloak of their grief. But in every case, they chose to live again rather than hide from the pain.

I want to be courageous like them.

I like what Iris said about Gage choosing to spend whatever time they have left with her, even knowing there's a chance he could lose her prematurely.

Even if Tom had never had a heart attack, there's no end to the list of things that could befall him on any given day. Oddly enough, that thought brings me a measure of comfort.

If I've learned anything from Jim's illness and death, it's that living life to the fullest means managing the pain of loss. There's no escaping it. I like the saying I learned from my widow friends that life is a fatal illness, because none of us is getting out of here alive.

I take a deep breath and release it slowly, comforted by the reminder that we're all going to die eventually. Some of us will get much less time than others, which will never seem fair or just, but there's nothing we can do about that other than appreciate each day for the gift that it is.

As I turn on my side and try to find a comfortable position, I close my eyes and hope for sleep, so I won't be a wreck tomorrow. While sleep remains elusive, all I can think about are the things Tom said to me. I hear the words in his voice, and I smile.

Life doesn't come with guarantees. I know that all too well. But I want the same thing he does, and as soon as the time is right and he's feeling better, I'll tell him so.

Tom and I spend the entire weekend together. We laze around watching movies and relaxing after the stressful week. We don't talk any more about serious stuff for now, and I get the sense that he's processing it all, the same way I am. I have no doubt we'll discuss it again when we're ready to.

Cora and her family are in and out between soccer games on Saturday, and Lydia and Rick come by on Sunday morning for a last visit before they return home to Minnesota.

They bring fresh berries and bagels with cream cheese for breakfast.

The four of us sit around Tom's dining room table for an

hour, chatting about everything other than what brought them to town before they get up to leave for their noon flight out of Dulles.

Lydia hugs Tom for a long time, and when she pulls back, she has tears in her eyes. "Don't do that to me again, you hear me?"

"I hear you."

"Thanks for saving his life, Lexi," Lydia says when she hugs me.

"Happy to help."

Tom gives me a sweet smile when I say that.

He shakes hands with Rick, promises to talk to them soon and then waves them off when they leave in their rental car.

"Phew." Tom comes slowly up the stairs to the living room, where I've settled with a fresh cup of coffee. "That's one less supervisor to put up with around here."

"She loves her baby brother."

"And I love her, but she's a lot." He settles in the recliner and turns to face me. "Not that I blame her for that. She had to step up to help with me when our dad died, so it became almost second nature for her to mother me."

"It's very sweet how much they care about you."

"It is. Don't get me wrong. I'm very thankful for both of them, but I'm also fiercely independent, so having them hovering over me for days has been stressful."

"I get that. You just want things to return to normal."

"Yes, that's it exactly, and I want them to leave us alone so we can hang out without them in the middle of it."

My face heats when his meaning registers. He wants to be alone with me, without fear of his sisters popping in. "What do you think is going to happen, tiger? You're only a few days removed from a heart attack and stent procedure."

He flexes his considerable biceps. "I'm feeling stronger every day."

"All well and good, but you're not doing a single thing to exert yourself until you're medically cleared."

"You could do all the work."

"Tom!"

His laughter is cut short by pain that makes him groan. "You're not supposed to be making me laugh."

"Then quit saying outrageous things."

"How is that outrageous?"

"Behave. You're still recovering, and all you're going to do is sit in the chair and watch movies. If you're very good, I may even allow some football later."

"What would constitute being very good?"

This new flirtatious side of him is all new to me, and I can't deny I'm enjoying sparring with him, even if I'm still a little frightened about where it's heading. The thought of having sex with someone who isn't Jim has been overwhelming since it first became clear that his life would be cut short, and I'd be forced to go on without him.

"Earth to Lexi, come in, Lexi. I need to know how I'm going to earn some football around here."

"By relaxing and resting and not talking about things that aren't going to happen today."

He gives me a sweet, tender look. "But they may happen at some point? If I'm very good?"

"Tom..."

The footrest on the recliner drops so suddenly that it startles me. He gets up and comes over to sit next to me on the sofa. "Lexi."

"Yes?"

"You're beautiful and sweet, and all I think about is kissing you."

"That is not all you think about!"

"It really is." He reaches out to caress my face, and the soft swipe of his fingers over my skin sets off a body-wide reaction.

Tom Hammett wants to kiss me. From deep inside the recesses of my soul, teenage Lexi is doing handsprings.

"How is that possible when you're recovering from a health emergency while continuing to run your company?"

"It's a problem, as you can imagine. There are other things I should be thinking about, but every thought in my head is about you."

"That sounds like a serious problem."

"It's very serious, and it might be good if we just, you know, kissed or something so I could start thinking about something other than how much I want to kiss you."

I'm very much aware that everything will change if I lean in to give him what he wants. And let's be honest, I want it, too. But do I want everything to change? Do I want to cross that invisible line between friendship and romance, knowing that once it's done, it can never be undone? In the "before," a kiss was a simple thing between two people who were getting to know each other. In the "after," it's so much more complicated than that.

I lean in ever so slightly, no more than an inch closer to him.

He does the same, leaving less than an inch between us now, his piercing blue eyes conveying a wealth of emotion and affection, all of it directed at me. "It's gotta come from you, Lex." His voice is gruff and sexy. "I'll never push you for anything you're not ready for."

"I have coffee breath."

His huff of laughter breaks the tension that's built to concerning levels inside me. "Ask me if I care."

"Do you care?"

He shakes his head. "Not about coffee breath. About you? I care very much."

"I haven't kissed anyone since Jim."

"I know, and I get that it's a big deal. If you're not ready, that's totally fine."

"Is it?"

His gaze shifts to my lips. "Yeah, it is. You're the boss. We're on your timetable."

"I want to kiss you."

Now he's looking into my eyes again. "You do?"

"Yeah."

"Like, um, now?"

"Now would be good."

"Your move, sweetheart."

I appreciate, more than he'll ever know, that he's left the ball completely in my court, which proves that he not only understands what a big deal this is for me, but he respects my right to decide when and where and with whom. I place my hand on his face, and his eyes close as he seems to absorb the impact of my touch, as if it's something he's longed for.

I call on every bit of courage I can find to close that final inch that stands between friendship and romance. Every minute we've spent together runs through my mind like a beautiful story that's played out one meal and one cup of coffee and one conversation and one laugh at a time. This man has been there for me. He's made my life easier and better by offering me a place to be when I needed one so badly. But more than that, he's given me himself, time and time again, with no pressure or expectations or anything other than exactly what I needed.

Nothing is certain in this thing called life. Our time together could be brief, or it could span decades. No one ever knows what they're going to get ahead of time, and even knowing what I do now about his family history and the near miss of his heart attack, I want to be with him.

I touch my lips to his, giving him the lightest brush of lip against lip.

He sucks in a sharp deep breath, and his eyes open, as if he doesn't want to miss a second of this. "Lexi."

"Yes, Tom?"

"Do it again."

This time when I press my lips against his, I linger, taking in the sensations that course through me from the barest of caresses.

His left hand joins the right one on my face, tipping my head to improve the angle as he takes over, sliding his lips over mine.

Like a spark landing on dry tinder, I'm a wildfire of emotion and need as the feeling of desire comes back to me in a tsunami. I'd forgotten what it was like to want this, to need it, to crave it.

I curl my hand around his neck and part my lips, inviting him to take more.

"Lex. Are you sure? You're okay?"

"I'm okay. Are you?"

"I've never been better in my whole life than I am right now."

That's a pretty great endorsement for a girl who hasn't been kissed in years. I give a gentle tug to bring him back to me.

This time, our mouths are open, his tongue is teasing mine, and I'm completely lost to him.

I'm not sure how or when we end up stretched out on the sofa, arms wrapped around each other as we kiss like two people who've been separated for years and have finally come back together.

Should he be doing this? Not even that thought can convince me to stop the loveliest thing that's happened to me in a very long time. I trust Tom to know his own limits, and judging by the way he's kissing me, he's not thinking about limits. I lose track of time and place and everything that isn't his lips and tongue and the way his hand slides down my back to cup my ass and pull me in tight against his erection.

That's when I come to my senses. "Tom."

"Lexi."

"That's enough."

His groan against my neck sends shivers down my spine as he kisses every bit of skin he can reach. "Not enough."

"You shouldn't be worked up this way."

"Never felt better."

"Tom."

He sighs as he rests his head on my shoulder. "I knew it would be like that with you."

"Like what?"

He keeps his head on my shoulder when he says, "My whole life, I've heard people go on and on about how crazy they were about their spouse or girlfriend or boyfriend or whatever. I've never experienced that. For me, it was always kind of transactional. Sex is fun, so let's have sex and have fun. I never understood why people made such a big deal about it. But that... with you... Now I get it."

I feel like I've been wrapped away in storage or something, waiting to be wanted and needed this way again, and now that it's happening, I'm set free of the worries and fears that have kept me from taking this next step with him before now. I wrap my arms around him and hold him close while we try to catch our breath.

"I hope it's okay to tell you that."

"It's very okay."

"I used to think I was crazy for thinking about a girl I never even knew back in school, knowing you were married and off-limits. Now I know there was nothing crazy about it except for how right I was back then."

"I never stopped wondering about you, even after I was married. I was afraid to ask about you because it felt dangerous to go there. But I thought of you."

"I can't believe I'm finally holding you, that I got to kiss you and that it was the best kiss of my whole life."

"It's pretty surreal."

"I'm going to want to hold you as much and as often as I can for, well... ever."

"Easy does it. While you're recovering, we're not getting worked up like that again."

"I'm already worked up like that again."

"Tom! Stop."

His snort of laughter makes me smile.

"I read that people who have sex after a heart attack are less likely to die than people who don't."

"You're making that up!"

"I'm not. I swear to God. There was a study over twenty-two years or something that proved it."

"I'm going to need to see that."

"I'll send you a link."

"Excellent."

"Have I been good enough to earn some football this afternoon?"

"I suppose so, as long as you keep your hands to yourself and your heart rate down."

As if I've issued a challenge, his hand travels up from my waist to cup my breast and tease my nipple. It feels so good that I want to purr, but then I remember why he shouldn't be exerting himself this way. "That's it, mister." I give a careful push to move him so I can escape from the sofa before I forget why we can't do everything right this minute.

"I'm so glad I didn't die before I knew what it was like to kiss Lexi Nelson."

Eleven

Tom

I'm exhausted, but I don't want to sleep while Lexi is stretched out next to me on the sofa while we watch a movie. She insisted I relax all day, which is what I've done, but my mind is anything but relaxed as I relive the hot kisses that've kept me on edge ever since.

I've waited so long to be close to her. In some ways, I feel like I've waited most of my life for this chance, and of course, it happens after I have a heart attack that has me at about fifty percent of my usual energy and fitness levels.

Timing, they say, is everything. Without the heart attack, we might've gone on as we were indefinitely as friendly roommates who did nice things for each other and spent quite a lot of time together but were stuck firmly in the nothing-romantic zone. Not that there was anything at all wrong with that. I've loved every minute I've spent with Lexi. It's just that I've always suspected we could be something special as a couple.

Now I'm sure of it.

Kissing her was the best thing ever, but then, I knew it would be. However, here's the thing... It was *way* more than I expected. Kissing is almost always pleasant and fun and leads to all sorts of good things. But kissing *her* was different. It was like a full-body experience, like sex would be with someone else. Not that I've thought about sex with anyone but her since the night we connected in that bar. My friends with benefits were immediately forgotten the minute I saw her sitting on the barstool next to me.

Now that I know about her high school crush, I believe that night was fated. How else to explain two people who yearned for each other years ago meeting up in the same place at the same time when they were both free to finally have their first conversation and anything else that might follow?

It was fate. I'll always believe that.

Just like it was fate that I asked her to move in and then she was the only person due home when I was fighting for my life on the living room floor. Without her as my roommate, I wouldn't still be here.

"Do you believe in fate?" I ask her.

"What?"

I twirl a length of her curly hair around my index finger. Now that I'm allowed to touch her, I don't ever want to stop. "You heard me. Are you a believer?"

"I mean... I guess so? Are you?"

"I am now."

"What do you mean?"

"I've had a lot of time to think this week, sitting still for the first time in a while, about how if fate hadn't brought us together that night in the bar and I hadn't asked you to move in with me, I'd be dead right now."

"Tom... Don't say that."

"Why not? It's true. You saved my life. If you didn't live

here, I'd have been long gone by the time anyone realized I was in trouble."

"I can't even think about that."

"It was fate, Lexi. We're fated. Everything has been leading to this for both of us, even the bad stuff. Without that, you wouldn't have needed a new place to live. I wouldn't have had any reason to offer that to you. I'd have been living alone when I had a heart attack. It would've been game over if fate hadn't brought you into my life when it did."

"I suppose all of that is true, but do you think it was prearranged by the universe or something?"

"I've never been a super religious person, but I do believe there's something at work here that's bigger than us."

"Maybe it's Jim. He was so worried about what would become of me after he died, especially because his illness created such a massive debt for me. He suffered over that."

"I'm sure he did. It must've been hell for him that he couldn't do anything to fix that for you."

"It was. I often think it was the worst part of it for him, knowing he was leaving me with a huge mess to clean up."

"Have you spoken with a debt counselor? There're consolidation loans and stuff like that. You might also be eligible for some federal relief programs."

"You think so?"

"You won't know if you don't ask. I have a guy who's savvy about this stuff. I'll hook you up with him."

"Wow, that'd be amazing. I've sort of accepted that I'm going to be in debt for the rest of my life, which is fine because I wouldn't have done anything differently. I wanted Jim to be as comfortable as possible. My very last thought at the time was the cost."

"I get that. I'd be the same way for someone I loved. Whatever it takes."

"Back to your original question, it wouldn't surprise me to learn that Jim arranged for us to meet up. He was adamant about me doing whatever it took to be happy and to have a meaningful life. That was all he cared about the whole time he was ill. Even after he couldn't talk anymore, he would look at me, and I would know what he was thinking because it was so important to him."

"That's a precious gift to give the person you're leaving behind, the peace of mind to know you'd approve of them having a new life with someone else."

"It is. Some of my widow friends don't have their late spouse's implicit blessing because they died suddenly without ever having had those conversations. They can only presume that their late person would've wanted all good things for them."

"I'd always want that for you, just so you know."

"Stop. I refuse to have a contingency plan for you not being around."

"It just seems practical to mention it."

"It's not practical. It's morbid. You're fine, you promised me you're going to be fine, and that's all we're going to say about it."

She makes me smile even when I'm being morbid. "Is that your final word on the matter?"

"It is, so don't go there again."

I'm in love with her.

That thought strikes like lightning from above, electrifying me with the realization that, for the first time in my life, I'm truly in love.

As I watch Lexi walk into the kitchen to refill my ice water, I now know that no one else would've done it for me the way she does. Lying on a sofa with her and watching a movie is more exciting than anything I've ever done with another woman.

If Lexi walked away from me, I'd never forget her.

I'll do everything I can to make sure that never happens.

Lexi

TODAY HAS BEEN LIKE A DREAM. An entire day to laze around with Tom, watching movies, eating healthy food and experiencing the ever-present hum of desire for the first time in years. I'd forgotten what that was like, to know something is going to happen with a man and that it's only a matter of when.

His words from earlier have stayed with me all day: *I'm so glad I didn't die before I got the chance to kiss Lexi Nelson.*

Swoon—and hello, don't talk about dying! I can't bear to think of what a close call he had. It makes my hands shake and my knees go weak.

If he hadn't recently had a heart attack, I would've wanted to take those kisses to their logical conclusion, which is a startling thought for a widow to have for the first time since her husband died.

I haven't had sex in more than five years and haven't wanted it even once in all that time. Until Tom Hammett kissed me and reawakened me to things from another lifetime. Once upon a time, Jim and I had sex almost every day. We had incredible chemistry, and sex was a big part of our relationship, along with many other things that made our life together so fulfilling. He loved to go antiquing as much as I did, which I used to tease him about as I dragged him along on another weekend adventure to some random place to look at old dusty shit, as he liked to call it.

We enjoyed finding a treasure and bringing it back to life. Most of that stuff is long gone after we were forced to sell our home and most of our possessions to pay for his care.

I haven't thought about our antiquing adventures in ages. It makes me sad that my first thoughts of him are always the sick version and not the vital, active, funny man he was before disaster struck.

"What're you thinking about?" Tom asks.

While I was on a trip down memory lane, the movie ended. He switches the TV over to local news because he wants a sports update. As his roommate of nearly a year, I've learned he's obsessed with all the DC-area teams, and that's the only reason he ever watches the news.

"A lot of things," I say in response to his question.

"Anything you want to talk about?"

"Today was a really nice day."

"Yes, it was. Thank you for letting me watch hours of football. You took one for the team."

"I enjoyed it. I haven't watched it in years. I don't want to say I missed it or anything…"

"Haha, lest you have to watch it all the time?"

"Something like that."

"Today was a great day for me, too. I love being in the same room with you, but sharing the same sofa is way better."

Our legs are intertwined, and his arm is around me. I wasn't sure if it was okay to rest my head on his chest until he insisted I do so. "Nothing hurts," he assured me.

"I like snuggling with you."

"Lexi," he says on a long exhale. "I *love* snuggling with you. In fact, the more I do it, the stronger and healthier I feel."

That makes me laugh. "Now you're just being shameless."

"I'd prefer to think of it as truthful. I want you to know how I'm feeling so you won't have any doubt about how important you are to me."

"You've been showing me who you really are from the first night we met up and every day since then."

He reaches over to caress my face before he gently touches his lips to mine. "All I can think about is kissing you again. I have no idea what just happened in that movie or whether the Commanders won or if it's even still Sunday."

His words go straight to my heart. "You know the Commanders won."

"That was very low on the list of cool things that happened today, and a Commanders win is never low on my list of priorities, except for when you're snuggled up to me and filling my head with so many other thoughts."

"What other thoughts?"

He turns on his side to face me, but his fingers continue to glide over my face, setting off fireworks inside me. "Things you're not ready to hear."

"Maybe I am."

"I'm trying so hard to be respectful of how hard it's been for you to even think about starting over with someone new."

"You've been nothing but respectful, and just so you know, I haven't given the first thought to starting over with anyone but you."

He grins. "Don't say stuff like that. My fragile heart can't handle it."

I playfully scowl at him. "We're not talking about your heart being fragile."

"My apologies. I won't let that happen again."

I can tell he's surprised when I place my hand on his face and lean in to kiss him. "No more until you're better."

"But kissing you makes me better."

"Sure it does."

"No, really. I haven't felt as good as I do right now since it happened."

"You need to rest and relax, not get yourself worked up."

"I'm talking to my cardiologist about this tomorrow."

"He will tell you that you need to wait six to eight weeks after the stent procedure."

"That's not true. Where did you see that?"

"I checked online while you were napping earlier."

"I need to see this for myself."

"I'll send you a link."

"There's good news and bad news."

"Huh?"

"The good news is you were looking up how long we need to wait to have sex. The bad news is that it's six to eight weeks. I don't think I'll make it that long now that I know how great it is to kiss you and hold you." He nuzzles my neck and sets off more pyrotechnics inside me, making me wonder how I'll last that long either.

"There's more good news," I tell him. "The same site said that kissing and snuggling and hand-holding is fine, as long as we don't put any strain on your heart. And it said that you should be the passive partner at first."

His whole body goes taut. "Oh my God, the images that just flashed through my mind nearly gave me another heart attack."

"Tom!" I sputter with laughter, even though it's not funny. "Cut that out."

"Sorry, but it's true. The thought of Lexi Nelson 'tending to me' is the hottest thing I can imagine."

"Lexi Nelson is seriously out of practice, so don't get too excited."

"Too late. I'm already excited."

I tell myself not to look, but I can't help it.

Gulp.

"Is that good for your heart?"

"My heart has never felt better than it does right now." He takes my hand and places it over the bulge in his sweats that extends all the way to his abdomen. Holy moly. Tom Hammett is huge.

Like a kid set loose in a candy store, I want to feel every bit of him, but then I regain my sanity and pull back my hand.

He groans loudly.

"I'm so afraid of doing something to set back your recovery."

"Leaving me in this condition will set me back."

"It will not."

"Yes, it will."

I feel like I'm discovering a whole new side to him since our relationship moved from friendship to romance. This flirty, sexy version of him is chipping away at any defenses I had left where he was concerned.

"I should get to bed. Back to work tomorrow." Nothing can ruin a mood faster for me than thinking about the job I hate.

"Come sleep with me. Snuggling is good for my recovery."

I want to. God, I really want to, but I'm so afraid of him overexerting himself. "Not tonight. Let's save that for when you're back to full strength."

"I promise I won't get worked up."

That makes me laugh. "That's an empty promise."

"It's far from empty, as I just demonstrated."

I give him a gentle nudge to let me up, even though the last thing I want to do is end this perfect day.

He releases me, and I get up, straightening hair that has become a wild nest of curls from lying around all day. I offer him a hand up.

"I'm only accepting your help because I want to touch you, not because I need it."

"Noted."

When he's standing, he brings my hand to his lips. "Sleep well."

"You, too."

"I'd sleep much better with you tucked up against me."

"No, you wouldn't."

"Yes, I would."

"Wouldn't."

"Would."

Our "argument" continues as I go into the kitchen to put dishes in the dishwasher and set up coffee for myself for the morning. Since artificially stimulating his central nervous system and heart rate is inadvisable, he's off coffee for the time being. I feel for him and all the changes he has to make to keep his heart healthy, but I believe him when he says he'll follow every order given to him, except the one about sex, apparently.

Fortunately, one of us is thinking somewhat clearly on that front.

"I want to sleep in a bed tonight." He's spent the last few nights in his recliner.

"I'll walk you to your room." My room is over the garage, which is a different set of stairs from where his bedroom is.

"You don't need to."

"Yes, I do."

"All right, then."

He takes the stairs slowly, which is a reminder that he's not ready for any of the things he thinks he is. "God, this fucking sucks. I hate being feeble like this."

"Just keep telling yourself that it's temporary."

"I don't want you to see me like this."

"Tom, come on. I'm not judging you."

"I'm judging myself and coming up short. I hate putting you through another medical ordeal after you've already had a lifetime's worth."

"Please don't worry about it. All I care about is that you're on the mend, and in a couple of weeks, you'll be back to full strength."

While he uses the bathroom, I put his phone on the bedside charger, turn down the bed and fluff his pillows.

I tuck him in with a kiss.

"Are you sure I can't entice you to stay?" he asks hopefully.

"I'm sure. I might be gone when you wake up in the morning, but I'll check on you during the day, okay?"

"I'll look forward to that almost as much as I'll look forward to you coming home."

Smiling, I smooth the hair back from his forehead. "Today was a great day. The best day I've had in years. Thank you."

"Thank *you*. It was the best day I've *ever* had, other than the feeble part."

"You're not feeble. You're recovering from a heart attack. That doesn't make you feeble. It makes you human."

He continues to play with my hair. "I don't like it."

"Yes, you've mentioned that."

"I've hardly been sick a day in my whole life."

"You've been incredibly lucky. A few sick days won't kill you but overdoing it before you're ready just might. So don't do that. We don't want any setbacks."

"Right. No setbacks. So the website really said six to eight weeks, huh?"

"It really did, and if you read the instructions they sent home from the hospital, you'll find it says it there, too."

"You're a real buzz killer, you know that?"

"Grumpy Tom is cute Tom."

"I'm not grumpy."

"If you say so." I kiss him once more and get up to leave. "Call me if you need me during the night."

"What if I need another kiss?"

"Don't call me for that."

"Fine."

"Fine. Good night, Tom."

"Good night, Lexi. I miss you already."

I can't stop smiling as I go downstairs, shut off the lights and then go up another flight of stairs to my room over the garage.

My smile dims when I realize how far I am from him. What

if he really does need me during the night? When he slept in the recliner, he was located at the bottom of the stairs to my room. Now he's a whole house away from me.

Shit.

I change into pajamas, brush my teeth and bring my phone with the alarm set for the morning with me when I return to his side of the house.

He's scrolling through his phone when I appear in the doorway. "May I help you, ma'am?"

"It occurred to me that I'm really far from you over there, and if you needed something, it would take me a minute to get to you, and worrying about that will keep me awake."

"I believe I tried to tell you that."

I walk into his room and go to the far side of his king-sized bed. "No, you tried to tell me you needed me tucked up against you while you sleep, which isn't going to happen."

He watches me with keen interest. "What is happening, then?"

"I'm sleeping over here, and you're sleeping over there, and there will be absolutely no touching. Do I make myself clear?"

"Unfortunately, yes."

I bite back a laugh. He's so grumpy!

I settle myself into his comfy bed and pull the covers up to my chest. When I glance his way, I find that he's turned on his side to look at me.

"What?"

"Lexi Nelson is in my bed. You can bet your ass I'm going to enjoy this."

"Shut the light off, Tom."

"Not yet, Lexi. I need a few more minutes to commit this to memory."

I roll my eyes at him.

"By the way, the pajamas are adorable."

I have to think for a second about which ones I'm wearing.

Ah, right, the ones with the calico cats on them that Jim gave me years ago for Christmas because they reminded him of the cat we had to rehome when we moved in with my parents. We couldn't risk him falling over her, which was another heartbreak in a series of them.

"What just made you sad?"

"You're supposed to be sleeping."

"I can't sleep when Lexi Nelson is sad."

I love the way he uses my full name. "Jim bought me these pajamas because we had a cat who looked like the ones on the print."

"That's a sweet memory. Did it make you sad to think of it?"

"No, it made me sad to remember how we had to rehome our cat because we were afraid he might trip over her because she loved to be underfoot."

"Aw, Lex, I'm sorry. That must've been so hard."

"She was the first pet either of us ever had that was entirely ours, so it was heartbreaking to let her go. Luckily, she went to our friends, who brought her to visit us as often as they could. But it wasn't the same."

I haven't thought about Lola in a long time, and recalling the moment when I knew she had to go is as searing today as it was then.

"What was her name?"

"Lola."

"Is she still alive?"

"She died a year to the day after Jim did."

"Ugh, that's rough, sweetheart. I'm so sorry."

"Thank you." I look over at him. "Grief is such a bitch sometimes. Here we are having this perfectly awesome day, and you made a perfectly innocuous comment about my pajamas, and it brings back a whole bunch of stuff that still hurts."

He reaches across the bed to me.

I meet him halfway, and he links our fingers. I appreciate that he offers comfort rather than platitudes or any of the dumb shit people say to grieving people that makes us want to smack them.

"If I could have my way, nothing would ever hurt you again for the rest of your life."

"That's a very sweet goal."

"I'll do everything within my power to make it happen."

Twelve

Wynter

I can't stop staring at my daughter's perfect face.

I have a *daughter*. And she looks exactly like her daddy. At first, that was a huge shock. It wasn't like I didn't know that was possible. It was just hard to believe how much she resembles Jaden. His mother and I have talked about it a few times, how it's both the most amazing thing and the most difficult at the same time.

That's grief for you, always an asshole even at the best of times.

To look at my sweet Willow, you'd never know my DNA was included with his. My mother said she's him all over again.

Adrian comes into the nursery that we lovingly put together for her in what used to be the spare bedroom at his house. He's wearing only the formfitting boxer briefs that still make my mouth water with desire for him long after I first saw him wearing only them.

We were like bunnies in the weeks before Willow's birth. Pregnancy made me super horny, and Adrian was more than happy to oblige. Normally, the sight of him in nothing but those briefs (or even better—nothing at all) would get my motor running. But nothing like that is happening any time soon as I contend with stitches and other horrors after giving birth.

Hemorrhoids, for one thing.

What a nightmare! But hey, childbirth is the most natural thing in the world. My ass, it is. I'll never complain about anything having to do with Willow's birth, though. It ended with a healthy baby and mother, which are all that matter after Adrian lost his wife, Sadie, immediately following the birth of their son, Xavier.

"You're still up?" he whispers.

"Can't drag myself away."

"You're supposed to sleep when she does."

"I know, but I don't want to miss anything."

"Wynter, you have to get some sleep. Our little girl will need you to be well-rested. Let me put her in the bassinet."

I don't want to, but he's far more experienced with newborns than I am, so I hand her over to him.

"Come to bed."

"I'm coming."

I follow him into our room and watch as he tucks our sleeping girl into the bassinet that he used after Xavier was born. It feels weird to leave her uncovered, but I remind myself that she's wearing the equivalent of a blanket and will be fine. We were told to put nothing at all in the bassinet, to keep her safe while she's sleeping. Jaden's grandmother crocheted the most gorgeous blanket for her that I'm saving for when she gets a little older.

"Now, Mommy," he whispers as he guides me to my side of our bed and tucks me in. "Can I get you anything?"

"Just your arms around me."

"Coming right up."

I bite back a laugh at the frisky way he says that.

He gets in on his side of the bed and comes right over to me. Knowing how sore I am, he's careful when he puts an arm around me. "Is this okay?"

"Mmm, yes. Thank you for everything you've done to make this transition so easy for me."

"Watching you in mommy mode has been among the most exciting things in my whole life. I never got that with Sadie and Xavier."

"Is it making you sad all over again for what she missed?"

"I'll always be sad about that, but the joy over our sweet girl —and the relief that it's over and everyone is okay—outweighs the sadness."

"You were a trouper, love. I'm so proud of the way you overcame your fears to be there for me."

"I'm not sure I deserve that."

"You absolutely do. You never left my side for more than a few minutes the whole time I was in labor, and you treated me like a queen when I was pregnant."

He kisses my cheek. "You *are* my queen."

"Love you so much."

"Love you more."

"Nope."

"Yep."

It's still amazing sometimes to be in a bed with Adrian as his son and now my daughter are asleep under the same roof. I wonder where Jaden has gone, and I know Adrian still looks around, expecting to find Sadie. Life has marched forward since we lost our spouses almost two years ago, and now we have this whole new life together that's made us both so happy, even as we continue to mourn the ones we loved and lost.

"I can't get over how much she looks like Jaden."

"How do you feel about that?"

"I love it. I really do. It's just sort of... I don't even know how to describe it."

"The other day, Xavier made a face that was all Sadie. It was one of her trademark expressions that just appeared out of nowhere and flattened me for five full minutes. It was the craziest thing."

"You never mentioned it."

"You've been a little busy, babe."

"Still, you should've told me."

"It was a good thing. Everyone says he looks like me, but for that brief moment, he was all her, and I loved it once it stopped hurting like a bitch."

"Yeah, that's it... I love that she looks like him, but it hurts, too. Makes me miss him even more than I already do. He'd be flipping out over her, and he'd *love* that she looks like him."

"After seeing some of your Jaden videos, I can almost picture his reactions to her. I'm sure he'd be flat on his face in love with her the way we are."

"Thank you for loving my little girl."

"She's our little girl, and I'll always love her the way you love Xavier. He's so happy to have a baby sister."

"Life is so effed up and crazy and also beautiful and amazing, isn't it?"

"It sure is. Since you proved to me I have nothing to worry about with you and pregnancy and childbirth, we should have one together."

I groan as he laughs. "Talk to me about that when I can pee without wanting to scream from the pain."

"Will do."

"Look at you, conquering your fears and living your best life."

"Thanks to you and our babies. Love you so, so much, Wynter."

"Love you, too, Adrian."

. . .

Lexi

I HATE my job with a fiery passion. It's so boring! All I do for eight straight hours—with half an hour for lunch—is enter data into spreadsheets. I have no idea what the numbers mean or how the information is used by the organization. They don't include me in any of the meetings at which they crunch the data I import to make decisions. That's fine with me because I don't care what they do with the information.

I don't even understand the mission of this place. Something about connecting companies with qualified contractors or some such thing.

Whatever. I do my job and collect a much-needed paycheck every two weeks. Other than one woman who's become a sort-of friend, I barely talk to anyone over the course of a day, which is fine. I'm not looking to make more friends.

My boss, Erika, is nice enough, but I don't have much contact with her, except by email when she forwards the daily reports from which I gather the data that's then inputted into the spreadsheets. If I never see another spreadsheet, that'll be fine with me.

Earbuds are essential to my sanity. I listen to podcasts and music, which help me survive the long days. I think I've listened to every grief podcast in existence, which is both helpful and depressing at times. Whatever it takes to pass eight hours of drudgery, even if I'm sobbing at my desk. No one pays any attention to what I do, so I'm free to sob as needed.

I'm three hours into what promises to be another endless day because I'm tired after waking up every few minutes—or so it seemed—to make sure Tom was still breathing. He was fine, but I'm an anxious wreck. Worrying about him has triggered me. I decide to lean into it and let it be what it is until he's back to full health. After that, if the anxiety is still an issue, I'll reach out to the therapist who was so instrumental in getting me through Jim's illness and death. I haven't seen her in quite some time, which she says is a good thing. It proves I don't need her the way I once did.

Erika startles me when she suddenly appears in my cubicle. I haven't seen her in two weeks, so I'm taken aback.

I remove my headphones. "Hi."

"Hey, Lexi. Could I see you in the office for a minute?"

What the hell? I haven't been in her office since she interviewed me. "Um, sure." I save my work, because God forbid I should have to redo any of it and get up to follow her.

"Close the door."

After I close the door and take a seat in one of the chairs in front of her desk, she lets out a deep sigh.

"I'm sorry to have to tell you that we're facing budget cuts due to missing our targets for the last two quarters, so we're laying you off. Your medical insurance will be covered for three more months, and you'll receive a month's salary as severance. You'll also be paid for all your remaining vacation and personal days." She hands me two pieces of paper. "One of those pages outlines all your remaining benefits and compensation. The other is a reference I wrote for you. Please feel free to have any prospective employers call me. I'll be happy to recommend you."

I'm in shock. I've barely heard anything she said after "laying you off." I hate the job, but I need it. Badly.

"Lexi... Are you all right? I feel terrible about this."

When she called to offer me the job, I told her that I was a widow and there might be times when I seemed off. I wanted her to know why.

"I hate to do this to you on top of everything else..."

"It's okay." I want out of there before I lose my composure, so I tell her what she needs to hear. "I'll be fine."

If there's a silver lining, I'll never again have to spend eight hours putting numbers into spreadsheets that mean nothing to me.

A soft knock on the door sounds.

"Come in."

One of the guys is standing there with a box in his hands. I can't remember his name. We met on the first day, and I hadn't seen him since.

"Justin has packed up your desk and will walk you out."

I've heard of this kind of thing happening to other people, but until it happens to me, I don't understand how demoralizing it is that they don't trust me to pack up my own desk or to not be destructive on the way out.

I'd have to care to do something like that. I get up, take my box from Justin and brush past him on my way to the exit. I don't need him to show me the way since my favorite part of every day I've spent there is when I leave.

It's just as well, I tell myself as I walk out the main doors and head for my car. I hated every minute of that job, but it served the purpose of helping me make enough to pay down some of the debt.

At least they gave me severance and health coverage for a while, which is a relief.

For a long time after I stash the box in the passenger seat and get into the driver's side, I sit there and stare straight ahead, absorbing the latest blow.

What now?

It took months of applying for every job I could find to get this one, and as much as I hated it, I didn't want to lose it. Before Jim got sick, I was a third-grade teacher. By the time he died, the thought of supervising twenty eight-year-olds all day had lost its luster. Truth be told, it'd lost its luster long before Jim's diagnosis.

My phone buzzes with a text from Brielle. *Single ladies... Are we still on for dinner tonight? And, Lex, how is Tom doing?*

Brielle, Naomi, Hallie, Joy and I get together on our own sometimes, separate from the other Wild Widows who are in new relationships. We jokingly call ourselves the holdouts. I've been the biggest holdout with almost three years since Jim died without so much as a date.

Although, they argue I've been on a months-long date with Tom since I moved in with him, complete with romantic candlelit dinners most nights. I denied that emphatically, but now I'm not so sure. They may be right.

Almost losing him has shaken me out of my years-long stupor to be reminded once again that life is short, and we must live every day to the fullest. Being with him makes me feel good, and that's the best possible reason to make myself ready for him after feeling like total shit for so long. He's like a breath of much-needed fresh air in my life.

Tom is doing well, I respond. *Can I let you know later if I can make it? I want to make sure he doesn't need anything.*

Fine by me, Brielle says. *Usual place and time. Hope to see you!*

We go to the same Mexican restaurant every time—and every time, we talk about how we need to broaden our horizons, but then we end up back there the next time. Joy says there's no reason to tempt fate when we're happy where we are.

That reasoning applies to more than just the restaurant.

Why tempt fate, indeed. Like we don't have enough heartache without inviting in more.

Although now that I've lost my job, I have much bigger concerns than whether I have the guts to fall in love again. The massive debt isn't going anywhere, and being out of work for any length of time simply isn't an option.

I start the car and head for home, bringing the unsettled feeling with me, but glad I can be there for Tom while he recovers. His sister was going to stop in today to check on him. Hopefully, I'll have another job lined up by the time he's ready to get back to work.

When I arrive at Tom's, his truck is in the garage, and there are no other vehicles in the driveway. I hate the slight trepidation I experience as I grab the box of my work things and go inside, hoping to find him sitting in the recliner and not passed out on the floor.

As I come up the stairs to the living room, I notice his chair is empty. "Tom?"

"In here."

I follow the sound of his voice to the kitchen in the back of the house. "What're you doing?"

He's wearing sweats and a T-shirt, and his hair is wet from a shower. "Making a smoothie."

"I can do that for you."

"I've got it." He glances over his shoulder, his gaze settling on the box I'm carrying. "What're you doing home so early?"

"I got laid off."

His face falls with dismay. "Oh shit, Lex. I'm sorry."

I shrug. "At least I never have to look at another one of their spreadsheets again."

"There is that. Are you okay?"

"I will be. A little freaked out about the financial implications, but they gave me severance and three months of health insurance before they escorted me out, so it could be worse."

"I'm sorry that happened."

"Did you take a shower when you were home alone?"

"Maybe."

"Should you be doing that?"

"I'm fine. I swear."

"What if you weren't fine in the shower while you were home alone?"

My anxiety immediately spikes to the danger zone.

Seeming to sense that, he crosses to me and puts his hands on my shoulders. "I'm okay, Lex. Are you?"

"I, um... I came home once to find Jim had fallen in the shower. He... he hit his head and couldn't get up on his own. He was there for about three hours by the time I found him. The water had gone cold, so he was... He had a concussion and hypothermia."

"God, Lexi. I'm so sorry I did something to remind you of that."

"Y-you didn't. I just... I don't want something like that to happen to you."

"It won't. I promise. If I didn't feel strong enough, I never would've done it. I don't want to end up back in the hospital. Believe me." As he gathers me into his warm embrace, I realize I'm trembling from the memory of Jim's fall. That was when we realized we could no longer live by ourselves.

And then I wonder if maybe I'm trembling because Tom is holding me the way a lover would, and after the way he kissed me and held me yesterday, it's clear we'll be lovers before too much longer at this rate. Every nerve in my body is attuned to him as I breathe in the clean, fresh scent of his body wash.

"Hold on to me, sweetheart. I've got you."

Every muscle in my body has gone tense, so it takes a second to relax and give in to the comfort he's offering.

I'm not sure how long we stand there wrapped up in each other before we hear a car door closing outside and reluctantly separate.

He stares at me. "I, um... That felt good. Really, really good."

I can only nod.

"Let's do that again soon, okay?"

"Um, okay."

"Are you all right?"

"Yes. Thank you."

"You don't have to thank me for doing something that felt so good."

"Tom—"

"Morning!" Cora comes up the stairs carrying grocery bags, unaware that she's walking into an emotional firestorm.

At least, that's what it is for me.

"What are you doing home, Lexi? Thought you were working today." She starts unloading her bags. "Is everything okay?"

Tom glances at me as if he's uncertain whether he should tell her my news.

"I got laid off."

Cora stops what she's doing and turns to me. "Oh no. I'm so sorry."

"Thanks. I'm trying to see it as a blessing in disguise. I hated the job."

"Who do we know who's hiring?"

"Oh, that's okay," I tell her. "I'm going to take a second to figure out my next move."

"But surely we know someone."

"Cora," Tom says, "ease up. Lexi needs a minute to catch her breath."

"Of course. I'm sorry. It's the mom in me. I see a problem, and I want to fix it."

"Which is very kind of you."

"If you want me to pass on some leads to you, just let me know. Between all of us, we know a lot of people with businesses who are always looking for good help."

"I'll keep that in mind. Thank you."

Cora shifts her focus to Tom. "You look better today."

"I feel better."

"I'm so glad to hear that."

I don't know her very well, but even I can see that she's wound tighter than a drum and running off adrenaline after her brother's near miss. I can't imagine what kind of trauma his incident has resurrected in each of them after losing their father in a similar fashion.

Good old trauma, always in there, waiting to remind you that you're powerless against memories you wish you could forget forever.

"I'll be home until at least dinnertime," I tell Cora, "if you have other things you need to do today."

"I could use a day at home," Cora says. "My house is a disaster."

"Go ahead," Tom tells her. "We're fine."

"I bought ingredients for power bowls full of kale and quinoa and other things that are heart-healthy."

"Yummy," Tom says with a grimace. "Kale. My favorite."

I laugh at the face he makes.

"I know," Cora says. "It's gross but good for you."

Tom gives her a kiss on the cheek. "Thank you for everything. You've been amazing. But you can exhale. I'm going to be fine. I'm going to eat the kale and the quinoa and all the other good things to stay healthy so I can drive you all crazy when I'm a hundred and two and losing my teeth."

Cora laughs even as her eyes fill with tears. "I'll hold you to that."

Tom hugs her. "I have no doubt you will. Go home. Clean your house. Take a deep breath. Everything is okay."

"Fine. Be that way." She wipes tears off her face. "If you do this to me again, I'll never forgive you."

"I hear you."

Cora squeezes my arm. "Thank you for everything."

"I haven't done anything."

"Yes, you have. You saved his life, and we'll always be grateful to you for that."

"Oh, well... I'm glad I was here when it counted."

"We're all thankful for that." She grabs her purse and her

cloth grocery bags. "Okay, I'm gone. Call me if you need anything."

Tom walks her to the door. "We won't need anything but a visit after you've taken a few days for yourself."

"If you don't check in, I'll worry."

"I'll check in. Now go. Get out of my hair."

She smiles, kisses him on the cheek and walks out the door.

"Sheesh." After he waves her off, he comes up the stairs, taking them one at a time rather than two at a time the way he usually does. "I thought she was going to move in for a minute there."

"You're lucky to have her and Lydia."

"And I know it."

"I wish I had siblings. I feel like everything would be easier if I did."

"In some ways, it is. In others, it's a pain in the ass, but I'm always thankful for them. Never more so than this week."

"You need to be thankful for them all the time."

"I know." He smiles. "What do you feel like doing with this unexpected day off?"

"I have no idea."

"You want to go for a ride? I'm feeling a little stir crazy, and I need to take a look at a couple of job sites."

"You're not cleared to go back to work yet."

"I won't do anything but look."

"In that case, let's go for a ride."

Thirteen

Tom

I'm so glad to be out of the house. I put the window down to let in some fresh late-autumn air and let the sunshine warm my face. I keep thinking about what Lexi shared about Jim falling in the shower and ending up with a concussion and hypothermia after being stuck there for three hours.

What a nightmare for both of them.

I hate that I brought that memory back to the surface for her.

But I don't hate that I got to hold her, to comfort her, to be close to her again. God, it feels so good to hold her. She's so soft and sweet and gorgeous. It's all I can do not to stare at her when she's in the same room. I never get tired of looking at her or talking to her. She does it for me. She has for as long as I've known about her.

It was amazing to me how feelings I had more than twenty years ago were still there the first time I saw her again. Those feelings have only grown stronger as I've gotten to know her. In the past, she was a dream girl, a fantasy. In the nine months that she's lived with me, I've learned that the reality of her is way better than the fantasy ever could've been.

I love talking to her and getting her witty take on whatever subject we're covering. She always has something interesting to say or a facial expression that makes me laugh or want to cry when her grief surges to the surface. I'd do anything to take that ache away for her, but it's something she'll carry with her forever because she loved Jim so much. I'd be lucky to have her love me like that, and I know it.

I direct her to Fairfax County, where my company is constructing a new office building that's about half done and running a month behind schedule. We've recently ventured into a few commercial projects, and I already regret taking them on in addition to our booming home-building business. The last thing we needed was for me to go down with a heart attack at this crucial juncture. Fortunately, I have outstanding employees who are able to pick up my slack while I'm out of work. But I want to see for myself that things are progressing in my absence.

"Take the next right."

After she makes the turn, I direct her to the site in the back corner of a large business park.

"There it is."

"Wow. That's huge."

"Six stories."

"I can't believe you know how to build something like that."

"It's not that hard once you figure out the basics."

I direct her to park outside the trailer that serves as our on-site office and then text my foreman Ryan to come out.

With a hard hat tucked under his arm, he comes out of the office and down the stairs, smiling as he approaches the passenger side of Lexi's car. "Hey, boss. Good to see you out and about."

"Good to be seen."

"How're you feeling?"

"I'm still fine from when you asked me that three hours ago."

Ryan, who's tall, muscular and in his early thirties, grins. "Sorry. You gave us a scare, man."

"It's all good. This is my friend Lexi. Lex, this is Ryan, one of our foremen."

Ryan bends at the waist so he can see her in the driver's seat. "Nice to meet you."

"You, too."

"Things are looking good here," I tell him.

"Much better than a week ago."

"Thanks for taking on more than your share. I appreciate it."

"No problem at all. I'll keep you posted."

"Thanks, man."

Ryan waves as he walks toward the building under construction.

"So I thought you did homes. Thus the name Hammett Homes."

"Ninety percent of our business is houses, but we've taken on some commercial projects in recent years. I've been thinking about getting out of that sector, though. It's nonstop challenges from start to finish. I've grown to hate it."

"Then you should quit doing it. Maybe that's why your heart revolted."

"Wouldn't surprise me. The stress level on this one has been off the charts."

"That's not good for you."

"I know, and I'd been thinking about making some changes before the ticker incident. I have this one and two others in the works. After that, I'm stepping away from the commercial sector."

"Sounds like the right call."

"It is. I don't enjoy it the way I do the home building. That's much more fun, working with clients to pick out all the finishes to create their dream house."

"That would be fun. I love watching design shows and mulling over what I'd choose from among the various options. Most of the time, I wouldn't go with any of the things those designers like."

"I'm not much good with making those choices, but we have an awesome design team that walks our clients through the process."

"That would be a dream job."

He glances over at me. "They're always looking for help in that department if you're interested."

"What? No. I couldn't do something like that. I have zero training or skills."

"They would train the right person."

"I'm not the right person. I've never done anything like that in my life."

"But you know what you like, right?"

"I do, but I'd have no idea how to advise someone else on what they want."

"That's the thing. Most of them are looking for someone else's opinion to get them started, and then they take it from there."

"I'm sure the professional designers would be thrilled to have someone who knows nothing about their field working with them."

"You could have a conversation with them. That wouldn't hurt anything."

"I get what you're trying to do, Tom, and I appreciate it. But they'd hate having to hire the boss's friend."

"I still say it's worth a conversation."

"And I still say thank you for caring, but no. I'm not doing that. I'll find something that works for me, and this time, I won't settle for the first thing that comes along. Now that I know how soul-crushing it is to be in the wrong job, I'm going to hold out for the right fit."

"That's the way to be."

"After Jim died, I was so frantic about the enormous debt that I took the first job I was offered. I've learned since then that debt isn't going anywhere, so it doesn't matter if it takes a minute to find a fulfilling job rather than one that simply pays the bills."

"I'm sorry you were left with that burden. I'm not sure if I've ever said how much I admire what you did for him."

"Don't make me the hero of that story. He was. I did what anyone would do for someone they loved."

"Not anyone. I know people who put ill relatives in facilities the first second it gets to be too much for them. Hell, we did that with my mom when she started showing signs of dementia. None of us could give her the care—and supervision—she needed because of work and family demands. We felt sick about it but needed her to be safe."

"I've learned that people generally do the best they can in situations like that. You did the right thing for your mom, even if it felt terrible."

"Moving her in there was the second-worst day of my life. She was still cognizant enough to realize what was happening, and she begged us not to leave her there. It was horrible. All we could think of was how much she'd done for us after our dad died. She worked two jobs so we could have everything we needed, and now we were putting her in a home. I can't even think about that day without wanting to wail."

When we're stopped at a light, Lexi looks over at me and puts her hand on top of mine. "I'm so sorry you had to do that, but you know it was the right thing, don't you?"

"Yeah, but that didn't make it any less hellish at the time. She declined very rapidly after that and doesn't know us anymore, which is a blessing in light of recent events. Hearing I'd had a heart attack would devastate her after losing my dad that way."

She looks back at the road but keeps holding my hand. "She probably would've declined rapidly no matter where she was."

"We'll never know that for sure."

"I'm sure the mother who loved you so much wouldn't want you to feel guilty for doing what you felt was right for her at the time."

"She wouldn't, but I can't help feeling that way. My sisters do, too. We felt like monsters, even as we made sure she got the best care money could buy."

"Where does she live?"

"In Herndon."

"Do you want to go see her?"

"Like, now?"

"I'm not doing anything. Are you?"

"It's okay, Lex. We don't have to do that."

"I honestly don't mind. I'd love to meet her and for you to have the chance to see her, if you'd like to, that is."

"It's never easy to see her."

"I understand. Whatever you want to do is fine with me."

I think about it for a second, weighing whether I have the emotional energy to see my mother today. I don't, but then again, I never do. "I think I'd like that, if you're sure you're up for it."

"I'm up for it. Show me the way."

Lexi

IN TRUTH, I'm nervous about seeing Tom's mom, but I'd never say so to him. I want him to have the opportunity to see her, especially after what he's been through in the last week. But

I can feel the tension in him from the second I suggested the visit. I know all too well how difficult it is to witness the decline of a loved one, so I feel for him and his sisters. He's mentioned before that his mom has dementia, but he doesn't dwell on her situation, so I haven't asked about it.

"You know," I say to him after a long period of silence, "what you're feeling toward your mom in her current condition is a form of grief. Even though she's still living, you've lost the person she once was to you."

"Yes, that's true. It's been the most difficult thing in my life. She was such a life force, and dementia has reduced her to a shell of her former self."

"That has to be agonizing for you and your sisters."

"It has been."

"I'm so sorry, Tom." I feel guilty for focusing our entire friendship on my grief without realizing he was dealing with his own—for both his parents.

"Don't be sorry. I don't talk about it because it's easier not to."

After a long pause, I say, "May I speak freely?"

"Of course. You should know that by now."

"This is a tender topic, so I just wanted to be sure."

"I'm here for whatever you want to say—any time."

"Over the last few years since Jim died, I've delved pretty deeply into grief and how it works and how to manage it. I've learned so much from people who've been at it longer than me and have suffered greater losses than I have."

"Every loss is a great loss."

"True, but my friend Gage lost his wife and twin daughters to a drunk driver."

"Damn."

"Yeah, he's like our Yoda. We look at him and think, if he can do it, so can we, you know?"

"I can't imagine surviving a loss like that."

"Neither could he until he had no choice. He posts daily thoughts on grief on Instagram, and it's required reading for most of us."

"I'd love to check that out."

"I'll send you a link. What I really want to say is that by not talking about it, you're possibly making your journey harder than it needs to be. There are so many people out there who'd totally relate to what you and your sisters have gone through with your mom—and with losing your dad so young. I'm not saying you have to seek out strangers, but talking about it helps to make it a healthier experience, if that makes sense."

"It does."

"But?"

"No buts. It's just that talking about them and what happened to them is so painful."

"I know, but that's kind of the point. Giving life to the pain helps to lessen it."

"Does it really?"

"It does. Before I joined the Wild Widows, I was so deeply mired in the loss of Jim, the devastation, the injustice of it all. I couldn't see a way out. I hated talking about him and his illness and everything we'd endured for four horribly difficult years. I'd basically locked it all away inside, and I've come to see that was killing me. They've shown me how important it is to talk about it with people who understand what you're going through and how light can be found, even in the deepest darkness."

"That's really profound."

"It took me a while to believe it could work, but I've seen it change people's lives. My friend Wynter was twenty when she lost her husband to bone cancer. They'd been married for four days when he died, but together for years. She was the angriest, most bitter person you'd ever want to meet when her mom first insisted she attend our meetings. She didn't want to be there and didn't even try to hide that from us. But we stuck with her—and she stuck with us—and now she's a totally different person than who she was then, even if her heart is still as broken as it ever was over the loss of her Jaden."

"They were so young."

"I know. She's a trouper, though, and seriously one of the funniest people I've ever met. At first, I honestly thought I wasn't going to like her because she was such a pain in the ass. Now she's one of my favorite people ever. The night of your incident, I was coming home from visiting her in the hospital after she gave birth to her daughter with Jaden."

"Oh wow."

"She found out a year after he died that he'd banked sperm before his cancer treatments. He didn't tell anyone about it. His parents found the paperwork in his things."

"That must've been one hell of a surprise."

"Totally. She was shocked and immediately intrigued by the possibility of having his child. At the same time, she was caring for our widower friend Adrian's young son, Xavier. His wife died right after she gave birth to Xavier. Now Wynter and Adrian are together and raising each other's children as a family."

"That's amazing. I'm so happy for them. They were part of your moving crew, right?"

"They were all there that day. They're the best friends I've ever had, and I think each of them would say the same. We love our other friends, but our widow friends... They're the ones who put us back together, you know?"

"I can see that. I'm so glad you have each other."

"So am I. I can't imagine where I'd be without them and their courage or optimism. You can't be around them for long without being inspired by their stories."

"Before I connected with you, I never once gave a thought to the young-widow experience."

"Why would you? Most people are lucky to not know any young widows."

"One of my college friends lost his wife a few years ago to breast cancer. They had two little kids."

"How's he doing?"

"I'm not sure. I haven't seen him since her funeral."

"You should reach out to him. I'm sure he'd love to hear from you."

"He wouldn't think I'm an asshole for not reaching out before now?"

"Probably not. If I had to guess, he'd appreciate that you're thinking of him and wanted to check in. People tend to run away from disaster, which can be a lonely proposition for the people left behind. Jim and I had so many friends before he got sick. When things got really bad, we found out who among them were our true friends. Many of them disappeared, never to be seen or heard from again."

"That's lame."

"It is, but I get it. People can't handle it. They see something horrifying happening to someone and run from it out of fear of it happening to them."

"I'm sorry that happened with your friends."

"I was so bitter about it until my widows said the same thing happened to them and explained why. When people don't know what to do, often they do nothing."

"I've been guilty of that with my friend, but you're right that I should reach out to him, and I will."

"And you'll talk about your own grief? It doesn't have to be with me, but you should talk about it with someone. It's not healthy to keep it all bottled up inside."

"Would you mind if I talked about it with you? That wouldn't make your own grief harder to handle, would it?"

"Nah, it'd be fine. Sharing the common experience can help to lighten the load for both of us."

"I've found it so difficult to talk about what happened to either of them. When my dad first died, my mom tried to get us into therapy, but none of us was willing. We couldn't conceive of talking to a stranger about him. With hindsight, I wish she'd made us."

"It was a different time. People didn't talk about grief the way they do now."

"I suppose that's true."

"It's never too late to air it out, Tom. You've been carrying it around for a long time."

"For sure. Can I tell you something strange?"

"Sure."

"A few days after my heart attack, I remembered something that must've happened when I was out of it."

"Okay..."

"He was there. My dad."

"What?"

"While I was in the hospital, I woke up in the middle of the night with the memory of how I'd seen him and how it only could've happened when I was out of it. I know it sounds crazy, but he was there."

"Wow. Did he say anything?"

"He told me to go home, that it wasn't time yet."

"Tom. Oh my God."

"I've been afraid to say anything about it because it sounds nuts—even to me."

"What a gift, though. Are you able to see it that way?"

"Definitely, even if I was a bit spooked when I first remembered it."

"Anyone would be. I wonder if it was really him in spirit form or if it was a dream."

"It seemed different from a dream. I'm not sure how to describe it, but it wasn't like a dream."

"Will you tell your sisters?"

"I'm afraid it'll freak them out to know how close I came to joining him."

A huge lump settles in my throat as I realize the same thing he's trying to protect his sisters from. "Thank goodness he sent you back," I say when I'm able to speak again.

"I'm sorry. I shouldn't have told you that."

"No, I'm fine, and I'm glad you told me."

"When I'm not thinking about you and wondering when I'll get to kiss you again, that's all I've thought about since it happened."

My entire body goes warm at the thought of kissing him again, and I wonder if he can see it in my face. I feel like I'm awakening from a long slumber. I'm tingling in places that've been asleep for years.

Fortunately, we arrive at his mother's care home, and the cool fresh air helps to settle me.

As we walk inside together, his hand lands on my lower back. "I'm sorry if the flirting unsettles you. I can't seem to help it."

"It doesn't unsettle me."

"Are you sure?"

I force myself to look at his handsome face. "I'm sure."

He stops short of the main door and turns to face me. "Then what is it?"

"I'm feeling... things... that I haven't in a long time, and whenever that happens, it comes as a bit of a surprise to me because I'd forgotten what it was like."

"What kind of things?"

I say the only word that comes to mind to adequately describe it. "Desire."

He takes a step toward me. "Lexi."

"Later."

"No, right now."

"Tom..."

His deep sigh says it all. "To be continued."

Fourteen

Lexi

The smell of the place reminds me of a rehab Jim was in for a time while we were still trying to figure out what was wrong with him. From the start, he feared ALS, but one doctor after another told him not to jump to conclusions until they knew for certain.

He was sure of it a long time before they finally confirmed it.

Tom checks in at the reception desk and gets guest passes for us. As we walk toward his mother's room at the end of a long hallway, he casually reaches for my hand, as if that's something we do every day. Maybe it will be.

"Remember that she won't know me. It can be upsetting, even for people who don't know her."

"I understand." At least, I think I do. Thankfully, I don't have much experience with dementia.

He knocks softly on the door before he enters a bright, cheerful space with one bed, a TV mounted on the wall, family photos in frames on another wall and a view of a garden that must be lovely in the summer. His mother is seated in a comfortable recliner chair, looking at the TV, and doesn't react to our arrival.

Tom releases my hand and moves into her line of vision. "Hi, Mom. It's your son, Tommy, and I've brought my friend Lexi to meet you."

His words sear me. Imagine having to introduce yourself to your own mother.

"My son passed away."

"No, Mom, that was Dad. I'm still here."

"No, Tommy died."

I can't bear this for him, so I step forward. "Hi, Mrs. Hammett, I'm Tommy's friend Lexi. He brought me to meet you."

She takes a careful look at me and then shifts her gaze back to him. "Tommy didn't die?"

"No, Ma, I'm right here."

She begins to cry.

When he gets down on his knees to comfort her, my heart is completely lost to him. If a man is judged by how he treats his mother, he gets an A-plus.

"Tommy, I want to go home."

"They take such good care of you here."

"I hate it here."

"I know, Ma."

"What's your name?"

"I'm your son, Tommy."

I ache for him. It's unbearable, but he's nothing but patient with her as he answers the same questions over and over.

A nurse pushing a wheelchair comes to collect her for dinner.

I check my watch. It's only four thirty, but everything is earlier in here. I remember that, too, from when Jim was in a similar facility for a time.

After Tom and the nurse help his mother move to the wheelchair, Tom leans in to kiss her cheek.

"I'll see you again soon, Ma, okay?"

She gives him a blank look. "Okay."

The nurse smiles at me as she rolls Mrs. Hammett out of the room.

I go right to him and hold out my arms.

He steps into my embrace, drops his head to my shoulder and holds on to me.

"You're such a good son."

"No, I'm not. She's living in a place she hates."

"She's safe and clean and well fed and has a beautiful private room that I'm sure you pay extra for. I have no doubt you and your sisters have done everything humanly possible to make her comfortable."

"I wish it could be more."

"I know that feeling, all too well."

"Yes, you do." He raises his head and gazes into my eyes. "Thank you for coming and for stepping in to help when I needed it."

"I'm very glad to have gotten to meet her." I force a small smile. "Tommy."

He gives me a side-eyed look. "That's reserved for my ma and my oldest friends."

"Is that right?"

"Uh-huh."

"I've known you for twenty years. That makes me one of your oldest friends."

"Wait a minute..."

With a laugh, I turn to leave the room, relieved to have been there for him when he needed me. It feels good to give back to him after his extraordinary generosity over the last nine months.

Everything about this feels good, if I'm being honest. That's both scary and exhilarating, I decide as I drive him home. I'm still hoping to see the girls tonight. I need to talk it out with my people, the ones who understand the enormity of this moment better than anyone.

Tom

I'm WRECKED after the visit with my mom, but that's nothing new. Seeing her always devastates me. That she thought I was dead made this time extra difficult. Did she somehow sense that I had a close call? Lexi was amazing, the way she stepped in and tried to help. Having her there to hold me afterward made all the difference.

She makes everything better.

When we get home, I head straight for the chair, exhausted by the outing and the emotional wallop that always comes with seeing my mom.

"Can I get you anything?" Lexi asks.

"I'm good. I might take a nap."

"Do you mind if I run out for a bit? Some of my widow friends are getting together for dinner."

"Of course not. Go ahead and have a nice time."

"You'll be all right?"

"I'll be fine."

"And no showers while you're home alone?"

"I won't do that again until I'm fully healed. I promise."

"Thank you. Can I bring you back some dinner?"

"I'll pick at what we have here." I can tell she's torn about leaving me. "It's all good, Lex. Go have a nice time with your friends. I'll be right here—in the chair—when you get home."

"Too soon, Tommy. Far too soon."

I cough out a laugh that makes me instantly regret it. I'm ready for the full-body soreness to let up any time now.

After she goes up to her room to get ready for her dinner

out, I doze through *SportsCenter*, coming to when she appears next to me—looking and smelling too good to be true. "You're gorgeous."

"Thank you."

I love her shy smile and how she's easily embarrassed, although she has no reason to be. I'm so gone over her, and relieved that I can finally show her how I feel without having to worry about scaring her off. If the heart attack and stent procedure didn't scare her off, that is. I hate how she still looks at me with fear of what might happen if she leaves me alone.

Hopefully, that will pass in time, because I want her to look at me the way she did outside the nursing home earlier when she admitted to feeling desire for me. I want more desire and less fear.

When she's put on her coat and grabbed her purse and keys, she hesitates at the top of the stairs, as if she's still worried about leaving me.

"Go, will you? Sheesh, I can't get you out of my hair for five minutes."

"Okay, tough guy. I'm going. Call me if you need anything."

"I'm not going to need anything except for you to come home after you've had a great time with your friends."

"I'll see you in a bit."

"Drive safe."

A short time after she leaves, I get up to look for my discharge paperwork. There's one detail in particular I'd like to revisit. The paperwork is half an inch thick and full of dos and don'ts for patients recovering from the stent procedure. On page twelve, I find the item I'm looking for.

Resumption of sexual activity can take place between two and eight weeks following the procedure, depending upon the patient's pain level and general rate of recovery.

"Yes!"

That's way better than six weeks or ninety days or some other random number they might assign to my condition.

Since I'm feeling stronger every day, I can work with the two-week parameter. One week down. One to go. I can't wait to tell Lexi this news.

Lexi

TRAFFIC IS THE USUAL DISASTER, and I'm about fifteen minutes late to meet the girls, but they won't mind. I've had friends in the past who'd be annoyed if someone was late, and once I was caring for Jim full time, those same friends fell by the wayside, unwilling to be inconvenienced by the slow-motion catastrophe unfolding in my life.

Plenty of others were right there, pitching in as they could and never turning away from the horror of his illness. I still hold them close, even if I don't see them as much as I did before everything changed. These days, I find myself gravitating to friends who are in the same season I am, putting shattered lives back together one day at a time. Although I see my other friends, I find it hard to relate to their soccer-mom lives, their upwardly mobile career challenges, their husband gripes and all the regular-life stuff that they're understandably annoyed by.

I usually find myself biting my tongue in their presence, wanting to say, *Shut up already. I never got to have kids because my husband was too sick to have sex, and since he's been gone, I can't afford kids because of the millstone of debt around my neck that I'll never be rid of.* I want to remind them to count their blessings, even on days when their lives are out of control, when their kids are melting down and their husband has gone golfing —again. They have no idea how lucky they are to be so annoyed by regular life.

But who wants to hear that?

No one does, and since I find myself biting my tongue almost every minute I'm with them, I don't see them very often.

My widow friends, on the other hand, never annoy me the way the others do. They dwell in a place of gratitude and optimism after having survived the worst thing. They never gripe about normal-life stuff because they know all too well how quickly a normal life can be ripped apart. They take nothing—and no one—for granted, and they don't sweat the small stuff like someone being fifteen minutes late.

"Oh, hey, you made it." Joy jumps up to hug me when she sees me heading for our usual table.

I return her tight embrace. Joy gives the best hugs. "I made it."

Brielle hugs me and moves over to make room for me on the bench seat. "We're so glad you did."

"How's Tom?" Naomi asks.

"He's doing great. I took him for a ride today to check some of his work projects and to see his mom at her care facility. She has dementia."

"Didn't you have work?" Hallie asks as she dips a chip in salsa.

"Well... I did until I got laid off."

"Oh no," Joy says. "Shit."

"What does it say about the job that I'm relieved more than scared?"

"You hated that job," Brielle says bluntly.

"I'm not sorry to lose it, because it will force me to find something that doesn't make me feel like I'm dead inside after every day I spend there."

Joy raises her margarita in a toast to me. "That's the spirit. You're going to find something wonderful. I know it."

"Enough about me. Tell me everything that's going on with you guys."

"Oh, no, no," Brielle says. "I want more deets on what's happening with the high school crush."

"He's become my adult crush. There might've been some kissing over the weekend."

"Lexi!" Naomi says dramatically. "His heart can't take it."

"He tells me his heart is never better than it is when I'm close by."

Their chorus of *awwwws* is too cute.

"I like him so much for you," Joy says. "The way he stepped up for you when you needed a way out of your parents' basement and how he's taken such sweet care of you for all these months without an ounce of pressure for anything more has earned him a permanent place in my heart."

"Mine, too," I tell her with a smile. She's the most loving, generous person, and when she says she wants only the best of everything for all of us, we believe her. "What about you and the new guy?"

"Well... I might've had a sleepover the other night."

This is huge news. She hasn't been with anyone since Craig died.

Once again, we all speak as one. "*And?*"

"Mama got her freak on." Despite the way she says that, her eyes are full of tears.

"Aw, sweetie." Brielle puts an arm around Joy. "Are you okay?"

"I am. I really am. And, you know, that's the problem. Everything about it feels so wrong, and yet, it felt so right at the time, and I just..." Joy takes the napkin I hand her. "It's such a mess."

"It's an important step forward," Hallie says. "You know that, right?"

"Yeah, I do," Joy says with a sigh. "But it's made me miss Craig more than I have in a long time. I mean, I always miss him something fierce, but it's been worse lately."

Naomi nods in understanding. "Which is also completely normal."

"What even is normal anymore?" I ask the question before I think too much about it. "I look at my life today, and it bears no resemblance whatsoever to how it was before Jim got sick. I mean... I got laid off today, and I don't even care when I desperately need the money."

"That's because you know there're far worse things that can happen than losing a job you hated to begin with," Hallie says.

Brielle nods in agreement. "Ain't that the truth?"

"You're right," I tell Hallie. "I'm numb to disaster."

"This doesn't even count as a disaster," Joy says. "In the grand scheme of things."

"No, it doesn't. It's a wrinkle, and I'll figure it out. How are things with Robin, Hallie?"

"So far, so great," she says with a grimace. "Leave it to me to find someone who fits just right who also happens to be battling metastatic breast cancer. That's a heck of a chapter two."

Joy puts her hand over Hallie's. "Nothing says you have to take on her battle, love."

"Oh, I know, but I seem to be having a problem walking away from it—and her. She's lovely and fun, and the other day, I met her kids, who are also wonderful. They were so nice and welcoming."

"How old are they?" Naomi asks.

"Eleven and thirteen."

"Not usually the most welcoming ages," Joy says.

"Nope, but these kids have watched their mother fight a disease that could've killed her years ago. They know what matters and what doesn't. They want her happy, even if that means dating a woman after leaving their father."

"Are they still close to their dad?" I ask.

"Very much so, but they can see both parents are happier apart than they were together, so they're cool with it."

"They sound like great kids."

"They really are. It's all good, except for the part about how she could die and leave me devastated again. You think there's something wrong with you for not caring about being laid off, Lex. What level of masochist does it make me to get involved with her knowing what may be coming?"

"Ah, hell," Joy says. "It's coming for all of us."

"See, I know that," Hallie says. "And I think about what happened to my Gwen and your Craig as an example of how lightning can strike at any time, without warning. It's all a risk. Every fucking thing is a risk. But some things are riskier than others."

"Very true," Brielle says, "which means you have to decide if you can handle it if the worst happens again."

"I'd probably handle it better than I did the first time around. At least this time, I'd have some warning, you know?"

Gwen's suicide left Hallie shocked to her core. It's taken her years to even think about dating again.

"Knowing it's coming doesn't always make it easier to accept."

"Lexi is right," Joy says. "My grandmother was sick for years before she finally passed, and I was flattened by it anyway. And that's not the same as losing a significant other."

"Loss is loss," Brielle says. "And it all sucks. I'd rather talk about when Lexi is going to start getting busy with Tom Terrific."

Her nickname for him makes me laugh. "Where'd that come from?"

"That's how I've thought of him since he offered you a place to live and wined and dined you for the better part of a year while he waited for you to be ready for him."

"Is that what you think he's been doing?"

"Duh, honey," Joy says with a grin. "We've all thought that."

"Really?"

"Lexi, sweetheart," Naomi says, "no man makes dinner for a woman six nights a week and serves it with candles while making her lunch and coffee and doing whatever else he can to make her life easy and sweet without hoping she might someday see him as more than a platonic roommate. You aren't so far out of the dating loop that you can't see that, are you?"

"No, but..."

"No buts, my love," Joy says. "The man is crazy about you and has been from minute one. I only met him on moving day, but I'm crazy about him for the way he's cared for you without expecting one single thing in exchange. If you ask me, he's given the master class on how to successfully date a widow without her knowing she's being wooed."

Her assessment makes me laugh. "I'm so dumb."

"No, you're not!" Brielle laughs along with the others. "You just weren't ready to see it until you almost lost him and had to ponder life without him, too."

"I used to be quick on the uptake. Once upon a time."

"Didn't we all?" Joy asks. "Chalk it up to widow brain. It's a real condition."

We order dinner, and they get more margaritas since they're Ubering. I stick with water because, clearly, I need to keep my wits about me for when I get home to Tom Terrific. That nickname cracks me up. I love that Brielle calls him that, and she's right that he's earned it.

My chicken enchiladas are delicious, but I end up boxing half the meal to take home. The servings at this place are enormous, and I've never finished an entire meal in one sitting. I'll have to hide the enchiladas from Tom, who loves all things Mexican and will be drooling over them.

The girls have given me a lot to think about as I drive home through drizzle and fog that has me taking it slower than usual.

Fifteen

Lexi

When I get home shortly after ten, Tom is watching more *SportsCenter*, his favorite thing.

"Hi, honey, you're home."

"I'm home." I stash my leftovers in the fridge and hang my coat in the hall closet before going in to check on him. "How're you feeling?"

"Much better since my gorgeous roommate came home. Did you have a nice time?"

"We always do. Lots of laughs. I'm going to run upstairs and change. Be right back."

"I'll be here."

Upstairs, I brush my teeth and hair, remove my makeup and change into comfy pajamas. I debate bra on or off and then decide to go without it. I zip a sweatshirt over my T-shirt. I wish I had something more interesting to put on, but all that stuff is long gone now. Maybe it's time to go shopping.

Oh wait, you lost your job today, so no shopping for you.

I keep forgetting I got laid off, which is comical. You'd think

I was independently wealthy rather than in debt up to my eyeballs. But a funny thing has happened in the nearly three years since Jim died. The debt has become just another thing to be dealt with. It doesn't define me the way it did initially, and that's thanks in large part to the change in scenery Tom provided with this new place to live.

Anywhere else would've run a credit check, required first, last, damage, all of which would've kept me in my parents' basement indefinitely. Because of the enormous favor Tom did for me, I no longer obsess about the debt the way I once did. That doesn't mean I'm not still worried about it. I am. Very much so. But it's not the first and last thing I think about every day anymore, which is a huge relief.

Tomorrow, I'll get busy looking for a new job. For now, I want to go hang with the man who is slowly but surely changing my life once again.

And I'm letting that happen, eyes wide open to the potential implications. I found the conversation about Hallie's new friend, Robin, interesting. Hallie is going into that relationship knowing that Robin could die prematurely and doesn't seem to be backing away. The same might be true for Tom. Then again, he might live another fifty years. And if he does, would I want to spend those years with him?

I think maybe I would. Living with him for the last nine months has given me a perspective I couldn't have had otherwise. He's shown me over and over again who he really is, and I believe he's as genuine as he appears.

Even with a perfectly healthy partner, no one ever knows if they're going to get one year or fifty. Anything can happen at any time. Life is all about choosing how to spend whatever time you have in a way that makes you happy. Tom makes me happy. The very thought of him has made me happy since I was about fifteen years old. The reality of him has proven to be far more exceptional than even my vivid teenage imagination could've hoped for.

I go back downstairs, eager to be with him, to maybe kiss him some more, to see where we might go together.

He's moved to the sofa and seems to be waiting for me.

I sit next to him and take the hand he offers me. "Missed you while you were out."

"I missed you, too."

"How are your friends?"

"They're good. Fun as always. I found out they have a nickname for you."

"For me?"

"Yep."

"Are you going to tell me what it is?"

His expression makes me laugh. "I'm not sure if I should. It might inflate your ego."

His eyes crinkle at the corners as his smile slowly unfolds. "Lay it on me."

"Tom. *Terrific*."

"Huh. Well... I suppose that's better than Tom Terrible."

That makes me laugh. "As if you could ever be terrible."

"You know what this means?"

"I'm afraid to ask..."

"You must've told your friends some pretty good stuff to earn me that nickname."

"I might've said a thing or two about the dinners, the lunches, the coffee, the overall TLC."

He brings my hand to his lips. The brush of his lips over my skin sets off a reaction I feel everywhere.

"They also pointed out that we've been 'dating' for quite some time without me realizing it."

He turns my hand to kiss the tender inside of my wrist. "Did they now?"

"Uh-huh."

"That'd be pretty sneaky on my part."

"That's what I said!"

"I wasn't trying to sneak anything by you, Lex. I was simply enjoying having you here with me and getting to know you better—and hopefully vice versa."

"You did everything right."

"Did I?"

"You did. You gave me the time to grow into the idea without overwhelming me or putting pressure on me for something I wasn't ready for."

"I hope you know that even if I realized it wasn't going to happen, I wouldn't have done anything differently, and I wouldn't have any regrets about asking you to move in."

"That's what makes you so terrific."

"I really do dig that nickname."

"I had a feeling you might."

"I have some good news for you. At least, *I* think it's good news."

"What's that?"

"While you were out, I took another look at the discharge paperwork and found where it says sexual activity can resume within two to eight weeks, depending on how the patient is managing any pain remaining from the procedure."

"Oh. Well..."

"It's already been a week."

"Has it?"

He nudges me with his shoulder. "You know that. I'm feeling pretty damned good."

"Easy, stallion."

He turns so he's facing me. "Does the thought of that freak you out?"

"Not like it would with someone else."

"Do you have other candidates in mind?"

"Stop it! You know I don't."

His low chuckle makes me smile. "I love when you get feisty."

"There's no one else, and you know that."

"I do. I know. I worry about us taking things to the next level and whether it's something you want or something you feel pressured to do, which is the last thing I'd ever want."

"I don't feel pressured. I feel... I mean, I'd be having sex with *Tom Hammett*." I use my free hand to fan my face. "Fifteen-year-old Lexi is losing her mind over that."

Still smiling, he says, "How does thirty-five-year-old Lexi feel about it?"

"She feels pretty good whenever you're around, and she has for quite some time now."

"That's the nicest thing anyone has ever said to me."

"No way."

"It is!"

"Before we, you know, take this to the next level," I say, forcing myself to look at him, "there're some things you should know."

"About what?"

"Me."

He links our fingers as he gazes at me with pure affection and interest. "I want to know everything there is to know about you."

"Some of it is weird."

"That's often the best part of someone. The weird stuff."

I eye him skeptically. "Said no one ever."

"No, it's true. The weird is what makes us different from everyone else."

"Okay..."

"Tell me, Lex. Tell me anything and everything."

"All right, then... Remember, I tried to warn you."

"It's all good."

And because I know that's true, it's not hard to tell him

about the things that hurt me. "For as long as I can remember, I've had an irrational fear of my dad dying. I'm not sure where it came from. There was no inciting event or anything like that. It was just this thing inside me that took over for a while. I remember being very small and creeping into their room in the middle of the night to make sure he was still breathing."

"Aw, Lex."

"He was always robustly healthy. That's the strange thing about it. There wasn't anything at all wrong with him."

"Same with my dad until he was dead."

"What happened to you was my greatest fear. That he'd go off somewhere and never come home. He traveled a lot for work. I wouldn't sleep for all the time he was gone."

"Lexi... Seriously?"

"The whole time. A week once."

"What did your mother say?"

"She doesn't know any of this. Neither of them does. I've hidden it for years."

"How did you hide the fact that you weren't sleeping for a whole week from your mom?"

"I'm not sure how I got away with it, but I did."

"You had severe anxiety."

"I know that now, and I'm medicated for it these days, but back then... It wasn't as common of a thing for people to recognize in others. One time, his flight was delayed, and he didn't make it home when he was supposed to. He called my mom to tell her, but I didn't know that. I was sure he was dead."

"I just want to wrap my arms around young Lexi and hold her tight."

That's the sweetest thing he could say. "I've never really outgrown this fear, but I've learned to manage it better. And what's ironic is that while I was so busy worrying about him, my mom ended up with skin cancer while I was in high school. Then I had to worry about both of them."

"She's doing okay, though?"

"She is, but for the five years after her treatment, I was sure it would come back. I was a wreck over that. All this is one of the reasons why it was so upsetting when we weren't getting along after Jim died. I love them so much. I never wanted to fight with them."

"They know that."

"I was so busy worrying about them that it never occurred to me that I needed to be worried about Jim. Not once, in all the years we were together, did I ever stress out about him dying the way I did my parents."

"Why would you? He was young and healthy and should've had decades left to live."

"I was so busy being happy with him that it simply never occurred to me to add him to my list of panic-inducing worries."

"I love hearing that you guys were so happy."

"We were. He was the best. Every year when I got my class list, he'd ask for a copy of it, and he'd memorize the name of every kid. He knew all their little quirks and the things they struggled with. At dinner, he'd ask me about them. Like, 'How is Emma's reading coming along?' Or, 'Did Clifton come back to school after his grandfather died?' Or, 'How is Daisy's speech?' On the last day of school for each of the years I taught, he'd pick me up in his restored Mustang convertible and take me for a ride to Skyline Drive with the top down. I've never felt so free as I did on those rides, knowing I had the next two months off."

"That's such a sweet tradition."

"I'd look forward to it all year long."

"What did he do for work?"

"He was a mechanical engineer and ran a machine shop out by Tysons. He'd come into school once in a while to read to my kids, and they loved him. He did all the voices and brought every character to life. He would've been a wonderful father."

"No doubt. Did you plan on having kids?"

"We were talking about it when the first sign of impending disaster struck."

"What happened?"

"I was in a faculty meeting after school one day when one of the admins came to the door and signaled for me to come out of the room. I thought she must be talking to someone else, but she was pointing at me. Of course, my first thought was that my father had died." I give him a wry smile. "Old habits die hard. I gathered my stuff, apologized to the others and left the room. In the hallway, Linda, the admin, told me the police had tried to call my phone, but it was muted for the meeting, so they called the school. Jim had fallen down a flight of concrete stairs leaving work.

"Linda said he wanted me to know where he was and that they were taking him to the hospital. She asked if she could drive me there, and I told her I could probably do it myself, but that was a mistake. I'd driven about two blocks when I realized I had no business driving, because my hands were shaking so hard. I kept thinking it was good news that he was well enough to tell someone to call me, right? He had given them my number, told them where I worked.

"I took comfort in that as I drove through traffic that just wouldn't move on the way to the hospital. Somehow, I managed to call my parents to tell them Jim had fallen down the stairs at work, and my mom said they'd meet me at the hospital. I told her they didn't need to. I thought, how bad could it be? He was conscious and talking and was able to tell them how to reach me. I told my parents not to come. I didn't want to inconvenience them. I actually thought about how they wouldn't want to miss *Wheel of Fortune* and *Jeopardy!* Not to mention the *Nightly News*, which they watch every night.

"For some reason, it never occurred to me to try to call him. I thought about that afterward. Like, why didn't I try to call *him*? I figured he must be busy if he was injured enough to go to the hospital. I didn't know what to think, honestly. I couldn't imagine what'd happened. Jim wasn't one to fall over things or trip over his own feet. That was my thing. I was actually known for it among our group of friends. If there was something to fall over, Lexi was the one going headfirst over it. Never Jim. I figured somebody must've pushed him or tripped him somehow or gotten in his way. I thought maybe he was in a rush to get out of work to beat the traffic to get home before me for once. Not for one second did it ever cross my mind that the fall would be the end of our life as we knew it, even if that wasn't clear for a while afterward."

Tom hands me his Stanley cup with the ice water I poured for him earlier.

"I'm sorry. I'm talking too much."

"No, I want to hear it. Tell me the rest."

I take a deep breath and release it slowly before I continue. "He was a bloody mess. His head and face were cut. He had a concussion and was black and blue all over. When I asked him what happened, he said he wasn't sure. One minute, he was on the steps leaving work. The next, he was on the sidewalk, surrounded by people who'd rushed to his aid. A woman who was behind him and saw him fall said it looked like his left leg had given out.

"When I heard that, my heart dropped into my stomach. His left leg had been giving him trouble for a while by then. He'd had weakness in his calf and weird tremors in his thigh. Every so often, it would just give out, and he'd stumble. This was the first time he'd gotten hurt, though. And it was the first time I wondered if there was something seriously wrong with him—and the doctors were asking the same questions.

"He was in the hospital for four days. They ran every test

imaginable, all of which came back inconclusive. They ruled out a lot of scary things. He didn't have MS or Parkinson's. It wasn't a brain tumor. I remember being relieved as each of those things was knocked off the list of possibilities."

"Of course you were."

"After they'd run all their tests, they sent him home without an answer, and once he was recovered from the fall, we sort of picked up where we left off. We went out to the beach for a week that summer and had friends over for cookouts and went sailing on the Chesapeake with one of his college friends. It was a lovely summer, other than the ongoing challenges he was still having with his left leg. He worked out like a demon, trying to strengthen it. He even did two triathlons that summer, but he was upset that his times were way off from the year before, and he couldn't understand why."

"That had to be so frustrating for him."

"It was. He was always super fit, and to be losing ground so quickly was upsetting. He was hard to be around during that time. Very cranky and out of sorts. We fought more during that year than all the other years put together. Every little thing set him off, and I tried to tell myself he wasn't himself, but that didn't take the sting out of being the one he took out his frustrations on. Then he fell again—this time off his bike in traffic, narrowly missing being hit by a truck."

"Oh God."

"Yeah, that was bad. You know what's worse?"

"What?"

"That sometimes I wish the truck had hit him and spared him what was coming."

"That's not bad, Lex. I totally get why you'd wish for that."

"I felt terrible later when I realized that as bad as that would've been, it would've been better than the long, drawn-out nightmare he endured."

"That you both endured."

"My suffering had nothing on his."

"Sure it did. Don't discount the enormity of his illness for you, too."

"He was the hero of that story."

"I have no doubt whatsoever that you were every bit as heroic."

"I don't know about that. Anyway, a few months after the fall off his bike, he fell in the shower, and that's when shit got real. His PCP was the first to suggest ALS. Jim had been thinking it was that for a while by then, but he'd never mentioned it to me. Let me tell you... Googling that acronym was the biggest mistake of my life."

Tom winces.

"But as I read through the information, it started to add up to what'd been happening for almost two years at that point. He got an official diagnosis Christmas week of that year, shortly after the fall in the shower. My parents suggested we might want to move into their basement so we could have all one-level living. We were in a two-story townhome at that point, with our bedroom upstairs. Jim cried when I said we ought to accept their offer because we were also going to need their help."

I haven't told the full story since the first time I joined the Wild Widows. I'd forgotten how exhausting and devastating it is to revisit that time. "At least we had an answer, though, you know? Even if it was the worst possible answer. We weren't flying blind anymore. There were resources available through the ALS Association, which was just a lifesaver. I've stayed involved with them since he passed. They do such incredible work for people dealing with the most hideous diagnosis."

"When did you move in with your folks?"

"In March of that year. It was a difficult few months spent adjusting to the reality that our time together was going to be cut short. I was struggling to finish the school year before I took a leave of absence. Jim insisted on still going to work for as long as he could. After the doctors suggested strongly that he not drive anymore, which was a terrible loss for someone who loved to drive, one of his colleagues, who lived near us, made it possible for him to keep working for a while longer by driving him every day. Everyone was so incredibly nice."

I wipe away a tear, the first one to show up during the telling of this story, which is remarkable. The first few times I told it, I sobbed the entire time. I cried for months after the diagnosis. Every time I was alone, I'd dissolve all over again.

"You know what the kicker is?"

"What's that?"

Sixteen

Lexi

"Even in the middle of this massive crisis, I still worried about my dad dying."

"Anxiety is ridiculous that way. One of Cora's kids has had a rough time with it."

"It sure is, and I'm sorry to hear that."

"She's doing better than she was. Good meds help."

"They sure do."

"So you moved in with your folks."

"We did. All our friends helped. The hardest part was getting rid of things Jim had loved but would never use again, while he was still alive, like his baseball glove, his hockey skates, the Mustang. That was gut-wrenching. I did it after we'd moved him to my parents' house so he wouldn't be there to see it go."

"That must've been awful for you."

"When I look back at the entire nightmare, that day definitely stands out as one of the roughest. We were dismantling his life while he was still here. One of my friends is a whiz at selling things online. She sold everything and got as much as she could for all of it, which was such a blessing at the time, as we were faced with both of us being out of work."

"Thank you for sharing that with me. It means a lot to me that you'd trust me with your story."

"I'd understand if my neurosis and grief are too much to take on."

"It's not too much. You know what came through loud and clear to me as you were sharing that?"

"What?"

"How deeply you love the people you care about. How lucky your dad is that you love him so much, you can't imagine life without him. How lucky Jim was to have a wife who saw to his every need and took tender care of him through a horrific illness. A lot of people would've run from that. You never blinked."

"I did, though. I blinked a lot. There were so many days when I thought I couldn't do it anymore."

"But you never ran from it. Not once."

"Maybe once or twice."

"Did you always go back?"

"Yeah."

"Then that doesn't count as running."

"I could never have left him for long."

"The people you love are very lucky, Lexi. I hope you see that."

"Thank you."

"I loved having that little peek inside your life with Jim and to know more about him. I keep going back to him memorizing the names of all your kids each year."

"The first time he did that, I was so shocked. He'd found the printout on my desk and committed it to memory. I think he had their names memorized before I did."

"That's the sweetest thing."

"He'd want me to tell you that he could also be a dick when he wanted to be."

Tom laughs. "I find that hard to believe."

"We had some spectacular fights. Mostly because, despite all his fitness, he still liked to drink like he did in college. That drove me mad. I hated it."

"I can see how that'd be a problem."

"He never had another sip of alcohol after his diagnosis. The doctors strongly recommended he not drink because that would only make him more prone to falls. He'd been badly injured three times in falls by then, so they didn't have to tell him that twice. He lost everything, one thing at a time."

"He never lost you, and I'm sure he'd say you were the most important thing in his life."

"Yes, he would've said that. I never had any doubt that he loved me madly."

"I hope you have no doubt by now that I do, too."

"Tom..."

"Maybe this isn't the right time to say it, but it's true, Lexi. I love you. I love hearing how much you loved Jim and how sweet your life was with him, and I want you to know that he'll always be part of whatever you and I are together. He's part of you, and I love every part of you."

By now, tears are running unchecked down my face as this man who's been such an extraordinary friend shares his heart with me. "I love you, too."

"You don't have to say that just because I did."

"I never would unless I truly meant it, and I truly do. What you said about Jim being part of us shows me everything I'll ever need to know about how you understand what it's like to be involved with a widow."

"I get it, Lex. He's as much a part of you as your curly hair and the sweet dimple that shows up right here when you smile big." He touches his finger to the spot. "He's in your heart and soul, and I love your heart and soul. I think I've loved you since I was eighteen years old."

"Tom…"

"I never forgot you. I thought about you far more often than I should have, even after I heard you'd gotten married. I wondered what might've been different if I'd defied my mother's orders and asked you out in high school."

"I probably would've wet my pants or something equally embarrassing if you asked me out then."

That makes him laugh hard. "I think you would've held up just fine."

"I would've melted down for sure. Ask any of my high school friends."

"I'll do that the next time we see them."

"They'll tell you… I would've been taken away in an ambulance if you ever even looked at me, let alone talked to me or asked me out."

"It was like that, was it?"

"Yeah, it was pretty bad."

"And now? What's the crush-o-meter reading looking like?"

"Definitely inching toward the danger zone. Some days, I still can't believe I live with Tom Hammett, that I'm friends with Tom Hammett, that I *kissed* Tom Hammett."

"You're *best* friends with Tom Hammett, and he can't wait to kiss you as much and as often as he possibly can for the rest of his life."

"That could be a long time."

"I hope it's so long that we're chasing each other around the nursing home someday and causing scandals with our outrageous behavior."

I lose it laughing at the picture he paints.

"Can I ask you something else?" he says when I quit laughing.

"Sure."

"Do you want to have kids?"

"Oh man, I used to want them more than anything, but now? I don't know anymore. After years of intense caregiving, the thought of taking full-time care of anything, even a pet, feels a bit overwhelming to me."

"That's fair enough."

"What about you?"

"I always pictured myself having a family someday, but as I inch closer to forty, I'm not sure I want to be sixty with kids in college."

"I hear sixty is the new forty."

"Sure it is. It also means working until I'm seventy to pay for it all."

"That's true."

"But if you were interested, I'd be down for it. I'd never want to deny you something you want."

"I haven't thought about that in such a long time that I'm not even sure how I feel about it anymore. It felt like one more thing that was lost to Jim's illness, you know?"

"I see what you mean, but we're both still young enough to make it happen if we decide to go for it. I'd work until I was eighty if it helped to make your dreams come true."

"Just so you know, whoever is writing your material is spot-on. They know just what to say to me."

"Haha, all my own original work, I'll have you know."

My phone chimes with a text from Iris. She rarely texts us this late. "Do you mind if I check that?"

"Of course not. Go for it."

The text is to the full Wild Widows group. *We've got two new people interested in joining our ranks. I thought it might be nice to do more of a mixer sort of thing where we bring friends and make it more social than widow-focused to introduce them to our group. Gage and I were already thinking about doing a get-*

together for everyone next weekend, so we could invite them to join us? What do you guys think?

Brielle has already replied. *I love that idea. That way, they can see how close and welcoming we all are, and the rest of us can get to know some of the new SOs. Hello, Tom Terrific, I'm talking to you!*

Iris responds: *Wait, Tom Terrific? What'd I miss?*

Joy: *Single-girl outing tonight, and a nickname for Lexi's "roommate" was born.*

Iris: *Oh, I do so love that! LOL*

Me: *So does he. HAHAHA. Love the idea, Iris. Count us in and let us know what we can bring.*

I turn to Tom. "How do you feel about going to a Wild Widows party on Saturday night?"

"I feel very good about that. I'd love to get to know your friends."

"They're very interested in getting to know Tom Terrific, too."

"That name is gonna stick, isn't it?"

"I believe so. And PS, you've earned it, so enjoy it."

"I plan to enjoy every minute of it."

Tom

TONIGHT WAS one of the best nights of my life, and all we did was talk after she got home from dinner with her friends. I've had more romantic dates with other women that ended up in bed, but no one has ever touched my heart and soul the way Lexi does. The things she told me about her relationship with Jim and what they went through during his illness will stay with me forever.

As we attempt to watch a movie that neither of us is all that interested in, I think about him falling down a set of concrete stairs and her getting that call while at school.

Her head is on my shoulder as I run my fingers through her curls. I love being close to her like this, even if all we do is snuggle. As I breathe in the scent that's so uniquely hers, all I want is more. I want everything with her.

I want to protect her from anything that could ever hurt her again, especially myself. I'll never eat another french fry or pizza again if it means staying healthy for her, so she never has to go through losing another man she loves. I'll hit the gym seven days a week. Whatever it takes to be there for her long term.

After I yawn, Lexi raises her head off my shoulder. "You should get to bed."

"Are you coming with me?"

"Only if you want me to."

"Duh."

I love that smile. I'll do anything to see it as much as I can every day. I want her smiling, happy, joyful, looking ahead to all we have to look forward to.

We disentangle from each other and get up to head to my room. Or is it *our* room now? I like the sound of that. I, who never wanted anyone invading my personal space, was ready to turn over the keys to my kingdom to her the day she first moved in.

She gets into bed while I use the bathroom and brush my teeth.

I get in bed and turn to face her. "You're too far away over there."

"You need your rest."

"I need you more."

She scoots closer, but not close enough.

I reach for her, and she moves into my embrace.

"Good?"

"Much better. If you kissed me, it would be better still."

"You're supposed to be resting and convalescing."

"Nowhere in the instructions does it say that kissing is forbidden."

"It says sexual activity is forbidden. Kissing is sexual activity."

"Say 'sexual activity' one more time."

"Stop!"

"Make me. There's only one way to shut me up, and you have the power."

"I suppose I have to do what must be done if there's any prayer of getting some sleep tonight."

"That's the spirit."

She's smiling when she raises herself on an elbow and presses her lips to mine. "There. Now shut up and go to sleep."

Before she can get away, I hook an arm around her neck and turn us so I'm on top of her, gazing down at her lovely face. "Not so fast, love." I skim my lips gently over hers, mindful that I'm the first man she's been with this way since she lost her husband. I want to make sure she's comfortable with what's happening.

I take it nice and slow until her arms come around my neck and her mouth opens to my tongue. Then it's game *on*.

Kissing her is like coming home to the place I was always meant to end up. I can't help the feeling of fate or kismet or whatever you want to call it that put us in the same place at the same time that night we first connected, years after we nursed fierce but secret crushes on each other.

Maybe it was her beloved Jim who steered her my way, knowing I would treasure her the way he did. Whatever it was that brought us to this moment, I'm deeply thankful for it.

"Tom."

"Hmm." I kiss her neck and gently nibble on the tendon at the base of her neck.

She gasps as her legs curl around my hips. "We shouldn't be doing this."

"I'm fine. I swear to God. I'm fine, and I'm going to *be* fine. Nothing has ever been better than being with you this way, Lex."

I can tell she's torn between wanting the same thing I do and making sure I'm not doing too much too soon. I'm going to follow the doctors' orders. There'll be no sex until at least the fourteen-day mark. But there's plenty we can do in the meantime.

Her hands are on my back, under my T-shirt, making me shiver with desire. "I promise I won't overexert myself, okay?"

"Okay."

I push up her T-shirt to reveal full breasts with dark pink nipples.

Sitting back on my heels, I pull my shirt over my head and then help her out of hers. "God, that feels so good." The feel of her breasts against my chest is like heaven, especially with my hard cock pressed against the heat between her legs.

This has got to be what heaven would feel like, I decide, as I run my tongue over her left nipple before tugging it into my mouth.

She grabs a fistful of my hair and lets out a sound that's pure need.

Christ have mercy. I want her like I've never wanted anything in my entire life.

Then her hands are inside my pajama pants, pulling me tighter against her as she chases a release that erupts from her like a sob as she says my name on a long moan.

Hottest thing *ever*.

I continue to move against her, riding the waves of her release but not allowing myself to follow her. I promised I wouldn't overdo it.

187

She takes a deep breath and releases it on a shaky-sounding exhale. "Wow."

"My thoughts exactly."

"You didn't... I mean, you probably shouldn't..."

I kiss her. "No worries. You can make it up to me later."

She laughs. "Are you going to keep a tab?"

"You bet your ass I am."

Lexi

I'M on edge the entire next day after the sexy interlude in Tom's bed last night. It's like I'm coming back to life after a long, cold, lonely winter. His touch sets me on fire, which, of course, I already knew, which is why I told him we shouldn't get too close in bed. I knew what would happen when I moved closer to him, but I can't say I regret it.

If only I wasn't so worried about him having a setback.

He starts cardiac rehab today and is going to drive himself, which I'm not sure I like, but he insisted he's perfectly fine and ready to get back to normal.

Watching him drive off in his truck reminds me of when Jim insisted on driving long after he shouldn't have been. It had taken a near miss with a minivan full of kids to get him to finally admit what I and others had known for a while by then —it wasn't safe for him to drive anymore.

Everything about Tom's situation is different. Unlike with ALS, where every loss was permanent, Tom is expected to make a full recovery. When he says he feels fine, I have to try to believe him and stop anticipating disaster. Anxiety is preprogrammed into my DNA. I need to keep in mind that this is not the same as it was with Jim, which is easier said than done.

To keep busy while he's gone, I do a load of laundry for

both of us and then get out my laptop to check my email and begin the dreaded job search once again.

I read the email from the HR director at my former company, detailing the same information about severance and benefits that Erika outlined during our meeting. I reply to thank the woman who sent it and then read an email from Nora, the volunteer coordinator at the local ALS chapter. I've done some work with the support groups and been involved with several fundraisers. The organization was such a lifeline to us when Jim was sick that I feel like it's the least I can do to pay back some of the kindness.

Hi, Lexi,

I wanted to let you know that I'll be leaving the organization at the end of this month to have my first children (twin girls— ack, wish me luck!). I'm reaching out to some of our more engaged volunteers to ascertain whether you'd have any interest in a job with us. We're actively recruiting for my position as well as several others that have opened up in recent months. Your contributions on both the support group and fundraising sides of the house have been substantial, and your firsthand experience with ALS would make you such a valuable resource to families just receiving this devastating diagnosis.

I read the paragraph twice because I can hardly believe I'm being offered a job right when I lost mine. Is that Jim at work on my behalf once again? I wouldn't put it past him. However, I'm just not sure I have the emotional bandwidth to immerse myself in an all-ALS-all-the-time life.

Nora acknowledges that possibility in her second paragraph.

I will totally understand if this opportunity is not for you. As someone who's lived this experience, it may be healthier for you to remain an occasional volunteer rather than a more active partici- pant. Either way, I want you to know how thankful I am for your many contributions and that your story—and your husband's—is one that will stay with me long after I've moved on from this position.

If you're interested in hearing more, please reach out at your earliest convenience. The board is hoping to have someone in place shortly before my last day as the need for what we provide unfortunately continues.

All my best,

Nora

I'm stunned and honored to have been asked, but also hesitant. I have no idea how to respond, so I save the message as new to deal with after I've had some time to think about how best to reply.

Seventeen

Lexi

W hile I'm online, I decide to do a search on something I want to know more about: the so-called widow-maker heart attack. I've heard the term before but never gave it much thought. Since Tom mentioned his father dying from one, it's been on my mind. As I type the question into the search bar, I'm aware that I'll probably regret this, but I press Enter anyway.

Google reports that "a widow-maker heart attack is a type of heart attack in which you have a full blockage in your heart's biggest artery. This artery, the left anterior descending (LAD) artery, sends oxygen-rich blood to your heart's left ventricle."

With my own heart in my throat, I scroll down to learn the survival rate is a measly twelve percent. I glance at Tom's discharge paperwork sitting on the counter, and before I can talk myself out of it, I get up for a closer look.

On page four, I find a description of his presenting condition: ninety-five percent blockage of the left anterior descending artery.

I draw in a deep breath. *Oh my God.* He had the same heart attack his father did. Does he realize that? He must. They would've told him that in the hospital when he—or his sisters—shared family history.

I knew his condition was extremely serious but reading that it was the exact same condition that killed his father has left me shaken and needing more information. I want to talk to him about it, but I'm not sure how I'd bring that up. *So, Tom, I was reading your discharge paperwork and realized you suffered a widow-maker heart attack like your father had. Did you realize that?*

I can't just ask him that.

My phone rings with a call from my mom.

"Hey, Mom, how's it going?"

"It's going. How about you? How's Tom?"

I push the words *widow-maker* out of my mind for now. "He's doing great. Took himself off to cardiac rehab this morning."

"Should he be driving yet?"

"He says he's fine, so what could I do? I keep having to remind myself that his situation is not like Jim's was. He's going to be fine eventually."

"That must be so challenging for you."

"It is, but he's going to be fine, so that makes it as different as night and day, you know?"

"I do, but it must still be stressful for you."

"It's been okay, actually. He's doing really well and is like his old self. The key thing is making sure he doesn't do too much too soon." *Including have orgasms.* My urge to giggle like a fool at that thought is tamped by the words *widow-maker* popping into my head again. I knew I shouldn't have googled it.

"I'm so glad to hear he's doing well. That's such a relief."

"It really is."

"Dad and I were wondering if you two would like to come for dinner tonight."

"We'd love to, but Tom is eating super healthy."

"I was going to make salmon with green beans and salad."

"That sounds perfect. He'll love it."

"He'd probably love a steak more."

I laugh. "He would, but he's on best behavior going forward."

"I'm glad to hear he's taking it seriously."

"He is. He says he has a lot to live for."

"Including you?"

"It seems like I might be on the list."

"That's wonderful, Lex. I'm so happy for both of you. He's such a nice guy."

"He's the best, and he's been so great about being a good friend to me even as he was hoping it would someday be more. There was never any pressure."

"Does he know about the world-class crush from high school?"

"He does, and guess what? He had one on me, too! He wanted to ask me to his senior prom, but his mother wouldn't let him because I was too young. So he didn't go at all."

"Oh my goodness. How sweet is that?"

"High school Lexi would've passed out if he'd asked her to prom."

Mom's laughter is such a delight to me. We went years without much laughter in our lives.

"How's the job search going?"

"Oddly enough, I've been offered the chance to apply for something with the ALS Association. Their volunteer coordinator position is opening up."

"Wow. How do you feel about that?"

"I'm stunned to have the universe show up for me this way,

and I can't help but wonder if Jim is making things happen for me."

"I wouldn't put it past him, but, Lex... ALS... I mean, how do you feel about that?"

"Extremely conflicted and not at all sure if that would be a good idea for me. On the one hand, I have a lot of experience that would be beneficial to others. On the other..."

"It's ALS."

"Right. I don't know what to think."

"You'd be great at it, but whether it would be great for you is the question."

"Exactly."

"Sit with it for a minute. See how you feel about it in a day or two."

"That's what I'll do. I'll reply to Nora, thank her for thinking of me and ask for some time to consider it."

"Sounds like a plan."

"What can I bring tonight?"

"Just yourselves. We've got it covered."

"Thanks for the invite."

"Looking forward to it. See you soon. Love you, honey, and in case I forget to say it every day for the rest of my life, I'm so, so proud of you."

"Aw, thanks. That means a lot. Love you, too."

After the call with my mom, I push all thoughts of widow-makers aside for now, update my résumé and log on to some of the bigger job searching sites where I still have accounts to see what else is out there. The offer from the ALS Association looms large in the back of my mind, but before I decide about that, I need to check my options. I apply to a few admin jobs, but only because there's no mention of data entry or Excel spreadsheets in the descriptions. There's an event assistant position that sounds interesting, so I apply for that, too, even though I'm not qualified.

Hopefully, my experience as a third-grade teacher is proof that I can handle just about anything a job throws my way.

Out of curiosity, I go to several of the websites for local school departments and note almost all of them are desperately seeking substitute teachers at all three levels. It's good to know that's a possibility. I wouldn't mind going back to teaching, but it's not my first choice anymore. I no longer have the emotional bandwidth to manage twenty children with twenty different sets of needs and learning styles. The door to that career closed when Jim was sick, and I'm not sure I could find the where-withal to push it back open.

But if all else fails, it's good to know they're hiring. When I was searching for my last job, I never even looked on the school sites, knowing I wouldn't have been able to handle the demands of being back in the classroom. I'm three years out from Jim's death and stronger than I was then, for sure. However, I'm a completely different person than who I was the last time I was in a classroom. I'd much prefer to start fresh in a new field than to revisit the past.

Besides, how would I ever again welcome a new class without Jim with me to memorize all the students' names and quirks? That'd be more heartbreak when I've already had plenty.

I apply to more than a dozen jobs in total. If what's past is prologue, I'll be lucky to hear from one of them.

By the time Tom comes in from cardiac rehab, I'm making a turkey sandwich for lunch. "Hungry?"

"Starving."

I make a second one for him, but I substitute carrot sticks for the chips he'd usually have.

"Thank you," he says when I put the plate in front of him at the counter bar.

"How was it?"

"It was fine. They hooked me up to an EKG and had me do

some exercise. I go back again the day after tomorrow, when I'll also meet with a nutrition counselor."

"How often will you go?"

"Three days a week, which will be interesting when I go back to work the week after next."

"Is that too soon to go back to work?"

"I don't think so. I'm feeling pretty good already."

"I'm still worried about you doing too much too soon."

"I know you are, but you don't need to worry. The last thing I want is another incident. Trust me." He takes my hand and brushes a kiss across the back of it. "I have much better things to do than be sick."

His meaning registers and makes me feel warm all over.

I'd forgotten what this was like, to be deep in the trenches of intense attraction, knowing what's coming—soon. The buildup is almost as good as the event itself.

"What're you thinking about?" he asks.

"Anticipation." What I'm trying not to think about are the words *widow-maker*. I'm already a widow. I can't go there. I just cannot.

He pauses midchew, brows raised as he reaches for his glass of water. "What about it?"

Pushing aside the ever-present fear of someday losing him, too, I say, "How it can be every bit as exciting as what comes next."

"Damn it, Lexi. Don't talk about it until you're ready to follow through. It's not good for my heart to have all these *highs* and *lows*."

I hold back a laugh when I realize he's not talking about his heart. "I'm ready. You're the one with restrictions."

"Now you're just being mean to me."

I lose it laughing, reminding myself that he's here, he's healthy and beautifully alive. I've learned as a widow that all we have is right now, and my right now is rather lovely, thanks to him. "How do you figure?"

"I have four more days to go."

"So that means I'm not allowed to talk about it until then?"

"That's exactly what it means."

"Then I guess no more kissing or other *preliminaries*."

"When did I say that?"

"You're being ridiculous. Not to change the subject or anything, but my parents invited us to dinner tonight."

"Good. Keep talking about your parents. That's the ultimate cockblocker."

I sputter with laughter. "I cannot believe you just said that about my parents." Suddenly, my eyes are full of tears as it occurs to me that the banter with him is reminiscent of my relationship with Jim, and I realize how much I've missed having that with a partner.

He slides his chair so it's next to mine, puts his arms around me and holds me close. "What's wrong, Lex? I was only kidding. I love your parents. You know that."

As I breathe in the scent of him, the scent that's become home to me at some point over this last year, I wave a hand in front of my face, embarrassed and overwhelmed at the same time. "I'm sorry."

"Don't be. What's going on?"

"The dumbest thing."

"No, it isn't. Not if it upset you. Was it what I said about your parents? I really do like them."

"I know you do, and they like you, too."

He kisses the tears off my face. "Then what, hon?"

"It's just that this, with you, reminded me of how Jim and I were together, and it made me miss him and appreciate you all at the same time."

"Aw, honey, I'm so sorry you ache for him the way you do. I wish there was some way I could take away the pain."

"You've made it much more bearable than it was before you came into my life. That's for sure."

"I'm glad to hear that, but I still wish it could be more."

"It's everything I need, Tom. *You* are everything I need. It's just that the two things coexist in this crazy mishmash of sad and happy and grief and joy. Sometimes the emotional overload gets to be too much. That's when the tears show up."

"The tears are part of who you are, and it's such a testament to who you are that you still weep for him after all these years."

"I'll always weep for him and how he was cheated of the long life he deserved. No one should have to endure what he did."

"No, they shouldn't."

I wipe away the remaining tears, thankful for his unwavering support and love. Being with a widow is never easy, but he always gets it just right by understanding that my love for Jim is eternal. "Speaking of ALS, the local chapter of the ALS Association offered me a job."

"When?"

"There was an email from them waiting for me this morning."

"Wow. That's some amazing timing, huh?"

"I thought the same thing."

"What's the job?"

"Volunteer coordinator for the Northern Virginia chapter."

"Lexi... That's amazing. You'd be great at that."

"You think so?"

"Definitely. Who better to help others than someone who's been through it herself? Although... it might be hard for you, right?"

"That's my biggest hesitation. ALS all day every day. I'm not sure I could handle that."

"Yeah, I can see how it might be too much. How did you leave it with them?"

"I asked for some time to think about it."

"Good idea. Either way, it's nice to have an offer."

"It does take the sting out of being laid off. I applied to a bunch of other stuff. I'll see what happens."

"I'm sure you're going to find something you love before too long."

"That'd be nice. The job search dragged on for months last time."

His phone chimes with a text that he quickly reads. "Gotta deal with some work stuff."

"Not too much, I hope."

"Nah, just stuff only I can do. They're waiting on decisions from me for a bunch of things. I promise not to overdo it."

"I'll hold you to it."

He gives me a soft kiss. "You going to be okay?"

"Yes, I'm fine. I promise. Grief makes me weird sometimes."

"You're not weird. You love with your whole heart and soul. That makes Jim and me lucky guys—and we know it."

"Thank you for understanding."

"I'll never fully understand what you went through or the depths of your grief, but I so respect the way you continue to honor him in everything you do. He'd be so proud of you."

"That's very nice of you to say, and I hope he would be. He told me all the time how proud he was of the way I took care of him and never wavered, even if it broke his heart that my life became all about taking care of him. He would've done the same for me, which is what I told him every time the subject came up."

"It takes a special person to step up for someone else the way you did for him."

"Hardest job I ever had, but also the most rewarding. I feel like we gave him time he wouldn't have gotten otherwise. We knew this other couple... The wife was diagnosed around the same time as Jim, so we ran into them occasionally at appointments. At first, the husband was totally on Team Jan, but over time, he disengaged. They ended up divorced. She told us he couldn't handle it."

"Poor baby."

"That's what I said, too, but Jim said it was too much for anyone to handle, and he didn't blame him, even if he'd make different decisions. We talked a lot about how no one knows what they'd do in any situation until they're confronted with it. We all like to think we know, but we don't."

"I know without a shadow of a doubt that you'd be there for me if I ever needed you like that, and I can assure you I'd be there for you, too. You don't leave the people you love when shit gets hard. That's when you double down and dig in."

"That's the goal, but I've found it's not always achievable for some people, no matter how much they want to do the hard stuff."

He kisses my forehead and then my lips. "I'll never leave, no matter how hard it gets. That's not something you ever have to worry about."

I want to tell him the same goes, but the words *widow-maker* pop into my brain before I can say anything.

"Off to work I go. What time do we need to leave for your parents' house?"

"Five thirty."

"I'll be ready." He steals one more kiss and an apple from the bowl on the counter and heads to his office while I watch him go, really wishing I'd never done that search.

Eighteen

Lexi

My anxiety is through the roof all afternoon. I reach out to the therapist who helped me through Jim's illness and the first year of widowhood. I went for as long as my insurance would pay for it and stopped only when it became too expensive.

However, Antonia, who goes by Toni, has continued to check in regularly with me since we stopped our regular appointments.

I send her a long text, updating her on recent events and how I made the huge mistake of looking into the widow-maker term.

She texts me back an hour later when I'm in my room getting dressed after a shower.

Can you talk?

Yes!

She calls.

"Hey. Thank you so much for calling."

"Of course. Wow, I can't believe what happened to your friend Tom. Is he doing okay now?"

"He is and expected to make a full recovery, which is a bit of a mind-bender for me after living with someone who would never recover."

"I can imagine it takes a different mindset to approach Tom's recovery."

"I'm working on that."

"What the heck were you thinking with the Google?"

I laugh at how she phrases that. "I know! I'm the one who tells others to stay off Google when they receive a diagnosis of any kind." Jim and I found that the more information we had about his illness, the more terrified and anxious we became. We made a vow to limit the influx of info to only what was needed in that moment. It was a good policy and one I should've stuck to with Tom's situation.

"Of all the things for it to be called, too. Ugh."

"Right?"

"Lexi, you know that he's not in any immediate risk of having that kind of heart attack again, right? The problem that caused the first one was corrected, and he's being closely monitored and will continue to be going forward."

"Yes, I know, and still, my anxiety is crazy."

"It could be that what almost happened is fully sinking in now that the crisis has passed."

"That's possible. Things with him have gotten more involved since his heart attack. We've said and done some things that're leading toward a relationship."

"Are you feeling ready for that?"

"I want to be. I think it's safe to say I'm in love with him, and vice versa."

"That's so wonderful to hear, Lexi. I'm thrilled for you."

"I want to be thrilled for me, too."

"Then you need to stay off the Google!"

I laugh. "I know. Trust me. Huge mistake."

"If you ask me, you're reacting to fully understanding how serious his heart attack was and how close you came to losing him. Before you did that search, his condition was more abstract. Sure, you know a heart attack is serious, but a widow-maker is a whole other level."

"Yes, I'm sure that's what's causing the anxiety."

"Would you feel comfortable talking to him about this?"

"I don't know."

"You might feel better if you told him what you were thinking and feeling."

"I'm trying to imagine starting that conversation when all he wants to do is move on from it."

"Would he want you to be suffering from your worries over him?"

"Not at all."

"You should talk it out with him. It'll probably ease your mind."

"Sometimes I wonder if I'll ever have normal reactions to anything again."

"Do you define normal as how you would've reacted before Jim's illness and death?"

"I guess so."

"Then no, you won't, because you can never go back to who you were before that happened. You're a new version of yourself in this aftermath, so your reactions are normal for who you are now."

"That's an interesting perspective."

"I see a lot of patients in my practice who are very eager to return to the life they had before their traumatic event. They want to go back to the simplicity of that time when they were still untouched by loss or grief. I have to gently bring them around to the simple fact that they can never go back to who and what they were before."

Her profound words bring me to tears. "How do you always know what I need to hear?"

"That's sweet of you to say. I'm sorry that my words apply to your situation."

"This has helped me immensely. Thank you for being there for me."

"I'm happy to talk any time you need it, Lex."

"You have no idea how much that means to me."

"Take good care of yourself and try to focus more on the new love and joy in your life than worries about how it might end."

"I'll do that. Thank you again, Toni."

"Any time, my friend."

I put down my phone and go into the bathroom to finish getting ready while picking over the conversation with Toni.

Tom would want to hear about my anxiety, even if he's the cause. I just hate to add anything else to his plate when he's probably dealing with his own fears following the near miss.

"Hello up there! I'm coming up! Are you decent? Please say no!"

And he makes me laugh like I haven't laughed in many years. "Sorry to say I'm fully dressed."

"Damn it." He comes quickly up the stairs, not at all like a man recovering from a... *Don't say it, Lexi. Don't even think it.* "You look beautiful as always. I love your hair like that."

It's pulled back into a clip because I didn't have an hour to straighten it. "It's a mess."

"Doesn't look like a mess to me." He tips his head and looks at me more intently. "What's wrong?"

"Huh? Nothing."

"Don't lie to me, Lex. You've been wound tighter than a drum since I got home earlier. What's going on?"

There's been only one other person in my adult life who *sees* me the way Tom does. When I lost Jim, I wondered for a time if

I'd ever have that again. Now that I do, the thought of losing it again is so overwhelming to me. "I did something earlier that I shouldn't have done."

He steps closer to me, running a hand over my bare arm and setting off a chain reaction that I feel everywhere. "What did you do, sweetheart?"

"I googled widow-maker heart attacks."

He winces. "Why'd you do that?"

"I wanted to understand what it was. And then I looked at your discharge paperwork and saw that the description of your incident matched the definition."

"And now you're freaked out about it."

"I don't want to be, because I know the problem has been fixed, and you'll be closely watched going forward..."

He puts his arms around me and draws me in close to him. "I'll be very closely watched, and I'm willing to change everything about my life if it means staying healthy so I can be with you for so many years, you'll wish I'd drop dead."

"Tom! I'll never wish for that."

"Never say never."

"I am saying *never*."

"I'm so, so sorry to have done this to you. I wish I could take back every burger, french fry and pizza I ate that clogged my artery. I wish I'd paid closer attention to what happened to my dad, so I could've been more proactive with my own health. And more than anything, I wish it hadn't been you who came home to find me in distress."

"I'm so glad I was here to find you, even if it was traumatic."

"I'd never want to be the source of more pain for you when you've already had way more than your share."

"It's not your fault."

"Sure it is, but from here on out, I'm all about healthy

living. We've got a lot of stuff to do, and I want to be here for all of it."

"What do we have to do?"

"Romantic dinners, a ton of great sex, lazy mornings in bed, long hikes in the woods, lots of cool trips, and maybe someday, when the time is right, we'll have a baby together. Then maybe we'll like that first one so much, we'll want another one."

I'm laughing even as tears wet my cheeks. The life he describes sounds like paradise.

"Where in the world have you always wanted to go but have never been?"

I answer without hesitation. "London."

"Don't hold back on me now."

More laughter. "I'm a freak for the royal family and all things British."

"Then we'll go to London as soon as we can."

"Just like that?"

"Just like that. Whatever my love wants."

"Sometimes I feel like this is all a dream, since the night we met up in that bar where I'd hardly ever been before then."

"It was fate. Or maybe it was your Jim, bringing you someone who could love you and care for you the way he did."

"I'd like to think he had something to do with it." I remember something right then, something that's been buried in the deepest recesses of my memory, overshadowed by the trauma that consumed our lives in his final years. "I told him about you once." I struggle to piece together the details. "We were out to dinner one night talking about people we'd crushed on in high school and how we'd been convinced then that no one would ever notice us because they didn't."

"Point of order. Yours definitely noticed you."

Smiling, I say, "I didn't know that then." He's gazing down at me with tenderness and affection that soothes my anxiety. For right now, he's here, he's healthy and he's mine. "It's funny to think that maybe Jim knew exactly who to send my way."

"I almost drove by the bar that night. I was late getting home, starving and didn't feel like cooking."

"I'm so glad you didn't drive by."

"Even with all this widow-maker business?"

"As long as you don't make me a widow any time soon, it's all good."

He holds me tightly. "I'm sticking around for a good long time because I've finally got Lexi Nelson in my arms. And nothing has ever been better than that."

MY MIND IS much calmer after my talk with Tom. The rest of me, however, is abuzz with anticipation of the rip-roaring love affair he's promised me as soon as he's allowed to partake in such things. It's amazing to realize that when Tom and I first connected, the thought of having sex with anyone who wasn't Jim—even the former man of my dreams, Tom Hammett—was still unimaginable.

But a funny thing has happened one dinner at a time, one conversation at a time, one day at a time living under the same roof with the man I once thought I loved with all my heart. I didn't love him then. I didn't even know him. But now I know him, and I love him for real this time.

Before I started living with Tom, I hadn't been on a date or even thought about joining a dating site or anything like that. Friends offered to fix me up "when I was ready." I was never ready. I rarely ever even thought about anything like that unless one of my widow friends was starting something new, and then I might wonder for a second or two if that would ever happen for me.

Then Iris and our other friends pointed out that Tom and I

had been "dating" for months. No man makes dinner for a woman every night if he's not interested in being more than roommates with her, they've all said at one point or another. The keen observations were like a light going on. I started to pay closer attention to the way he tended to me. And I started to see what Iris saw from a distance.

He was interested.

Very much so.

I wasn't ready then.

Now, though...

Now, I'm ready, or at least I think I am.

"Whatcha thinking about over there?" he asks as he drives us to my parents' home in his truck.

"About timing and how everything revolves around it."

"How so?"

"What you said before about what you pictured for us?"

"I hope it was okay to lay it out there like that."

"I loved hearing how you see things unfolding going forward. I was thinking about how I wasn't ready for any of this when we first met up and how our friendship has evolved into this new and exciting thing."

"If you're still not ready, there's no rush, Lex. I hope you know that."

"I do, and that means so much to me. I think I am ready, but only because it's you that I'd be taking this step with."

His scowl is adorable and comical. "I should sure as hell hope it would be me."

"It is. Don't worry."

He glances over at me, seeming uncertain.

"What?"

"I want you to know that for all this time, I was hoping for where we are now, but I also was willing to step aside if you ended up falling for someone else. I never would've gotten in the way of that."

"That's very sweet of you to say."

"But I would've wanted to have him killed."

My shout of laughter echoes through the cab of his truck. I howl with it. I've forgotten what it was like to lose my shit laughing and how good it feels.

"Just so you know," he adds after I catch my breath.

"You crack me up."

"I like when you laugh."

"I do, too. It's been a minute since anything made me laugh like that."

"Glad to be of service."

"Keep it coming. Laughter is good for the soul."

It's also good for my anxiety, which is much better than it was earlier. Talking and laughing help. I need to remember that going forward. When Jim was ill, there wasn't much point in talking it out, because there was nothing anyone could say to make his situation better for either of us, and there sure as hell wasn't much to laugh about.

Not that he and I didn't occasionally revel in the morbid humor that'd been so much a part of who we were before disaster struck. But it wasn't as funny when the situation was dire and becoming more so all the time.

My parents are thrilled to see Tom and greet him with hugs and praise for how good he looks and how happy they are that he's set to make a full recovery.

Like me, I don't think they could've withstood another loss, even if they're nowhere near as close to Tom as they were to Jim. They know he's an important friend to me and appreciate the way he stepped up for me, even if they were a bit skeptical at first of his offer of a place to live. However, in the months since, they've seen him treat me the way any parent would want their daughter to be treated by a friend and a man, and they love him for it.

So they would've suffered, too, if we'd lost him.

They're the cutest couple ever. They met in Puerto Rico when my dad, Carl, was in the navy. My mom, Valentina—or Val, as everyone calls her—was twenty years old and fell madly in love with the handsome sailor who was five years older than her. I get my light brown skin, curly hair, brown eyes and fluent Spanish from her and the athleticism that made me a track star in high school from him.

I always wanted a marriage like theirs—loving, fun, full of laughter and adventure, and I had that with Jim. Maybe one day, I'll have it again with Tom. That thought would've overwhelmed me a year ago. Now, it doesn't seem so implausible, which is an amazing revelation in and of itself.

The salmon is tasty and tender, the green beans straight from their garden and canned last summer, and the salad crispy and delicious.

"This healthy-eating thing isn't so bad when the food is so delicious," Tom says.

My mom beams with pleasure. She used to love to cook for Jim, who we joked ate anything that wasn't nailed down. The first time he stayed at our house when we were in college, she offered him six different kinds of cereal for breakfast. He said, "Sounds good." She asked which one. "All of them," he said. We laughed about that for the rest of his life.

"What's so funny, Lex?" Dad asks.

"I'm thinking about Jim wanting *all* the cereal." I share the story with Tom and note both my parents watch him anxiously, no doubt wondering what his reaction will be to hearing a story about Jim.

Tom smiles. "I love that. A man after my own heart. My mom used to say I kept Kellogg in business when I was a kid."

My parents seem relieved by his easy acceptance of a story from our shared past.

"Guys..." I feel the need to put this out there. "Tom knows how much I'll always love Jim and how happy we were. He also knows it's important for me to be able to speak freely about him."

"I like hearing about him," Tom adds. "I'm sorry I never got to meet him. I think we would've been good friends."

There's nothing he could've said that would've meant more to me or my parents.

"I think so, too," Dad says softly.

Mom raises her wineglass in a toast. "To our Jim."

Tom and I touch our water glasses to their wineglasses. "To Jim."

Nineteen

Lexi

We send my parents into their cozy den to watch the news and their favorite game shows while we do the dishes. With the dishwasher loaded and the table wiped, I turn to Tom. "I'd like to show you our place downstairs, if you'd like to see it."

"I'd like to see anything you want to show me, but are you sure you feel up to that?"

I recall telling him how I never wanted to see that basement again after I moved out. "There're a few things I left here that I'd like to have, so I suppose I need to do it at some point."

"I'll be right there with you."

"Why do you think I waited until now to do it?"

He leans in and kisses me softly. "Lead the way."

I take his hand and walk toward the basement door, which is in the hallway of my parents' ranch home. In the den, I can hear them discussing something about Iran and Russia as the news drones on in the background. When Jim was first sick, I tuned out current events, and I still haven't tuned back in. I lack the bandwidth to take on anything more than my own load. After having been raised in a home where the news is read, watched and discussed daily, I suppose I'll get back to paying attention at some point, but not today.

Tom and I go down the most familiar flight of stairs in my world. If I had a dollar for every time I've run up and down those stairs, especially during the years we lived here, I'd be able to pay off my debt.

I flip on the light at the bottom of the stairs as a million memories flood me all at once. Maybe I'm not ready for this after all. Everywhere I look, I see him. In his recliner by the windows where he enjoyed watching the birds at the feeders my father kept in seed all year so there'd always be activity for him. In the wheelchair that made it possible for us to take him outside to get some sunshine on his face or to medical appointments in the wheelchair-accessible van that we could call on as needed for rides. The rides were four hundred dollars a pop, so we tried not to need them very often.

I see him in the specially outfitted bathroom that made it so we could bathe him with assistance from his devoted fraternity brothers. I hated them when we were in college but love them like family now after the way they stood by us through every step of the journey.

"Lex? Talk to me. Tell me what you're thinking."

"I'm thinking about how much I hated Jim's fraternity brothers when we were in school. You couldn't find a bigger bunch of douchebags than they were—Jim included when he was with them."

Tom laughs. "I knew a few frat guys at school. They weren't for everyone."

"No, they weren't, but oh, how they stepped up for us when we needed them. They took turns coming every day for two years to help Jim shower. Some of them drove two hours

SOMEONE TO WATCH OVER ME

each way to get here. There was no job that was too much for them. They were my heroes—and his."

"Wow. That's amazing."

"They were such a blessing, and I love them all like brothers to this day. Funny how people change, huh?"

"Life changed them. When their buddy got the worst possible disease, they grew up to be what he needed."

"That's exactly what happened. When I think about those years, they stand out like the brightest lights in a sea of darkness. The guys he played softball with came every week to play cards with him, even long after he couldn't manage his own cards anymore. My sorority sisters from UVA brought meals to us every weekend. Our neighbors, my parents' friends, cousins, extended family... They did what they could to make an unbearable situation easier than it would've been otherwise."

"I'm so glad you had that kind of support."

"It made all the difference." I blink and realize we're still standing on the bottom step. "I was going to show you..."

"Don't do it if it's too much. Your mom can get anything you need, can't she?"

"Yes, but I want to do this. I need to. I left him here, you know? I feel like I need to say hello or something."

"Whatever you want."

"Thank you for rolling with all my widow weirdness. I know it's a lot to ask of you at times."

"I don't mind at all. I'd say I understand, but I don't, so I'm following your lead here, sweetheart."

He touches me so deeply with his kindness and his understanding. No, he hasn't experienced what I have, but he holds the space for me to be exactly who and what I am—a widow who still deeply loves the man she lost to a cruel, relentless disease.

I curl my hand through the crook of his arm. "Right this way." I lead him into the big open living area and point to the kitchen my dad put in for us that includes a refrigerator, sink, oven with a stove on top and a microwave that made it so we could be more independent. "My dad showed up one day with an appliance delivery. He and two of his friends had it put together in about four hours. He'd planned it all out to be as quick as possible so they wouldn't disturb us for too long. While the guys were here, they also adapted the bathroom.

"Through the back door over there, we could take Jim to the driveway in his motorized wheelchair, which is why living here made so much sense. We had a way out."

"Things you never think about until you have to."

"Exactly. When I was a teenager, my friends and I used to hang out down here, and we'd sneak in more people through that same door. Not once did I ever imagine how critical that door would become to me in the future."

"That just gave me a chill."

"I'm sorry. I don't mean to be overly dramatic."

"That's not why it affected me that way. Your story about the door summed up the struggle you faced so perfectly. How it played a part in different eras of your life."

A lot of people pretend to understand. Few actually do. Maybe it's because he suffered his own tremendous loss when he was far too young to cope with such a thing. At least I had the benefit of maturity to guide me through the uncharted waters of young widowhood, for all the good maturity did me when I wanted to smash things.

"Jim said he missed looking at photos, so one of our friends put everything in a YouTube video we played on the TV. It was set to all his favorite music, and he'd watch it on repeat, reliving his childhood, ski trips, fishing trips, high school football and basketball, college, our years of dating, dancing at our wedding, our honeymoon, first apartment, the cat we adored and had to rehome."

He winces at that last part. "It's great that you found a way to make the photos accessible for him."

"It was, until he asked me to turn it off one day because he couldn't bear to remember everything he was missing out on anymore. He never watched it again."

"That makes me so sad for a man I'll never know in person."

"You'll know him through me."

We wander farther into the area that Jim and I called home for his last two years and where I lived for almost two years after he died. My parents had turned the extra upstairs bedrooms into a craft room for her and an office for him. I didn't have the heart to ask them if I could take one of them back, so I stayed put in the basement. It killed me to be there when he was ill, and it killed me all over again after he was gone.

"How did you deal with the stress?"

"I ran. Every day. Miles and miles and miles. My mom would come down every afternoon at three, when Jim was usually napping. She'd turn on *General Hospital* and send me on my way, telling me to take my time, that she could handle whatever came up. I'd tell her to call me if she needed me. I had my phone with me and figured I could grab an Uber to get home fast if need be. But she never once called me, even a few times when she probably should have."

He releases a deep sigh.

"There were times when I thought about not coming back." I stare at the print we bought on our honeymoon and had framed. We loved the sunsets in Jamaica and wanted to remember them always. I grew to hate that photo and everything it represents. The other trips we'd never get to take. Sex we'd never have again. The boring monotony of looking at the same photo day after day after endless day. I left it behind on purpose when I moved out.

"But you never acted on that impulse."

"And I never would have, but every single day, I thought about what it would be like to just keep running and never look back."

"Anyone would've felt the same way. You know that, right?"

I shrug. What do I know about how other people feel?

"I don't know if I could've done what you did."

"None of us think we can until we have no choice."

"I suppose that's true. I'd want to be there for you the way you were for him."

"I hope I never need you like that—and vice versa."

I turn on the light in the bedroom. "I mostly slept alone in here, always with the door open so I could hear him if he needed me." I'm not sure why I keep talking, but since he doesn't seem to mind listening, I continue the story. "Within three months of us moving in, Jim was sleeping in a power recliner that would help him up during the night. By then, it had become difficult to get him in and out of bed. It was too low for him. We bought that bed as newlyweds, along with the matching bedside tables. There were two of them and a dresser. We sold the rest of the set because we didn't have room for it here. For a while there, it seemed like we lost something new every day. Whether it was our precious cat or a possession we'd treasured or a friend who couldn't deal with the tragedy of it all or yet another function we all take for granted, such as brushing our own teeth or swallowing or speaking. It was like this endless doom spiral that seemed to have no end and no bottom to how low it could go."

Only when he brushes his fingertips over my face do I realize I'm crying.

I offer a shaky laugh. "I'm sorry. I probably shouldn't have come down here after all."

"Why don't you get whatever it is you need so we can go back upstairs?"

"Yeah, that'd be good." In the bedroom closet, I retrieve the running shoes and gym bag that contains leggings, sports bras, the thermal shirts, hat and gloves I need to run this time of year. Anything associated with Jim's illness was too painful to go near after his death, including my favorite form of exercise. I've been wanting to get back to it lately, but everything I needed was here, left behind in my haste to vacate the scene of our disaster. "That's everything."

He takes the bag to carry it for me, not because I need him to, but because he's always finding ways to lighten my load.

We make our way upstairs, and I put my things by the door, so I'll remember to take them with me. Widow brain is not to be trusted, even with the most obvious things.

When I turn, he's right there to wrap me in a warm embrace that I badly need. The visit downstairs has left me feeling unmoored and rattled. The sight of that space was enough to trigger a trauma tsunami.

I luxuriate in his tenderness for a few minutes before I finally break the silence. "I'm sorry to put you through that."

"You didn't put me through anything I can't handle. Everything you share about your life with Jim makes me see more of *you*. Your strength and courage are an inspiration."

"He was the hero of our story."

"Who would *he* say was the hero?"

I can't help but grin. "You think you're so clever."

"Nah, I'm just pretty certain he'd say you were the heroic one."

"He would, but I'd fight him on that. What he went through... No one should have to endure that. We're kinder to our sick animals than we are to human beings. Why can we send a dying dog mercifully to his or her rest, but Jim, who knew what was coming and had all his faculties, couldn't opt for a peaceful, painless death? It's obscene."

"Did he consider that?"

"We talked about it, and he seriously considered it. However... After years of baffling symptoms, his major decline happened somewhat quickly. Even in the states that allow it, he had to be able to administer the medications himself, which ruled it out for him long before we were prepared to make that kind of decision."

"We always think we have more time."

"Isn't that the truth? Jim said if he'd known he was going to die young, he would've skipped college and gotten out there and lived the second he turned eighteen. So much time wasted on classes he'd never need or use. He really struggled with all the time he felt he'd wasted."

"Hindsight can be awful that way."

"But he always added that if he hadn't gone to college, he never would've met me, so it was worth it for that alone."

"Are you kids ready for dessert?" Mom asks.

We release each other as if we've been caught doing something forbidden. Teenage habits die hard.

"Didn't mean to interrupt anything," Mom says with a laugh. "Whenever you're ready, I've got frozen yogurt. I thought that would be healthy, right?"

"That's perfect, Mom. Thank you."

"Yes, thank you," Tom adds. "I appreciate it."

"We need to keep you around for a good long time, young man. We can see how happy you make our Lexi."

She's gone before her words register. "Ugh. No pressure much."

"It's fine. She's lovely, and of course she wants you to be happy. As do I."

"Thank you for listening just now. It helps to be able to talk about it with you, to feel as if Jim is safe with you."

"You both are. Always."

On Wednesday, I head to my Wild Widows meeting with the brownies I baked earlier to share. I also made a veggie stir-fry for Tom to have when he gets home from spending two hours at his office after cardiac rehab. He swore to me that he's not overdoing it and that he'll nap when he gets home.

I can't help worrying about him, but I learned in the early days of Jim's illness that it was important for me to follow his lead and for him to feel like he still had agency over his situation. The last thing he wanted was for his wife to become his mother. Tom doesn't need that either, so I'm careful to keep some of my thoughts to myself so he won't feel like I'm hovering.

The caretaker mindset is hard to shake, especially when you spent years in the trenches.

Tom doesn't need a caretaker. He wants a partner to share his life, not to fret over his every move.

I'm working on that, but it takes real effort to bite my tongue when I want to tell him to sit on his ass and *rest*.

Iris is telling us about our two new members tonight before we meet them on Saturday. As much as I look forward to our Wednesday meetings, I adore the times we get together with the full crew, including all the kids I've come to love like the nieces and nephews I'll never have as an only child. Jim has brothers who haven't married, so maybe I'll get a few from them someday. His family continues to include me in every event, but there's some distance there now that he's no longer part of us.

His parents check in frequently, and I have lunch or brunch with them at least once a month, but my relationship with them was strained by the demands of caregiving and a few decisions I made on his behalf that they didn't agree with. They didn't like ceding their next-of-kin role to me, his chosen partner. Everything I did was with his best interests at heart, but at the time, you couldn't convince them of that.

They added stress to an already horrific situation, and while I've forgiven them for that, I'll never forget that they made things harder on me than necessary. And they know I won't forget it. We pussyfoot around each other, wanting to maintain the contact, but aware of the underlying tension that'll always be part of our relationship now.

Everything is weird in the after. Every. Single. Thing. I always had a great relationship with them until they started to question me at the worst possible time. I deeply resented the intrusion, even from the people who'd given him life. One of the last things Jim said to me when he could still speak was to always do what I thought was right and to not worry about what anyone else had to say about it. That gave me tremendous freedom from feeling guilty for doing what I felt was best for both of us, even if it angered his parents.

Jeez, I haven't thought about that stuff in an age. It feels like part of a distant past that belongs to someone else's life. I try to stay focused on the good with his family, the way his parents and brothers came running to help any time I asked for it, how their visits brought him joy and how deeply they grieved his death.

I'm the first to arrive at Iris's. It's a treat to have her all to myself for a minute, as Gage is upstairs showering, and her kids are with her mom for the night.

"What's new and exciting?" She pours me a glass of wine and gives me a careful once-over. "You're glowing."

I place my hands on my face. "I am?"

"You are. Is that thanks to our friend Tom Terrific?"

That nickname still makes me chuckle. "In part. Things with him are great and getting greater all the time."

"Oh, I *love* when that happens!"

"It's been fun. We've been sleeping together in his bed every night lately."

She raises a brow. "Just sleeping?"

"And some other stuff, but nothing major for him because he's not allowed until Friday."

"So is Friday like D-Day or something?"

I laugh at her phrasing. "I think it might be."

"How do you feel about that?"

"I feel good about it. I'm ready. I think..."

We share a grimace over how difficult it is to know such things for certain until they happen.

"You'll be fine. He's been showing you his heart for months now, and you know you're safe with him."

"I do, and that makes all the difference."

"I feel like I need a diploma to present when our members move into a chapter two. If I had one, I'd be giving you yours tonight."

"That's actually a fun idea for the future."

"I'll give it some thought. But a diploma doesn't mean you move on from us, you hear me?"

"I'll never move on from the best friends I've ever had, who put me back together piece by piece and helped to get me ready for what's ahead."

She reaches out to grasp my hand. "Love you so much."

"Love you more."

"No way."

"Yes way."

"What are we fighting over, ladies?" Gage joins us fresh from the shower with his wet hair combed back off his handsome face. True story—the first time I ever saw him, I thought he was hot, which came as a huge surprise to me because I hadn't had that thought about anyone other than Jim in years.

"We're arguing over who loves who the most," Iris tells her fiancé.

"Iris loves everyone more than any of us. Her heart is the biggest one in town."

"I can't take issue with that, so you win," I tell her.

"You guys... Cut it out."

Gage pats her ass and gives her a kiss. "Truth hurts, love."

I send a smirk her way. "What he said."

Twenty

Lexi

The others begin to arrive, first Brielle, then Naomi, Roni, Derek, Joy, Christy, Kinsley and Hallie.

"Are Wynter and Adrian coming?" I ask Iris.

"Not tonight, but they'll be here on Saturday."

"Oh good," Joy says. "I need some baby snuggles."

"Dylan loves his Aunty Joy snuggles," Roni says of her young son.

"Aunty Joy's got enough love for all the babies, sugar."

We fill our plates and form the usual circle of chairs in the living room.

Iris begins the meeting. "I mentioned that we've got two new members joining us, and I thought I'd tell you about them tonight so you're aware of their stories before Saturday." She glances at Roni.

"The first one is my boss's sister Angela," Roni says.

Her "boss" is the first lady and badass homicide detective Sam Holland Cappuano. Her brother-in-law's sudden death at

Camp David during the holidays last year made for shocking headlines around the world.

"Sam connected Angela and me a while ago," Roni continues, "and we've kept in close touch since her husband, Spencer, died from an accidental fentanyl overdose."

It's been big news that he bought a lethal dose on the street to treat unrelenting back pain after being cut off from pain medication by doctors. Sam and her team hunted down the dealers and charged them with multiple murders tied to the tainted product.

"His death was such a tragedy," Christy says.

"Yes, it was, and Angela has been left with three young children to care for on her own, which, as many of you know, is the hardest part. Her son, Jack, was very close to his dad, and managing his grief has been a nearly full-time job for Angela."

"I feel that," Iris says. "It's so hard. I'm glad Angela has decided to join us."

"She's wanted to for a while," Roni says, "but wasn't ready until now."

"I'm looking forward to meeting her and doing whatever I can to help," I say as the others nod in agreement.

"You guys will like her," Roni says. "She's one of us."

"I think you'll also like Luke," Iris says. "His son Beckham is in school with my Tyler. Luke's wife died from colon cancer a year ago, leaving him with four young kids. Beck is the oldest."

"Oh Lordy," Joy says. "That man needs us."

"He really does," Iris says. "I'm so glad we were able to convince him to give us a whirl. Gage was instrumental in that, letting him know there'd be other guys and other single dads."

"That helped," Gage says.

"We'll take good care of him," Kinsley says.

"It's amazing, isn't it," I offer hesitantly, "how with the power of hindsight, we can all see that joining this group was the best thing we ever did for ourselves, but at the time..."

"It was the scariest thing," Brielle says. "What in the world did I want with a group of widows when it was all I could do to keep my own head above water?"

"Exactly." I smile at Brielle. "I had to be talked into it, but once I was here, the benefit became immediately clear to me. Finally, I was with people who got it, who understood how hurtful the 'at least you never had kids' comments were, or 'he's in a better place.'"

Everyone groans. We hate that one. The only place he—or she—belongs is with us.

"Could I get your advice on something, guys?" I ask tentatively.

"That's what we're here for, sugar," Joy says. "What's going on?"

"I told you how I was laid off."

"Thank goodness for that," Gage says. "That job was killing you."

"I'm trying to see it as a blessing."

"It is," Gage says. "You wouldn't have left because you needed the job, but now you have the chance to find something you feel passionate about."

"That's where I need your advice. I've been offered a position by the local ALS Association."

"Oh," Iris says on a long exhale. "How do you feel about that?"

"On the one hand, it would allow me to make a difference for people who really need what they provide. They were so, so critical to helping us when we needed it the most. The volunteer coordinator oversees support groups and things like getting equipment to patients. I'd also be making sure we have volunteer support for fundraising events. As you know, I've volunteered at several of them already, so I have a sense of what's involved." They all attended one of the fundraisers last year.

"But, honey," Roni says gently, "it's ALS."

"I know. That's what my mom said, too. I'm not sure I can handle that kind of daily exposure to the disease that killed my husband. But... I keep thinking of the many ways I could help those who are just starting out on their journey."

"You'd be an outstanding resource," Iris says. "That's not even in question. The only issue is whether it would be good for *you* to give to that cause every day."

"The only way to know," Gage says, "is to try it. And think of it this way: At least you'd be giving your time to something you care about rather than putting numbers in a spreadsheet that means nothing to you all day."

I agree. "Anything is better than that."

"You're much stronger than you were when we first met you," Christy says. "You were in such a fog then, emerging from the exhaustion of years of intense caregiving mixed with deep grief. You didn't have much to say back then. I used to worry more about you than anyone."

"You did? Really?"

"Oh yeah. You were so fragile. But now... You're like a butterfly spreading your wings, ready to fly."

I'm moved to tears by her kind words. "Only thanks to all of you."

"And yourself, Lex," Derek says. "You did the hard work."

"I suppose I have without even realizing it."

"That's how it goes," Iris says. "You move forward because you have no choice, but at some point, you start to spend more time looking ahead than back."

"You have such a gift for summing it up so perfectly, Iris," Brielle says.

"I couldn't agree more," I add.

"Aw, thanks. I suppose it's become my thing to wallow in widowhood and help others, even though that was the last thing I saw myself doing when Christy, Taylor and I began this group.

When Taylor met her now-husband, she said she couldn't deal with staying immersed in widowville any longer, but I couldn't imagine giving this up even after Gage and I got together."

"Same," he says with a smile for her. "I keep writing my Instagram posts because I know they're helping people, even if my first thought every day is no longer about how shitty my life is or how unfair my loss was, even if that's still true. It helps me to help others, so I'll keep doing it."

"You both make great points. Either of you could've moved on from this group a while ago and been fine, but you choose to give back in an area that's caused you hurt in the past. If you can do it, maybe I can, too."

"You definitely *could*, Lex," Kinsley says. "It's just a matter of whether you *should*."

I take a second to choose my words and get my emotions under control, which is the one thing that hasn't gotten easier over the years. "When things first got bad with Jim, the people from the ALS Association swooped in and made us feel less alone with our devastating new reality. I'm still good friends with a couple of the volunteers we saw the most often. They made such a huge difference for us, and the thought of being able to do that for some other family feels meaningful, you know?"

"Absolutely," Joy says. "Who better to step up for a new caregiver or patient than someone who's been exactly where they are and knows exactly what they need most? And has a heart of gold to go with the TLC."

"Totally," Brielle says. "You'd be great at it, and maybe by giving back at that level, the disease itself will lose some of its power over you. Your experience with it will change to something more positive for yourself, even if it isn't for the people you work with."

"Wow, I never thought of it that way before. You guys are

the wisest people I've ever met. Truly. Thank you for this insight. I think I'll give the job a whirl and hope for the best."

"And we'll keep a close eye on you to make sure it's not too much for you," Roni says.

"I wouldn't have it any other way."

"Now for important business," Iris says with a salacious grin. "What's happening with Tom Terrific?"

Leave it to Iris to make us all laugh.

"That's the nickname the girls have given Lexi's 'room-mate,'" Iris adds for those who don't know.

"If the shoe fits," Joy says with a gleam in her eye.

"The shoe definitely fits," I tell them.

"So wait, did you, like, do it with him?" Derek asks haltingly.

We lose it laughing over his embarrassment.

"Sometimes I hate you people," he says.

"You do not," Iris says.

"Yes, I really do."

When I've caught my breath from laughing at the faces he makes, I put him out of his misery. "Not yet, but it feels... imminent."

"Now, was that so hard to just say?" Derek asks with exasperation that sets us off again.

"You said *hard*," Gage says with a grin.

Derek glares at him. "I expect better from you."

"I'm doing what I can with him," Roni says with a smile for Derek. "Work in progress."

Her beloved gives her a scowl that only adds to the laughter.

"We've lost control of this meeting, love," Gage says.

"When did we ever have control?" Iris responds.

"Good point."

"Lexi," Gage says in his stern dad-of-the-family voice, "how do you feel about sex with Tom Terrific being imminent?"

More laughter ensues.

"I feel good about it. He is, in fact, terrific and has been just what I've needed over this last year as I put myself back together and started to stick my head back out into the world a bit."

"I've absolutely adored hearing about how he's taken such beautiful care of you without expecting anything in return except friendship," Iris says. "I've been on Team Tom Terrific from the start."

"We need T-shirts!" Brielle says.

"Oh my God, yes!" Joy says with a fist pump.

"*Oh my God, no!*"

They crack up at my emphatic reply.

"Are you happy, Lex?" Naomi asks softly.

"I'm as happy as I've been since Jim died, but there's one thing hanging over everything."

"What's that?" Hallie asks.

"Tom's health. He's doing well now, but technically, he survived a widow-maker heart attack, and those words strike unreasonable fear in me."

"I get that," Hallie says. "The more involved I get with Robin, the more I question my sanity allowing myself to fall for someone with stage-four breast cancer."

"You understand better than anyone the spot I'm in."

"I do, but," Hallie adds, "what I'm discovering is that the heart wants what the heart wants, and if the worst were to happen again, I'm much more prepared to manage it this time. I have resources in place, such as all of you, a kick-ass therapist and a support system that was sorely lacking when Gwen died so suddenly. It wouldn't be the same as it was then. It'd still hurt like a mother-effer, but I'm confident in my ability to survive it—and I'm confident in your ability to survive, too, if the worst should happen, which God forbid it does."

"Hallie's right," Gage says. "When Iris was first diagnosed, y'all know I didn't handle it the way I should have for the same reasons that have Lexi worried about being with Tom." He glances at Iris with a warm smile. "But when I think about what I would've missed by being afraid of what *might* happen... That would've been a damned shame."

"Yes, it would have," Iris says suggestively.

"My little spitfire."

"Do you two need to get a room?" Derek asks to more laughter.

"We got one," Gage says. "Right upstairs and no kids in the house. We're heading there as soon as you people get out of our house. And it's going to be *loud*."

Iris covers her face with her hands. "Make it stop."

After that, we descend into full-on chaos with drinks being refilled, dessert served and much more laughter as the talk of Team Tom Terrific T-shirts continues unabated.

I love them all so freaking much, it's not even funny.

Tom

IT's boring without Lexi in the house. I, who lived on my own for years with no problem, now hate being home alone. Everything is better when she's here, which I realized almost immediately after she moved in. My eighteen-year-old self knew exactly who he wanted, and not much has changed in the ensuing twenty years.

I take a call from Cora, who's kept her promise to back off and give me some breathing room in recent days.

"Yes?"

"How about hello?"

"Okay, hello, dear sister, what do you want?"

"You're a jerk."

"You love me."

"Do I, though?"

"Was there a purpose for this call?"

"To see how you're doing, but it's clear you're fine."

"I told you to quit your worrying."

"Easier said than done."

"Lexi and I stopped in to see Mom."

"How was she?"

"The usual. Agitated and confused."

Cora's deep sigh says it all. We often wonder if the heavy burden Mom took on after Dad died led to her dementia. We'll never know for sure, but we have our theories. "It was good of you to go."

We all hate going there, knowing it won't make an ounce of difference to her, but we do it anyway, no matter how much it hurts every time.

"How's Lexi?"

"She's good. Out with her Wild Widows tonight."

"She has wild widows?"

"It's a support group. The name comes from the Mary Oliver poem that asks, 'What is it you plan to do with your one wild and precious life?'"

"Oh, I love that. I'm so glad to know there's support like that for people who need it."

"The young-widow experience is unique, and the group has been a tremendous resource for her. They're her best friends."

"It's funny how I never think about what it would've been like to lose Paul when we were first married, and the kids were still little."

"It would've been a completely different life. Several of her widow friends have young kids."

"I can't begin to know how hard that must be."

"Be thankful you'll never have to find out."

"Indeed. Well, I'm glad you're back to your feisty, obnoxious self. It's a relief, believe it or not."

"I believe it. All is well. Go live your life. I'll text you tomorrow."

"Promise?"

"Yes, Cora, I promise."

"Good night, Thomas."

"Good night."

I love her. I really do, and if she'd been the one to have the heart attack, I'd be losing my shit like she is. The incident has sparked a lot of latent trauma in all of us, and I don't blame either of my sisters for being extremely rattled by it. Hell, I'm still rattled by it. Nothing like a heart attack to wake you up to how life isn't a dress rehearsal, and yes, I know none of us gets out of here alive, but I'm not ready to exit stage left, especially right when things are getting interesting with my dream girl.

Speaking of her, I see headlights outside and hear the rumble of the garage door opening.

My love is home, and my heart gives a happy leap in anticipation of seeing her.

I've never once, in my entire life, had a thought like that or had that sort of physical reaction to any woman but her.

Others have gotten the predictable rise out of me, but there was never this kind of emotion involved.

"Hi, honey, I'm home," she says as she comes up the stairs from the garage.

"Hi, honey, I missed you. How was your meeting?"

"It was great. Lots of laughs tonight."

"Not the first thing I expect to hear about a Wild Widows meeting."

She takes off her coat and hangs it in the hall closet and then comes to sit next to me on the sofa, curling her legs under her. "We laugh more than we cry. At least we do these days. When it's new, there's more crying."

"Tell me the truth. Did you talk about me?"

"I didn't, but they did. There's talk of Team Tom Terrific T-shirts."

"Stop it. You're joking, right?"

She holds up her hands as she tries not to laugh. "It wasn't my idea, but I'm not opposed in principle."

"For fuck's sake."

Now she laughs—hard. "I thought you'd want a warning if someone actually goes through with this idea."

"Warning is good, but I think I might be busy Saturday night after all."

"You are not. Man up. You can handle a bunch of wild widows."

"Can I, though?"

She reaches for my hand and curls her fingers around mine. "Did you eat?"

"Yes, ma'am. The stir-fry was excellent. Thank you."

"I'm glad you enjoyed it. I made enough to have leftovers tomorrow."

"I'll look forward to it all day tomorrow."

"Are you just saying that when you have lust in your heart for steak?"

"I have lust in my heart for you, and if it means eating nothing but veggies for the rest of my life and I get to spend that life with you, then I'm all in with the veg."

She fans her face. "You've earned the T-shirt with that comment."

Scowling, I tell her, "No T-shirts. I mean it."

"It's out of my hands, unfortunately."

"You don't look the slightest bit contrite about any of this."

"I can't help if your reputation precedes you."

"Can we go to bed? If I kiss you, maybe you'll quit being mean to me."

Her smile lights up her entire gorgeous face. She's quite pleased with herself, as am I. Herself is my favorite self in the whole world.

I often wondered if I'd ever fall truly in love. I've seen my friends go crazy over women, marry them, have babies with them and walk around with a blissed-out look on their faces that baffled me. I'll be honest... I was sort of thankful to have escaped that fate when one of them would tell me he couldn't golf because he had to go to a friend's baby shower, or another would say his wife wasn't feeling well and he didn't feel right leaving her for the day.

What? Okay. Whatever, I thought.

Now, though, as I follow her to bed... Now I get it. There's nothing I'd rather do than hang out with Lexi as much and as often as I can. The hobbies I enjoy, including golf, have nothing on her. I probably owe some of my married friends an apology for teasing them about their commitments to their wives.

Would Lexi get married again? I have no idea, but I'd really like to know. We've talked about kids, but would she want to be married first? I'm not sure, and suddenly, I need to know.

Tom

When we're in my bed, on our sides facing each other, hands intertwined, I decide I want to know the answer to that question. "Can I ask you something?"

"Sure."

"Would you get married again?"

"In general or to you?"

"Why do you have to torment me this way?" I'm endlessly amused by her, and I realize that the emergence of her playful side is something that's happened slowly since she moved in.

She laughs. "I'm sorry. I was just wondering."

"I'm not exactly advocating for you to marry someone else."

My exasperation makes her lips quiver with more laughter looming. "I loved being married to Jim, and if the right guy came along, I'd probably be willing to do it again."

"If the right guy comes along..."

"That makes all the difference."

"How did I not know you were so mean?"

She dissolves into laughter.

I love to see her happy and laughing. She's such a far cry from the quiet, solemn, wounded woman who first lived with me. I'm not taking any credit for that. She's brought herself back from that darker place through lots of hard work and determination to make a new life for herself after being widowed. I'm just glad to be here to enjoy the fruits of those labors.

"You're so fucking beautiful," I whisper, overcome with a million emotions that are all new to me since I've loved her.

"I am not."

"God yes, you are. You always have been." I love to wrap her curls around my finger. "I also watched a couple of your track meets back in the day."

"What? You did not!"

"I did."

"I would've *died* if I'd known Tom Hammett was watching me."

"Then I'm glad I never let it be known. I would've hated for you to die before I could hold you and kiss you and love you the way I wanted to then. And still do now." I draw her in as close to me as I can get her with my hand on her ass and kiss her neck. "You were so sexy with the way you ran like you were being chased, balls to the wall. No one could catch you."

"That and the flute were the only things I was good at back then."

"You were like the wind, and I was mesmerized watching you."

With her hand on my face, she draws me into the hottest kiss we've shared yet, full of longing and heat that leaves me feeling singed. I end up on top of her with her arms and legs wrapped around me as I kiss her with two decades' worth of desire and yearning for everything I have now with her. I've begun to wonder how I survived all this time without her in my arms.

We get carried away... Before my brain catches up to the rest of me, we're both naked and straining against each other.

"Lex... I want you so badly. I've never wanted anything the way I want you."

"It's too soon. You shouldn't..."

"The wanting is more dangerous for my heart than the having."

"How do you know that?"

I take her hand and place it over the pounding organ in question. "Feel that?"

She licks her lips, and my already-hard cock gets even harder. "Yes."

"That can't be healthy."

"You're being ridiculous."

"I love you. I want to make love to you. Right now."

"If anything happens to you..."

"It won't. I promise." I kiss her again and can feel the exact instant when she makes her decision. "Do we need protection?" I bought a box of condoms after cardiac rehab the other day, just in case. The absurdity of that sentence would've made me laugh under any other circumstances, but nothing can distract me when I'm about to make love to Lexi Nelson.

Finally.

She shakes her head. "I have an IUD. I haven't been with anyone since Jim."

"I know. I haven't been with anyone since the last time I was tested. And I haven't been with anyone since the night I found you at that bar."

She grimaces. "You gotta say it like that?"

"Well... That's the story of us, right?"

"I guess that's where it all began."

I shake my head as I gaze down at her lovely face. "It began decades ago with a crush for the ages that's turned into the love of my lifetime."

We kiss again and strain against each other, both of us wanting more, which is exactly how I always hoped it would be if we got to this moment. It had to be on her timeline, not mine, but now that we've arrived, I want it to be so good for her.

I kiss my way from her neck to her breasts, teasing both nipples as she drives me crazy with the sounds she makes and the way she nearly pulls the hair out of my head. I love it. I move down, making her quiver with kisses to her abdomen and inner thighs. "Relax, sweetheart. Let me love you."

With her legs on my shoulders, I lean into her pleasure, using my tongue and fingers to bring her to orgasm twice. She's gasping and still coming when I move up and push into her, triggering another release for her that has me summoning every ounce of control I can find to keep this dream-come-true encounter from ending too soon.

I keep a close eye on her to make sure she's handling this first time since her husband died without any trauma. All I see is pleasure, thank goodness.

I make it last as long as I can before I give in to the need that pounds through me like an extra heartbeat.

Every second of this was worth the twenty-year wait to be with her this way. "Holy moly," I whisper as I kiss her neck and then her lips.

Her eyes are closed, her breathing is choppy, and her cheeks are flushed. "Mmm."

"Are you okay?"

"I'm very okay."

That's such a relief to hear.

Her eyes open as if she's suddenly realized she needs to be worried about me, too. "What about you?"

"Never been better in my entire life."

Lexi

SO THAT HAPPENED. I had sex with Tom Hammett, and it was incredible. I want to raise a toast to teenage Lexi, who picked him out of the crowd in high school and never forgot the heady feelings he inspired in her. She knew what she was doing when she set her heart on him, and she'd be freaking out to know she'd get to have sex—and lots of other things—with him in the future.

I can't ever regret the time I spent with Jim. I'm beginning to see, however, that I may have a whole other, longer life with Tom. A few years ago, I wouldn't have wanted that with someone else. But here I am, naked in the arms of another man I love and can see a future with.

"Well," he says, "now I can die happy."

My entire body recoils from that statement, even though I just made my own joke about dying over him as a teenager. It hits much differently coming from someone who just had a near-miss.

"Oh shit, Lexi. That was a very bad joke. I take it back."

I pull away from him and get out of bed, go into the bathroom and slam the door. I've gone from bliss to fury so fast, I'm shaking with it.

He knocks on the door. "Lex, honey, I'm so sorry. I didn't think."

No, you didn't. And that was the very last thing you should've said to me, of all people.

"Please come out and talk to me. Please?"

I put on a robe that belongs to him. It's huge on me, but I don't care as I throw open the door and make no attempt to hide my outrage.

"I'm sorry, love. I shouldn't have said that. I was in the moment—and it's the truth. Being with you that way made my whole life."

"I'm happy for you." I storm past him, gather my clothes and head for the door.

He's right behind me, gently grasping my arm. "Please don't go. I'm very sorry. I was in the moment and didn't think before I spoke. That was the worst possible thing I ever could've said."

"Yes, it was." I hate how my voice shakes and tears fill my eyes. I want to be strong in my fury, but his words have devastated me.

He puts his arms around me from behind. "I'm not going anywhere as long as I've got you to love."

"That's what Jim thought, too."

"I know, sweetheart, and in light of recent events, I never should've been flippant about dying."

"Don't ever be flippant about that with me again."

He drops his head to my shoulder. "I won't. I promise. I'm sorry I ruined our perfect night."

I start to relax a bit thanks to his sincere regret.

"Come back to bed."

I let him guide me back to the side of his bed that's become mine. He helps me out of the robe and tucks me in, leaning over to kiss me before he goes around to his side and snuggles up to me. "I want to tell you something that I hope will make you understand my gallows humor a bit better."

He slides an arm around me and rests his head on my shoulder. "After my dad died so suddenly, I didn't believe it for a long time. Even seeing him laid out in the funeral home didn't convince me that it'd really happened. So I started to make jokes about it with my friends, who laughed like the fools they were. Until one of them repeated some of my jokes in front of my mother, who was horrified by me. She immediately got me into counseling, where I was forced to talk about why I found my father's death so incredibly funny. Needless to say, it didn't take long with the counselor before I was sobbing my head off. It took me months to acknowledge what'd happened, and that could be the case now, too. If you joke about it, maybe you can pretend it never happened, you know?"

"I guess..."

"I know it probably sounds batshit crazy to joke about something so traumatic, and maybe it is, but everyone copes differently. Teenage Tom did not cope well with his father's sudden death. Despite that flimsy excuse for bad humor, it's something I never should've said to you."

"I know you meant it as a compliment."

"I truly did. Making love to you was like coming home to the place I've always been meant to end up."

"If only you'd said that instead of the other thing."

"Let's erase the other thing and go with that as the first words I said to you after the best thing to ever happen to me, okay?"

"Okay."

"I'd also add, I love you, Lexi."

"I love you, too."

After I say that, he seems to breathe a sigh of relief that the crisis has passed. I can't recall the last time I've been that pissed off about anything, and I suppose it's a healthy thing that he can make me mad like that and we can work it out.

Jim used to make me so mad sometimes, and he sucked at working it out. He'd walk away until I "got over it" or was tired of being mad. It was one of the things we really struggled with, especially as newlyweds.

Tom's approach in immediately acknowledging his error and profusely apologizing is vastly superior to what I'm accustomed to. I'd like to think that Jim would've evolved into that sort of husband if he'd lived long enough, but I'm not sure he would have.

I don't like to compare them because that's not fair to either of them, but I want Tom to know that I appreciate his immediate ownership of the situation.

"Thank you for what you did when that happened."

"You mean after I put my foot firmly in my mouth?"

"Yeah," I say, smiling, "that. You owned it, and you apologized right away, and that means a lot to me."

"I never want to say or do anything to upset you or add to your grief. I hate that I did."

"It's okay. I suppose we were bound to hit a snag at some point."

"I wish it hadn't happened after the best thing ever."

I squeeze the hand he's placed on my belly. "It doesn't take anything away from that."

"I didn't even get to ask you how you were feeling about it all before I screwed it up."

"I'm feeling okay. I've heard other widow friends say it's a relief to get the first time with someone else out of the way, but this didn't feel like a box being checked or anything like that."

"That's good, I suppose."

"It's very good. Some of my friends have had casual hookups to check the box, but I never could've done that with someone I didn't care about. I've never been casual about sex. Jim was my first, and you're my second."

"I wondered if that was the case."

"Now you know."

"Does that mean I have to share my history with you?"

"Absolutely not! Dear God, don't you dare."

He laughs at my emphatic reaction. "Phew."

"I'm sure it's in the high double digits."

"It's not even in the teens, so put your claws away, Cujo." He turns so he's above me, looking at me like a man in love. "And not a one of them could compare to Lexi Nelson, the ultimate dream girl. Or I should say woman. The beautiful, sexy dream girl grew up to be one hell of an amazing woman."

"Okay, if you insist. I'll do it with you again."

"Is that all it takes?"

"Pretty much."

He moves so he's fully on top of me, our bodies aligned as he gazes into my eyes. "That's good to know."

WE SLEEP late in the morning as neither of us has anywhere to be since his cardiac rehab is canceled today for staff training. Who said being laid off and in recovery from a heart attack didn't have a few perks? My ringing phone wakes us shortly after ten.

The caller ID shows Joy's number, which is odd. We mostly talk by text. I experience a moment of trauma-fueled anxiety as I take the call. Please God, don't let anything be wrong. "Hey. What's up?"

"Sorry to disturb you, but I was wondering if I could stop by for a minute. I have something for you."

I'm ridiculously relieved that there's nothing wrong. "Um, sure. What time?"

"In about thirty minutes?"

"That sounds good."

"Fantastic. See you then."

"What's going on?" Tom is facedown on the bed, his face crushed into the pillow.

"My friend Joy is going to stop by in half an hour. I'm going to take a shower."

"Want some company?"

Like a lightning bolt summoned from the heavens, I instantly recall showers with Jim.

Because he gets me, Tom says, "Feel free to say no."

"I'm not saying no. Just taking a second to remember other such showers."

He reaches for my hand. "If you've made enough new memories for a while, that's totally fine."

"I'm ready to make some more new memories, but we need to hurry up."

He pushes himself up with his arms and is off the bed with the speed and agility of a cheetah. "I can do quick."

I remember when Jim could move like that. It makes me sad that I rarely think of him as he was when he was healthy.

I've heard several of my widow friends talk about the insane push-pull of grief, balancing the life we had with the one we're building now, and how the most innocuous thing, such as a strong, virile man pushing himself up and out of bed, can trigger an avalanche of painful thoughts.

Rather than dwelling on those thoughts, however, I choose to focus on the fact that Tom feels strong enough to push his way out of bed like that, especially after we got busy four days before he was supposed to. I wish I could ignore the pang of worry that has my stomach aching as I join him in the shower.

He insists on washing me while he kisses my neck and gives my breasts extra attention.

By the time he's finished with me, I'm quivering with desire that I don't have time to deal with right now.

"Rain check, baby." He gives me a soft, sweet kiss. "Go see your friend. I'm gonna shave."

Twenty-Two

Lexi

I'm not sure I trust my legs to carry me out of the shower and into the closet to put on a pair of sweats and one of his Hammett Homes zip-up sweatshirts. I love the deep burgundy color and might have to keep this one for myself. I've got coffee going when the doorbell rings.

I dash down the stairs to greet Joy.

She comes in smiling and dressed to the nines in her work clothes. She's the most well-put-together woman I've ever known. Every detail is impeccable. Her nails and lips match her sapphire blue blouse and heels. "How do you manage to look like you just stepped off a Hollywood set so early in the morning?"

"Baby, it's almost eleven. I've been at it for six hours already. Not everyone can loll around in sudden unemployment, you know."

And she makes me laugh as I lead the way upstairs to the kitchen and the blessing of coffee to wipe the fog from my brain.

"Sorry to barge in on you and Mr. Terrific," she whispers. "Hope I didn't interrupt anything."

"You didn't. Last night, you might've."

"You jumped the gun!"

"I feel so guilty for letting him talk me into it." I pour coffees for both of us and grab the half-and-half from the fridge. "Not that he had to expend much effort to get me on board."

"Screw guilt. How was it?"

"*Sublime.*"

"Oh damn." She fans her face. "You're gonna get Mama Joy all hot and bothered just thinking about it."

"How's your new man?"

"He's becoming a problem."

"How so?"

"I like him more than I want to."

I laugh again. What a delightful—*joyful*—way to start the day. "Do you hear how stupid that sounds?" I love how it feels like we've known each other all our lives and can say any damned thing we want to each other without any worry of offense.

"Girl, of course I do. It's maddening, but I didn't come here to talk about me. I came to make a confession to you, my sweet friend."

I have no clue what she's talking about, but her smile tells me whatever it is isn't bad news. "A confession? About what?"

"I did something underhanded, unethical and borderline illegal, but for a very good cause."

"You're gonna have to fill in the blanks for me, pal."

"It's like this... You know I do a lot of social service work in my practice, helping people with housing issues, health concerns, child care, mental health. You name it, I've done it."

"You're a rock-star lawyer with a heart of gold."

"I couldn't imagine not using the gifts the good Lord gave

me to help people when I can. Not that your Mama Joy doesn't like making her some money, cuz she does."

"That's a given."

"Indeed. Anyway, through one of my clients and her case, I learned about a nonprofit that exists solely to assist people like you and my client who've seen a family member through a devastating illness and are left with equally devastating debt."

My mind goes completely blank as she names the foundation, talks about the founders and how they saw their parents through multiple illnesses that would've devastated them financially had they not been wealthy. "That led the siblings to ask what regular people do when it happens to them. They began a foundation in memory of their parents with that sole cause in mind, and well, I applied to them on your behalf—with your mother's assistance—and, well..."

She's positively giddy as she puts three pieces of paper on the table in front of me, all of them bearing familiar logos of local health organizations that are enough on their own to spark an instant wave of trauma. Except...

She points to my name and Jim's at the top of the pages and to the balances on each of them.

Zero.

Zero.

Zero.

"Joy..." I go mute with shock, and then I'm sobbing when it becomes clear she's eliminated a problem so massive that I long ago accepted it would outlive me.

"I'm sorry I was sneaky about it, but I didn't want to get your hopes up until I was sure it was going to happen, and then—"

I launch myself at her, nearly upending both cups of coffee on the table as I land against her full breasts, howling now with joy and relief and heartbreak and gratitude. More than anything else is gratitude to have such a friend.

Tom comes into the room. "Lexi, oh my God, what's wrong, honey? Is everyone all right?"

I'm so overcome, I couldn't speak if the house were on fire.

"I brought her some good news," Joy says.

He looks over her shoulder at the papers on the table and gasps when he sees the zeros. "Oh my God, Joy... *How?*"

She repeats the story of the foundation and how she asked for my mother's assistance to apply for relief from my medical debt. "Came through late last night, and it was all I could do not to march over here and wake y'all up."

I don't remind her that we weren't sleeping...

By the time I pull back from Joy, her gorgeous silk blouse has tearstains on it. I'm not sure if they're from my tears or hers, because she's crying almost as hard as I am.

She grasps my chin and looks at me with fierce love. "I see a lot of crazy-ass shit in my line of work, so many hard cases that don't end the way they should. I want you to know that doing this for you brought me as much happiness as it brings you, so thank you for letting me lie, cheat and pretend to be your lawyer to get this done."

Every part of me is trembling. "I'll never have the words."

"No words are needed. I love you. I wanted you out from under this burden, and now you are."

I hug her again, and at some point, Tom wraps his arms around both of us. I'm pretty sure he's in tears, too.

Joy has to go to work, so I walk her to the door.

"In my whole life," I tell her, "no one has ever done anything bigger than this for me, Joy. I'll never forget it."

"It made my year to pull this off for you—and for your Jim, who would've hated being the cause of such distress for you."

"It ate him up that I was going to be left with so much debt. That was his greatest fear about dying."

"I hope now he can rest more peacefully."

I hug her tightly for a long time. "Thank you."

"Love you."

"Love you more, and don't you dare argue with me."

She laughs, and when we pull apart, we're both wiping away more tears. "See you Saturday."

I wave her off and then go to find Tom.

He's waiting for me with his arms out.

I fall into his embrace, sobbing.

"I'm so, so happy for you, Lex. You deserve to be free and clear to enjoy your new life."

"I still can't believe it."

"What a friend."

"Right? I told you my widows are the best people I've ever known."

"They sure are."

My phone rings, and I take the call from my mom.

"Someone has been keeping secrets."

"I almost exploded the other night, knowing it was happening and not being able to say anything until Joy had the final receipts. Daddy and I are beside ourselves over this. You've got one hell of a friend in her."

"I know. I'm overwhelmed. It's going to take me a decade to wrap my head around this."

"What a relief."

"It sure is. Thank you for what you did to help her."

"I only told her who the biggest creditors were. She took it from there. She's a powerhouse, that one. They gave her some pushback, citing privacy laws and whatnot, insisting on talking to you. She wasn't having it and told them she had full authority to speak for you and let's get this done."

I'm in tears all over again imagining Joy going to war for me —and Jim.

"Daddy said this morning that Jim will rest easier now."

"That's funny. We just said the same thing."

"You must be elated. We couldn't wait for you to find out."

"It's such a huge load off my mind. I thought about it way more than I should have since I wouldn't have been able to pay it off in this lifetime or the next one."

"Now you can fully enjoy this lifetime, which is what Jim would want for you. It's what we all want for you."

"Thanks for everything, Mom. I know I say it all the time, but I never would've survived it without you guys, and Jim used to say the same thing. We were so lucky to have your love and support during the darkest days of our lives."

"We love you both, and we wouldn't have been anywhere else. And, Lex... We can see you have feelings for Tom, and we think he's a wonderful guy."

"I do, too."

"I hope you're giving yourself permission to be happy with him. Jim would want that for you, too. In all the years he suffered, all he cared about was what it was doing to you."

"I know." I look over at Tom, who's leaning against the counter, scrolling through his phone. "And I am happy. Happier than I've been since before..." I certainly don't have to define "before" for her.

He looks up, catches my eye and smiles.

After my mom and I say our goodbyes, I get up and go over to Tom, who puts his phone aside when he sees me coming. I slide my arms around him and rest my head on his chest. "You know what one of the best things about being laid off and out of debt and having your new guy being out of work on medical leave is?"

"What's that?" he asks, sounding amused.

"You could conceivably spend the whole day in bed and not have to feel one bit guilty about it."

He's immediately hard and ready for what I have in mind. "I'm really digging debt-free Lexi."

"You haven't seen anything yet, my friend."

Tom

You know how you can be sure you're in love with someone? When you're happier for them than you are for yourself. I've never been happier for anyone in my life than I am for Lexi after hearing her horrible debt has been cleared. After everything she did for her beloved husband during his illness, she's the last person who deserves to be saddled with that kind of burden for the rest of her life. I've been trying to think about how I might broach the subject of helping her with it, even if I knew she'd flatly decline such an offer.

What an incredible thing Joy did for her. I'll love her forever for that. I'm so glad Lexi has friends like her and the other widows who look out for one another in ways that go far beyond the topics of grief and loss.

And when she suggested we spend the day in bed, I nearly had another heart attack—the good kind, this time, the kind that seals the deal, not that our deal needed sealing. I'm all in with her and have been from the start.

I can already see the difference in her since Joy's life-changing visit. She's lighter, unburdened, freer to enjoy her new life now that her greatest worry from her past life has been resolved.

She stands next to my bed and whips her shirt over her head while I stare at her, still unable to believe that I get to have *this* with Lexi Nelson.

"Are you just going to stand there, or are you going to get naked?"

"Uh, definitely the latter."

"Well, hurry up already!"

"I'm a'hurrying."

We fall into bed, wrapped up in each other and desperate for more of the intense connection we shared last night. I can already see that unburdened Lexi is also uninhibited Lexi, as if she's been given a new lease on life, which, of course, she has.

Hands and lips and tongues and legs wrapped around hips —knowing we have nowhere to be and nothing to do other than fully indulge in each other has set us free to fully enjoy ourselves.

I push into her, loving the way she pulls me deeper, how her eyes close and her mouth opens on a silent scream of pleasure. God, she's beautiful, sexy, sweet and everything I could ever want. I raise myself up on my arms and move with her, letting her set the pace, which is fast and furious this time around. I'm down with that.

"Tom."

"I'm here, honey. What do you need?"

"Just this. Just you." She opens her eyes, and as her gaze collides with mine, I fall even deeper in love with her than I already was, if that's even possible.

We maintain eye contact as we chase the peak, crying out in unison from the power of what we created together. This goes way beyond anything I've experienced before. The difference between sex and lovemaking is finally clear to me.

"I have a confession to make," I tell her in the sweet aftermath.

"Do I want to hear this? I'm in a really good mood."

Smiling, I kiss her cheek and then her lips. "I think you might like this confession."

"Lay it on me."

"I have, at times, mocked the concept of lovemaking. Any time someone referred to it like that, I'd make fun of them. But now..." I kiss her softly. "Now I get it. For the first time in my life, I get why people call it that."

Her smile touches every corner of her sweet face. "You're right. I like that confession."

"I never knew it could be like this, or how much of a difference love would make."

"Thus the term *lovemaking*."

"Are you mocking me by any chance?"

"Would I do that?"

"Yes, I believe you would."

She loses it laughing. "Maybe I would."

"And here I was about to tell you how much I love you. But forget it."

"Please feel free to proceed."

"No, I'm mad at you."

She laughs some more, and the surge of love and tenderness and ever-present desire makes me light-headed—in a good way.

As I start to move in her again, I don't care that she's making fun of me or having such a good time doing it. I love her, I'm drunk on her, and I want this—I want her—for the rest of my life.

Lexi

TOM and I spend the entire day in bed, coming up for air, food and water before going back for more. I worry about him overexerting himself, but he says he feels great, and I decide to trust him. For the first time in years, I have nothing to worry about, no burdens to carry, no fears for the future. I'm free to fully wallow in the exceptional present and in my love for him.

I used to fear that I'd never have the kind of sexual connection I shared with Jim. That, too, has been resolved decisively after being with Tom.

I'm fully aware of how lucky I am to have found that twice in a lifetime, and I'll never take it—or him—for granted.

He's napping after we make love for a third time—and yes,

I'm still laughing at what he said about that term. I grab my phone from the bedside table and compose a text to my widows, wanting to tell them about the enormous thing Joy has done for me.

Their responses come flooding in.

Iris: *Joy... OMG. I'm in tears of joy for Lexi and for all of us to have a friend like you.*

Derek: *I'm so relieved for you, Lexi. Way to go, Joy. You're the best. What a thing to do for someone. So much love for both of you.*

Roni: *What Derek said. I'm mopping up tears at my desk! Joy... My goodness... You're a rock star.*

Brielle: *I've never had friends like you people. Joy, you are an exceptional human being. Lexi, I'm so, so happy for you. I hope you will fully enjoy every minute of your freedom from such a crushing worry.*

Kinsley: *I picture Jim smiling in heaven because Lexi has such an incredible friend who would do something like this for her. Well done, Joy!*

Wynter: *This is awesome! Adrian and I are thrilled for you, Lexi. And, Joy... There are no words. You're the best of the best. Love you all so much.*

Over the next few hours, Naomi, Christy, Hallie and Gage weigh in with elation for me and praise for Joy, who says, *I'm just coming out of court, and y'all have me in tears. This was the greatest thrill of my entire career. I'm so, so happy for Lexi (and for Tom Terrific... I hope he's benefiting from Lexi's newfound freedom from worry).*

My reply is two words that set off a furor: *He is.* <wink emoji>

Again, the replies explode my phone.

Roni: *GO, GIRL!*

Iris: *YESSSSSS*

Gage: *Go easy on the guy. He just had a heart attack. LOL *just kidding—I'm sure he's doing JUST fine**

Christy: *GET YOUR GROOVE ON!*

Derek: *Unsubscribe.*

That makes me laugh out loud, imagining the White House deputy chief of staff responding to such a thing from work.

Wynter: *I LOVE that laid-off Lexi is getting laid!*

Derek: *That's it. I'm out.*

Naomi: *I'm laughing my ass off.*

"What's so funny?" Tom mumbles.

"You'd have to hear the whole thing."

"Read it to me."

So I do.

"I can't believe you told them what we're doing," he says with a laugh.

"The widows tell each other *everything*."

"That's terrifying."

"Nah, I'll never go too far, don't worry."

"So 'laid-off Lexi getting laid' isn't too far?"

"Oh God, that's nothing compared to what we're capable of."

"I'd like to join Derek in unsubscribing."

Laughing, I tell him, "He's saying that from his office in the West Wing of the White House!"

"That's funny. You know what I never would've expected until I got to know you and your Wild Widows?"

"What's that?"

"How much you guys laugh."

"Oh jeez, if we didn't laugh, we'd never stop crying. Irreverence is our middle name."

"I like that for you, for all of you. That there's still joy and comedy to be found after what you've lost. Although, if I lost you, I'd never laugh again."

"Yes, you would."

"I don't think I would."

"Trust me... It's physically impossible to stay forever in the throes of early devastation. It's just not sustainable for a lifetime. Joy creeps in. It finds you even when you think it never will. It can be something simple, like a flower or a sunset or an exquisite butterfly hovering outside the window. Life is beautiful in so many ways. After the fog clears and you start to notice those things again, it becomes clear that you'll survive the seemingly unsurvivable, and you may even, one day, down the road, be happy again."

"That's beautifully said, Lex."

"I'm not saying it's easy, because it isn't. Jim's illness and death was the hardest thing I've ever been through, but I have gotten through it. I'll always love him, and he'll always be part of me, but his death didn't ruin my life as much as I thought it had for a while there."

"Because you didn't let it. You sought out support and found a way through it. That takes enormous courage."

"We have a saying in widow circles, when people tell us how they admire our strength, that you never know how strong you are until you have no choice but to be strong."

"I suppose that's true."

"When I was taking care of Jim, so many people told me they wouldn't have been able to do it, and that used to make me so mad because they *could* do it if they had to. They just didn't want to have to imagine a world where that would be needed of them, which is understandable. Who would want to picture themselves in a nightmare like that?"

"No one would, but I don't agree that anyone could do what you did. A lot of people couldn't and wouldn't do it. Please don't discount the extraordinary thing you did to make it possible for him to be at home for all that time."

"I don't discount it, but it's what most people do for the ones they love."

"I'll give you *many* people... Not most."

"Okay, I'll agree with that."

"You did an exceptional, selfless, kind, giving thing for him, and I hope you give yourself a ton of credit for what a difference you made for him at the end of his life."

"I do. In many ways, getting us both through that time in our lives is my proudest accomplishment, even if I hated that I couldn't change the outcome."

"Hearing about it has been enough to break my heart."

Smiling, I reach up to caress his face. "Thank you for today. It was lovely."

"Yes, it was. The first of many lovely days to come."

"Did you hear that my debt is gone?"

"I heard a rumor..."

"I still can't believe it. It's like a dream come true."

He drops his head to kiss me. "So are you."

Twenty-Three

Lexi

The next morning, I wake to a text from Hallie to the group: *Nine. One. One. Robin's ex-husband wants to move back into the house to care for their kids—and her. She says it's out of practicality and is not romantic, that she and I are still a couple, and nothing has changed. What. The. Hell?!?!?!*

My heart sinks for Hallie. The entire situation with Robin gives me a pit of dread in my stomach for my sweet friend.

Joy is the first to reply: *No. Just no. She can't have it both ways. She's either with him or with you.*

Roni: *WHAT JOY SAID x 1 million!*

Naomi: *x 2 million!*

I think about it for a second before typing my reply. *Playing devil's advocate here as a former full-time caretaker of a terminally ill person... Slow your roll, people. Is it possible that the ex is simply trying to do the right thing by the person he was married to for years and has children with? Is it possible he's acting in their best interest and not his own? Could he be involved with someone else, too? Are you willing, Hallie, to move in and care for her (and her kids) if it comes to that?*

Adrian: *I agreed with what Joy and the others said until Lexi weighed in, and now I'm not so sure. She makes very good points. What if Robin's cancer suddenly progresses? Does it make sense for the kids' father to be nearby if things get dicey? How far are you willing to go to be her caregiver if need be?*

Christy: *All good questions, Lexi and Adrian. Another thought... Robin has soon-to-be teenagers. Trust me... you don't want to be thrust into the game with them at this stage. I can barely handle mine, and I've known them for years.*

That makes me laugh. Christy's kids are great, and that's due in large part to how effectively she's managed their grief along with her own.

Wynter: *Why can't you all live together like one big happy family? He takes care of his kids. You take care of her?*

Gage: *What does it say about the rest of us that the youngest one has the best idea?*

Wynter: *That I'm smarter than all of you combined?!?*

Brielle: *Don't you have a baby to breastfeed or something?*

Derek: *Absolutely no talk of breastfeeding in this group text.*

Iris: <Laughing emojis> *Hallie, is this helping at all, honey, or have we made it worse?*

Hallie: *I sort of dig Wynter's idea...*

Wynter: *YES!!!! I win!* <fist bump emoji>

Hallie: *Except we're not even kinda ready for the move-in stage of the program.*

Kinsley: *From the cancer widow here... Things can change at any time, especially at stage four. If you've decided you're all in with her, which it seems as if you have, then be all in for the time you have left. Just don't give up your own home...*

Gage: *Very good advice, Kins.*

Hallie: *Thank you all for weighing in. When she told me*

this, my first thought was FUCK no. But you all make good points, and I feel better after talking it out with you.

Wynter: *Especially me.*

<Laughter emojis from everyone>

Iris: *Love you, Hallie. Let us know what we can do for you.*

Gage: *Ditto. Widow Movers is standing by ready to help.*

Hallie: *Thanks, guys! Xo*

"What's blowing up in widowville today?" Tom asks when he rolls over to find me on my phone.

"Hallie, who lost her wife, Gwen, to suicide, is dating Robin now. Hallie is Robin's first female partner, and Robin has two almost-teenagers and stage-four breast cancer. Her ex-husband is talking about moving back in to care for the kids—and Robin. Needless to say, that's not going over well with Hallie."

"Whoa. You guys don't mess around when it comes to complications, huh?"

"Sometimes it's messy. This is one of those times, and we're all terrified for Hallie in this situation, even if she assures us that Robin is lovely and all the things. It's a lot for Hallie, who's already been through so much."

"Surely Hallie is going into this with her eyes wide open."

"She is, but we wish it wasn't so complicated for her on the first time out after her loss."

"It's always complicated, isn't it? When it truly matters?"

"There's complicated, and then there's this situation. Wynter suggested that the husband move in to care for the kids and Hallie move in to take care of Robin."

"That sounds like the makings of an unfunny sitcom."

"I know."

"Come here."

I put down my phone and snuggle into his warm embrace.

"I love how you worry about your buddies, but I don't like that frown on your face when everything is going so well in your own life right now." He kisses the spot between my brows. "What can we do to turn that frown upside down?"

"This is the hard part of being one of the Wild Widows. We take on everyone else's problems and make them our own. And yes, we know that's probably not as healthy as it could be."

"It's very sweet the way you all take care of each other."

"I certainly wouldn't have been ready for you without their support."

"In that case, I'm very glad you have them."

"Me, too."

Hallie

MY STOMACH IS in knots as I wait for Robin to arrive. It's been in knots ever since she dropped the ex-husband-wants-to-move-back-in bomb on me earlier today. On the one hand, I appreciate that the ex wants to have everything in place for if and when her cancer takes a turn for the worse, which it probably will at some point in the not-so-distant future.

But to have him living in the house again? That might be a bridge too far for me.

In the years since Gwen took her own life for reasons that are still not clear to me, I've been in survival mode. The shock of that loss reverberated through every corner of my life, leaving me flattened with grief, regret and questions I'll never have answered to my satisfaction. It's taken me years to even think about dating again, and after a few first-date flops, along came Robin with her big smile and her zest for life that had me immediately dazzled for the first time since I lost Gwen.

However, then came the red flags that should've had me backing away slowly but certainly.

I would be her first female partner.

She has stage-four breast cancer, which is stable. For now, anyway.

Now, her ex-husband wants to move back into the house.

That latest flag has had me looking for my line in the sand, which has gotten foggy in this situation. I used to have hard-and-fast lines I'd never cross when it came to romantic partners.

At one point, I had a written list of things that were a hard no for me, such as homophobic family members who'd make our lives a living hell. I'd worked too hard on myself and my own family to take on bigots. If you're hiding who you are from the people closest to you, then I'm not your girl.

Experimentation was another. If you're "dabbling" in the lesbian lifestyle, I'm not the one for you. Either you're all in or you're not, which is totally up to you. But I'm not interested in one foot in while you keep your options open with men. Nope.

I walked away from people I felt a connection to because of these things, so these rules weren't just on paper. I lived them.

Robin has blown all my old rules to smithereens.

I was her first female lover.

She cried for an hour after the first time we had sex.

"I never knew what I was missing," she said. "How could I have lived all this time and not known?"

Those are heady words to hear from a new lover. She made me feel ten feet tall to have given her that experience and to have thoroughly enjoyed it myself, even if she had to be guided a bit on how to return the pleasure. I didn't mind showing her the ropes, so to speak, because she was eager to learn and even more determined to make it good for me, too.

She's gorgeous, funny, sarcastic, fatalistic about her dreadful illness and madly in love with her two children—a son, who's eleven, and a thirteen-year-old daughter. She cries when she talks about leaving them without a mother to finish raising them. My heart breaks for her and for them.

I've met her kids, and they're lovely. Sweet, polite, helpful...

Nothing at all like other kids in that age range, from what I've seen. They seem to understand their time with her might be short, and they're not going to waste it fighting with her over stupid shit. I admire them for that and for their kindness toward Robin—and me.

I can't imagine what it would be like to have my mom switch teams midway through my childhood, but Elias and River have welcomed me as their mom's special friend at this tender time in their lives. For that, I'll always have a place in my heart for them and the gift they've given their mother with their acceptance of her choices. I'm not under any illusions that it would've been so smooth without cancer in the mix, but I'm grateful for her sake that it has been.

And now, right when I was becoming as comfortable with a somewhat fucked-up situation as anyone could be with a stage-four cancer diagnosis hanging over a new relationship, the ex-husband reenters the picture.

By all accounts, he's a decent sort of guy. There was no big dramatic reason for their marriage ending, other than it running its course and Robin wanting more out of whatever life she had left than what she had with him. But the thought of the four of them all under one roof like a cozy family while I'm on the outside looking in is a hard no from me.

That is my bridge too far. My Wild Widows have given me the words to speak my truth to her, which I might've been afraid to do without their support. If I'm guilty of one big thing in all my relationships, it's that I tend to give more than I get. I did that with Gwen. I was constantly striving to make her happy, even if at times I sacrificed my own well-being for hers. I've had tons of therapy since her death, through which I've learned that there was nothing I could've done to change the outcome once she decided to end her life.

I've learned to live with that, even if I still revisit those final days far too often for my liking. I'm always looking for something I could've done differently, some sign that she'd made a decision that would shatter me, but there was nothing to find or see or do.

That's not the case with Robin, and I'm determined to stick up for myself this time around when my inclination would be to put her first, due to her situation.

I'm determined to stay strong and to make my case as important as hers.

To do that, I'll have to keep my emotions in check, which will be the hardest part. I wear them on my sleeve, or so I've been told my entire life. My mother used to tell me as a child that I could never hide when I was upset or anxious or happy or anything else. My face told the story, she said.

I take a deep breath and release it slowly, repeating the process until I find my inner calm.

A car door closes outside.

Here we go...

Robin comes in, carrying a bottle of the rosé we both love and looking a little beat up, as if she's been crying, perhaps. She's tall and blonde and so pretty, she makes me ache. The only outward sign of her illness is that she's thinner than she probably ought to be. She had a double mastectomy with reconstruction several years ago that retained her curves, not that it matters to me, but it did to her.

I wipe my hands on a dishtowel for something to do.

Normally, I'd greet her with a hug and a kiss, but today, I keep my distance.

"Hi," she says with a sheepish grin that turns my insides to putty. I love that little grin. "This is a fine mess we find ourselves in."

I laugh, and the tension is broken. I love that about her, the way she cuts through the crap with one sentence that sums things up.

"Indeed it is."

"I'm so sorry, Hallie. I know you're upset, and with good reason... I never saw this coming. I had no idea he was thinking about this or... Well, I didn't know he was worried about the kids."

I go to her because I can't not go to her.

We wrap our arms around each other.

"I was afraid I'd lost you over this one," she says softly.

"You haven't lost me, but I have thoughts."

"I'd be disappointed if you didn't. I'm not sure when it happened, but your voice has become the one that matters most to me. Your thoughts are the ones I most want to hear."

See how she does that? How can I not love her?

"Let's open this bottle of wine and talk it out."

She takes care of opening the bottle while I get the glasses.

We take them onto my back deck, where fairy lights are strung through nearby trees to create a magical atmosphere that Robin complimented the first time she saw it. We've spent many hours out here together since the first night she visited my home. The autumn scents of woodsmoke and decaying leaves are heavy in the air.

"Ah," she says on a long exhale as we land on the love seat and put our feet up. "I feel like I can finally breathe again. Today has been a lot."

"Yes, it has."

She looks over at me with liquid brown eyes full of emotion. "I'm sorry to have done that to you, but I wanted to be honest with you."

"Which I certainly appreciate. Don't think that's not the case."

"I know you do, but I wouldn't blame you for telling me to fuck off and get out of your life."

"I'm not doing that."

"Why not?"

"Because I care. I might even love you a little, and when you love someone, you don't cut and run when it gets hard."

She blinks when tears suddenly appear.

I hand her a napkin from the stack I brought out with the crackers and cheese we haven't touched.

"It's been hard from the get-go for you. Me and all my issues. Baby lesbian, recently divorced from a man, two young kids and terminal cancer. I'm one step away from being that toxic partner everyone warns you about."

Again, I laugh. "You're nowhere close to toxic. Trust me."

"What are your thoughts about Kevin moving back in? Please tell me the truth."

I take a second to get my thoughts together before I speak. "I know he's thinking practicalities and that it's not romantic."

"I can't speak for him, but it's not for me. That is long over. Even if I hadn't met you and had such an amazing connection with you, that would still be over for me. He's a good man and a wonderful father, but our romantic and sexual relationship had been nonexistent for years before we finally split."

She's told me that before, but it helps to hear it again, especially in light of current events.

"Thank you for saying that again."

"I mean it, Hal. I hope you know that."

"I do, and I believe you. And I think it would be good for the kids to have him there, if needed."

Her expression conveys confusion. "You do? Really?"

"Of course. Your health is precarious. He's concerned about his kids, as any good father would be."

"Okay, where's the *but*?"

"But... if he moves in to care for them, I move in to care for you."

She stares at me for a long moment before she blinks. "Really?"

"Really. I don't mind if he's there for the kids, but I do mind if he's there for you."

"So what you're saying is that…"

"We all live together like one big happy family for as long as we can."

"And you'd be willing to do that?"

"That's what I'm saying."

"Hallie…" Again with the tears.

I hand her another napkin.

"Are you for real? Why aren't you running away screaming?"

"I ask myself that question every day."

This time, we both laugh, even as she wipes away more tears.

"I hate that I'm doing this to you after what you've already been through."

"I think that what I've been through has made it possible for me to take this on, knowing how it might end."

She takes a sip of her wine. "How do you mean?"

"When Gwen died so suddenly, I didn't have any of the coping skills that I've acquired in the years since. That's not to say that losing you would be easier, because it wouldn't be. It would be different, though. I have a support system I didn't have then. I have knowledge about grief and grieving I didn't have then. Every loss is painful and difficult and so, so sad, and I'd feel all those things if I lost you. But I've shown myself that I can survive it and even eventually thrive again."

"You're the strongest person I know."

"No, you are. A lot of people would've snuggled into the status quo when faced with a diagnosis like yours. You blew up your whole life so you could live as authentically as possible in the time you have left. I think that makes you the strongest person there is."

"We can nominate each other."

"Fine. Be that way."

"I don't want to leave you sad and devastated."

"I'll be okay. I promise."

"You really want to move in with me?"

"You don't need me there right now. But if or when that time comes, I'll be there. In the meantime, if your ex is back at home and there's no need for me to move in any time soon, we have a built-in babysitter. You can come here after the kids are in bed."

She rests her head on my shoulder. "There is that."

I reach for her hand, relieved to have talked it out like adults and arrived at a solution that works for both of us.

"I love you, too, Hallie."

Her words bring tears to my eyes. I grab the napkin from her lap to deal with the tears.

"Thank you for sticking with me when anyone else would've run away from this ridiculous situation."

"I'm not going anywhere."

Twenty-Four

Lexi

I draft an email response to Nora, the woman who contacted me from the ALS Association. It takes me far longer than it should to write the four sentences that will send my professional life in a whole new direction, but this is no ordinary job or organization, so I take my time to get it right.

Hi, Nora,

Thank you for the time you gave me to consider your kind offer. As you know, the ALS Association was a lifesaver to my husband and me during his illness. While I believe aspects of the job would be difficult for me, it would be an honor to pay forward the many blessings we received from your organization for other patients and their families. Please let me know next steps when you have the chance.

Sincerely,

Lexi

I reread it at least six times before I press Send.

So... That happened.

I've officially tossed my hat in the ring for a job with the ALS Association. I can handle this. Right? I guess I'll find out.

I text the widows to update them.

Sent the email to the ALS group telling them I'd like to be considered for the position. Gulp. We'll see what happens.

They send congratulations and best wishes.

I'm proud of you, Lex, Wynter says in a private message to me. *There are so many jobs that would be easier, but few that'll make such a big difference for others.*

Aw, thank you, Wynter. That means so much. I'm proud of you, too, for so many reasons, but especially for the courage you showed in having Jaden's daughter. He'd be SO proud of you, too. Love you.

Quit making me cry. I'm lactating.

<laughter emojis>

"What's so funny?" Tom asks when he comes into the kitchen, where I'm on my laptop while sipping coffee.

"I applied for the ALS job."

"Okay… Where's the funny?"

I read my exchange with Wynter to him, and he laughs, too.

"She's a character, huh?"

"That's one word to describe her. She's the most hilarious person I've ever met. That message she sent me was so sweet. I've loved watching her mature over these last few years when she's gone from being so bitter at losing her beloved Jaden to a whole new life with Adrian and their kids."

"The more I hear about your widows, the more impressed I am by them."

"They're very special people. I'm looking forward to you getting to know them better at the party tonight."

My cell phone rings with a number I don't recognize. I take the call.

"Hi, Lexi, this is Nora. I got your email and figured I'd give you a call rather than typing a manifesto on next steps."

"Oh, cool. Thanks for calling on a Saturday."

"I'm trying to get my ducks in a row before my maternity leave starts, so there's no time to waste."

"Congrats on the babies."

"I'm in full-on freak-out mode with six weeks to go, if I make it that far."

The way she says that makes me laugh.

"I wanted to call you because I consulted with our director, Mina, and the board before I reached out to you. We all agree that the position is yours if you want it."

"Oh wow. Well... Yes, I want it. I think."

She laughs. "I get it, believe me. Well, I can't possibly understand it from your point of view, but I get your hesitation."

"A few years ago, I never could've handled something like this. But I'm stronger now, and I think I could be a resource for those who need it."

"I'm sure of it. You've been an outstanding volunteer, and we're thrilled to bring you into a more official role."

She states the salary and goes over the benefits. "You'll get three weeks' paid vacation, all the federal holidays, a week at Christmas when we shut down and another week of sick leave."

I'm still reeling from the salary, which is twice what I made at the data-entry job.

"Does all that sound good?"

"It sounds perfect."

"When would you like to start?"

Thanks to Joy settling my debt, I decide I want a little more time off before I dive into my new role. "How about I come in and train with you next week and then officially start on November first?

"That'd be great. I'll email you some details about next week and see you here on Monday around nine?"

"I'll be there. Thank you for everything, Nora."

"Thank *you*. I feel better knowing you'll be taking over for me."

We chat for a few more minutes before agreeing to continue the conversation on Monday.

Tom, who heard my side of the conversation, gives me a smile and a thumbs-up after I end the call. "Congratulations!"

"It's twice the money I was making before, too!"

"Do what you love, and the money will follow."

"Am I going to love this?" I'm still wary about the all-ALS-all-the-time aspect of this position.

"Maybe not every day, but I think you'll love knowing you're making a big difference for people who really need it."

"I will. For sure. So much more rewarding than data entry."

"That's a fact."

"We should do something to celebrate."

"What do you have in mind?" he asks.

"Champagne lunch followed by a nap before the party tonight?"

He comes to me, puts his arms around me and kisses me. "What kind of nap are we talking?"

"The good kind."

I'D FORGOTTEN what it's like to be newly in love, insatiable for more of him in bed and out of bed. Our lunch outing was full of laughter and excitement for my new job. The relief of having my debt settled continues to be a natural high, the likes of which I've never known. Even falling in love—twice—can't rival the massive feeling of liberation that comes from being free of that horrible weight.

Lying in his arms now, after making love again—I've lost track of how many times we've done it now—I'm as content as

I could possibly be in the "after," as widows often describe life following the loss of a spouse.

I'm in love again, and my future looks bright with promise.

"I'm going to want you to marry me, sweet Lexi. I hope you know that."

"I'm down with that."

"This isn't a proposal. That'll be epic. This is just a fishing expedition to make sure a proposal would be welcome."

I look up at him, so handsome and relaxed and happy. I like that I make him so happy. "It would be."

"And you'd say yes?"

I pretend to think about that long enough that he pokes my side and makes me laugh. "I'd say yes."

"Don't be mean to your future fiancé. It's not nice."

"I'm very sorry."

"Lying is also discouraged."

"I love this, Tom. Thank you for waiting for me to be ready for you."

"Sometimes it was hard to be patient, because I felt so strongly that we could have something great. And PS, I was right about that."

"Yes, you were, and I knew it, too. I've known it all along, in fact."

"You could've told me that!"

"What fun would that have been?"

"I'm not sure how I feel about mean Lexi."

Smiling, I move close enough to kiss him. "I wasn't ready, and I wouldn't have been doing either of us any favors by trying to be ready before I was."

"I get it, sweetheart. I'm glad it worked out the way it did."

"Just for the record, I could've done without the heart attack, however."

"Same. I'll always be sorry I did that to you."

"No need to be sorry, since you survived."

"I had the best possible reason to survive. Took until I was thirty-eight to really know what it means to be in love, and to be in love with *you* is the ultimate dream come true for me. I hope you know that."

Smiling, I kiss him some more. One kiss becomes two, which becomes six, and then we're straining against each other once again. Sometimes I still want to pinch myself that I'm rolling around naked in Tom Hammett's bed. Every time he pushes his hard cock into me, I gasp from the sheer pleasure that overwhelms me. I'd forgotten what it was like to be carried away by desire, and now I'm addicted all over again.

It's so good between us, so perfect, sort of like we both knew it would be way back when. But we had lives to lead before we found each other in this new chapter, and I'm incredibly thankful for what I have with him and how cherished he makes me feel all the time.

"God, Lex..." he whispers when he's deep inside me. "I can't get enough of you."

I hold him tight against me. "Same."

He pushes up so he can see me. "Love you."

I bring him in for another kiss. "Love you, too."

"Best words I ever heard from anyone."

I'M high on life after the best week I've had in years when we arrive at Iris's for the get-together with the new Wild Widows. I hope we don't overwhelm them with our sheer numbers, but Iris said both were interested in including their kids in the group. So we're taking our lead from them.

Tom is wearing a light blue polo shirt that makes his eyes look crazy blue, with khaki shorts in deference to the warmer-than-usual autumn we're having in Northern Virginia. He's handsome and relaxed after our afternoon in bed, and I can't wait for him to really get to know my best friends. Other than the day they helped me move into his place, he hasn't spent time with them. On the ride to Iris's in his truck, we reviewed each of them and their stories.

"Christy is the one who founded the group with Iris, right?"

I love how he pays attention to the details that matter to me the way Jim did with my students. "Yep. The third founder isn't active in our group since she remarried."

"Do people tend to stick around after they connect with someone new?"

"So far, only Taylor has moved on. I hope the others will stay with us. They're like family to me."

"So you'd stay involved even if we got married?"

I look over at him. "I always want to be involved with them. They're like the siblings I've never had. I hope you understand that even if I'm remarried, I'll always be Jim's widow."

"Of course I do. I was just wondering."

"Say what you want to say, Tom. It's fine. I promise."

"It's just that I worry about it being so heavy sometimes."

"That's life, though, right? Sometimes it's heavy. And like with the new job, I have wisdom now that I can share to make things easier for new widows. Not that anything can make it easy for them, but the support we've found in our group has been essential to each of us. I love them."

"I know you do, honey. And I'll always support whatever you want to do."

For a second, he scared me by making me think he might not want me to continue to be part of the Wild Widows once we get married.

"Don't be over there thinking I'd ever ask you to give up something that means so much to you. I wouldn't. My only concern is for you taking on the grief of others."

"I'll be okay. I promise."

He brings my hand to his lips for a kiss. "That's all that matters to me."

When we arrive at Iris's, bringing the buffalo chicken dip and brownies I made to contribute, we're greeted by a wild scene of screaming kids running through the house. I recognize Iris's three—Tyler, Sophia and Laney—as well as Derek's daughter, Maeve, Roni's son, Dylan, Brielle's son, Charlie, and a couple of others I don't know being chased by Christy's daughter, Josie.

"Josie, we paid you to watch them, not incite a riot," her mother calls from the kitchen.

Josie, whose dark hair is in a ponytail, gives me a sheepish grin and a shrug as she runs by me.

"Welcome to the loony bin," I tell Tom.

I get the usual feeling of homecoming that comes with every visit to Iris's home, where I get to be with my people.

Holding Tom's hand, I lead him to the kitchen, where Iris, Gage, Roni, Derek and Christy are with a few others I don't know.

Iris lets out a shout. "Oh my God! It's Tom Terrific *at my house*!"

When she comes toward us, I see that she's wearing a blue T-shirt that says #TeamTomTerrific in white letters across the chest, and I lose it laughing.

"Stop it," Tom mutters as Iris wraps him up in a big hug.

"Welcome to my home, to the Wild Widows family, to the craziest bunch of assholes this side of the nuthouse."

"Quoting *Christmas Vacation* might just get me to forgive you for the shirts."

"I didn't do it," Iris says, full of innocence.

"Why do I feel like none of you are going to take credit for it?" I ask Iris as I hug her.

"They just showed up in a box at my front door one day. What was I to do but unpack and distribute them?" She gives

Tom a big grin. "We already love you, so I hope you'll take the ribbing in the spirit in which it's intended and not run for your life from us."

"I think I can handle it," he says, "if it means I get to spend tonight and every night with Lexi."

Iris fans her face. "And you wonder why we had shirts made."

"You guys," Christy says, "this is Trey."

"I have to hug you," I say.

He holds out his arms to me.

"It's so good to finally meet you. We need #TeamTreyTerrific shirts, too."

"Don't give them any ideas," Trey says as he shakes hands with Tom. "I take it you're the terrific one?"

Tom grimaces. "You make a girl's coffee every day for a year and your reputation gets ahead of you."

"Well played, my friend."

"Tell him what *you* did, Trey," Christy says, beaming in a way I've seldom seen.

Her obvious happiness makes me feel emotional. I save Trey the embarrassment. "He's the one who volunteered with teens to get a better handle on how to relate to Christy's kids."

"Oh," Tom says, "that, too, was very well done. There should definitely be T-shirts."

"And here I thought we might be friends, man."

We all laugh as Joy comes in, carrying a massive pot that I hope is her jambalaya.

"Is that the magic stuff, Joy?"

"Would I bring anything else for you savages?"

"Yes!" I give her a fist bump. "You guys are in for a treat."

"Lexi and Tom Terrific, this is Angela Radcliffe," Roni says.

I hug Angela because that's what we do. "Welcome. I'm so sorry you're here."

Angela laughs as she returns my hug. "I'm sorry to be here,

too, but happy to meet you all. Roni has sung your praises, and from what I've seen so far, I'm going to love it."

"It's the worst club to join, but if you've got to be one of us, it's a good group to get through it with."

"That's what Roni has told me."

Iris has gone to the other room and leads a handsome man with four young kids following him into the kitchen. "Everyone, this is Luke Freeman and his kids, Nolan, Beckham, Clarissa and Phoebe." All of them have light brown hair and brown or hazel eyes. The girls have adorable freckles left over from the summer. The kids are seven years old and younger. Dear God...

We go around and give him our first names as he makes a valiant effort not to look overwhelmed.

Christy's son, Shawn, comes over to ask the boys if they want to play Xbox in the den.

They look relieved to take off with him.

"Josie, come see Clarissa and Phoebe," Christy calls to her daughter.

Josie comes into the kitchen, all legs and coltish beauty. "Hey, guys, you want to come hang with us? I'm trying to keep the little kids from destroying the house."

The sisters look at each other and decide to go with her.

"I'll be right here," Luke calls after them as they dash off to find some fun. "I know that was probably planned in advance, but I appreciate that you guys knew how to make them feel at home."

"We've got you, pal," Christy says.

His eyes fill, and he looks away, embarrassed.

Iris goes to him and hugs him.

"Thank you," he says softly.

"I'm Angela, and I'm new, too. Three kids—seven and under."

Luke shakes her hand. "Nice to meet you. I think."

They smile in solidarity at being new to the group and having seven young kids between them.

Gage gets a beer for Luke and a glass of wine for Angela.

"Are those your kids, Angela?" Joy asks.

"Yes, that's Jack and Ella. My youngest is at home with my mom."

"Let's go outside," Iris says. "It's so nice out, and Gage will light the fire."

Twenty-Five

Lexi

I love the outside of their house as much as the inside. Like everything with Iris, it's warm and inviting. We fill plates with crackers, cheese, dip and appetizers and land on the sofas that surround the firepit. Tom sits on a footstool next to me, his arm propped on my knee as he drinks from a water bottle he brought with him. He had a couple of sips of champagne at lunch earlier but has mostly given up drinking alcohol after the heart attack.

Naomi and Kinsley arrive together, followed by Adrian, Wynter, Xavier and baby Willow.

We make room on the sofas, and I end up next to Wynter and Willow.

"My goodness, she's pretty, Wynter."

"Isn't she? I know I'm not supposed to say that, but whatever. She's stunning."

"She really is, and you can say whatever you want about her."

"I agree." She nudges my arm. "So that's the new guy, huh? I hear he's quite terrific."

Tom, who was talking to Trey, Gage, Derek and Luke, turns back to us. "I can hear you."

"Oh, and he's cute, too," Wynter says.

"You must be Wynter."

"How'd you guess?"

"You're the one who says everything you think, right?"

"That'd be me. This is my daughter, Willow. I have a daughter!"

"Congratulations," Tom says, smiling. "She's gorgeous."

Adrian's son, Xavier, toddles over to Wynter, wanting her attention, and she deftly handles both kids, sending Xavier away happy with a small bag of Goldfish crackers.

"You're good at this mommy thing."

"You really think so?"

"I certainly do. You were a great nanny to Xavier, and you'll be an awesome mom to both your babies."

"We're going to make it official with adoptions. Willow will be a Hartley, because that's important to Jaden's family—and me. But Adrian will be her legal father."

"I love that for all of you."

"Sometimes it's all still surreal, you know? Jaden is gone, Willow is here, Adrian and Xavier are my family now... We're theirs."

"Life is strange and wonderful." I lean in closer to whisper, "I'm sleeping with my high school crush."

"Was it worth the wait?"

"Very much so, but I never would've skipped over Jim to get to Tom."

"I know that. You don't even have to say it. I suppose we can't do anything but fully enjoy the moment we're in while always remembering Jaden and Jim."

"Yeah, for sure."

We share a smile full of heartache, joy, grief and love.

When I first met Wynter, I never would've expected to one day consider her a close friend. She was so bitter, obnoxious and difficult. We gave her a ton of grace and space to mourn the loss of her young husband to bone cancer. She's repaid us a million times over by being a friend we all adore.

"With everyone here," Iris says, "let's introduce ourselves to Luke and Angela again."

"I'm Brielle. The little red-headed ginger inside is my son, Charlie. I was expecting him when my husband, Mark, was killed in a skiing accident while attending his brother's bachelor party."

"Naomi. My fiancé, David, died of lymphoma. I'll be forever thankful that this group allowed a not-quite-widow into the group."

"You're one of us, Nay," Iris says. "I'm Iris. My husband, Mike, who was a corporate pilot, died in a plane crash. My three kids are Tyler, Sophia and Laney. After a rough few years, we're all doing much better these days. And this guy is my fiancé, Gage Collier."

"I lost my first wife and twin eight-year-old daughters to a drunk driver."

"I love your Instagram account, Gage," Angela says.

Luke nods. "Me, too. A few weeks ago, I went all the way back to the beginning and fell down the Gage Collier rabbit hole. Your words have helped me more than you'll ever know."

"Thank you. That's nice to hear."

Iris smiles at Gage, who seems embarrassed by the praise.

"I remember being right where you are now." Gage's warm gaze takes in Angela and Luke. "I didn't have children anymore, but I was left to start over when I really liked the life I already had. None of the progress you see here, for any of us who've re-partnered, happened easily or quickly or painlessly."

"Gage is so right. I'm Derek. My wife, Victoria, was

murdered by Arnie Patterson and his band of thugs, who also held my one-year-old daughter, Maeve, hostage for a time. If you'd asked me then if I'd ever take another chance on love or romance or any of it, I would've said no freaking way. Maeve and I muddled through, thanks to my parents and some great friends and a wonderful nanny. Then we met Roni, who was pregnant with her late husband Patrick's son, Dylan, and now we're engaged and raising each other's children. Like Gage said, nothing about it was simple or painless."

"My husband, Patrick, was hit by a stray bullet on a DC street when he was out to lunch," Roni adds. "I met Derek long before I was ready for chapter two, which is what we call it in widow circles. He waited for me, and now I have a whole new life that I never wanted until I had no choice but to figure out a new path forward. Patrick and Victoria are very present in our new life. We speak of them often, and it's important that our children know that their biological parents loved them very much."

"I feel like I'm back in college and y'all are the professors," Luke says with a wry grin.

"You can call me Dr. Wynter," she says to laughter. "I'm the little kid of the crowd. I lost my twenty-year-old husband, Jaden, to bone cancer. We had one of those tragic hospital weddings that people have when time is running out. Later, I found out he'd frozen sperm before his treatment began, so I decided to have our little Willow." She glances toward Adrian. "I'm living with Adrian and his son, Xavier, and we're making a family together. And like the others said, it's all complicated and messy and perfect and all the things."

"One of these people once told me that life is what happens when you're busy making other plans," Adrian says.

"Compliments of John Lennon," Gage adds.

"Cheers to Lennon." Adrian raises his beer bottle to Gage. "I had other plans with my wife, Sadie, until she died suddenly right after having Xavier. I'll never get over that she didn't even get to hold the baby she'd wanted so badly. The best day of our lives became the worst—and best—of mine."

"I'm so sorry, Adrian," Angela says. "That's so sad."

"It was horrible, as was losing Sadie's mother suddenly just a few months later. She'd been like a mother to me, too, and was so critical in getting me through those early months with Xavier, and then she was gone, too. It was unbearable."

Wynter reaches for his hand.

He sends her a small smile. "We're doing better, but the sadness is always there for what Sadie missed, what we've all missed with her and her mom, who died of a broken heart, if you ask me."

"It's amazing that more of us don't die from the heart-break," Luke says. "Sometimes I wonder how it's possible to survive it."

Kinsley nods. "I feel that. My husband, Rory, died of pancreatic cancer forty-two days after he was diagnosed. I look back at that time as a whirlwind of bad news on top of worse news. It happened so fast, I'd barely adapted to his diagnosis when he was gone. I haven't met my chapter two, and it's possible that I won't, but watching my friends get there has been such a source of inspiration for me."

"Same," I say as I smile at Kinsley. "ALS widow here. My husband, Jim, endured four years of hell before he died three years ago. Tom Terrific and I have only recently gotten together, but we've known of each other since high school. We lived together as platonic roommates for almost a year before it became romantical."

Tom looks back at me in amusement. "Romantical. Is that what the kids are calling it these days?"

I shrug. "Whatever it is, it's working for me." I lean in to kiss him while the others catcall and act like fools.

"I'm Christy, and I lost my husband, Wes, to an aortic

dissection that happened in front of our kids, Josie and Shawn, who you met inside. We had a bunch of rough and difficult years, but we're doing better these days, thanks in large part to the wisdom of this brain trust that Iris and I founded along with another friend who's now remarried and not active in the group anymore. This is Trey, who recently talked me into a new relationship that's making me happy, even if I continue to mourn what I lost with Wes."

"Talked you into it, huh?" Trey asks. "You led me on a merry chase."

Christy smiles with satisfaction because that's true.

"I'm Hallie, and this is my partner, Robin. I lost my wife, Gwen, to suicide a few years ago and have recently started seeing Robin. We're taking it a day at a time and enjoying ourselves with many, many, *many* complications."

"She's referring to my stage-four breast cancer, my ex-husband, my tween and teen kids, among other things," Robin says. "But I'm thankful for this time with Hallie and to meet all of you. She speaks of you so lovingly."

"We're happy to meet you, too, Robin," Roni says.

"Tell me the truth. Are you terrified for Hallie?" Robin asks.

The rest of us exchange glances.

"It's okay," Robin says. "You don't have to answer that. Just know that I understand why you would be, and all I can say is I'm going to love her so much for however long I have left. And when I'm gone, I hope I can count on all of you to be there for her."

Damn it, the woman has made us all cry.

"Hell yes," I tell her. "We're here for her now and forever."

Joy is still mopping up tears when she says, "Absolutely. I'm Mama Joy, mother to all. At least in my mind, I am."

"You are," I say. "One thousand percent."

"My husband, Craig, died in his sleep at thirty-four from natural causes. Whatever that means."

"I'm an internist," Luke says. "It means they have no clue."

"That's what I've been told. I'm getting by thanks to this band of misfit toys."

"Hey," Naomi says, laughing with the rest of us.

"We're a ragged bunch of misfits," Iris says, "who love each other fiercely and will take you in, Luke and Angela, and make you part of us, if you'd still like to be after getting this up close and personal view of us."

"Before you decide anything," I say, "let me tell you a little story about how this group has been there for me. Mama Joy here took it upon herself to apply for a grant on my behalf that relieved me of hundreds of thousands in medical debt that my husband's insurance didn't cover. She's freed me from a lifetime of being shackled to the nightmare we endured during his illness, and she did it simply because she loves me, and she wanted to. I can give you countless other examples of how these people have stepped up for each other in big and small ways."

"That's incredible, Joy," Angela says.

"It made me happy to do it, and we're all about finding happiness anywhere we can these days."

"That's been a challenge for me," Angela says. "My husband, Spencer, died of an accidental fentanyl overdose, which I'm sure you all read about since it happened at Camp David with my sister and brother-in-law, the first couple."

"Oh damn," Luke says. "I remember that from the holidays last year, right?"

"Yes. Feels like a minute ago and a lifetime ago at the same time."

Luke nods. "I know that feeling. My wife, Isabella—also known as Bella—was diagnosed with colon cancer when we were expecting our youngest. She postponed treatment to see the pregnancy through. She died eighteen months after Phoebe was born. Even knowing it was coming..."

"Doesn't make the reality of it any easier," I say.

"No, it doesn't."

"Managing the kids' grief has been the hardest part for me," Angela says. "My son, Jack, was very close to his dad. It's been brutal."

"I agree. The kids have been the tough part. Well, hell, it's all hard. Bella and I were together for twelve years. I'm lost without her."

Josie, who's been in charge of the kids inside with Shawn, brings Charlie to his mother. "He was feeling a little sad."

Brielle takes her little boy and holds him close.

"How about some dinner?" Iris says as some of the others get up to help her.

"That was quite something," Tom says softly to only me.

"I'm glad you got the full experience."

"So am I. The courage, strength, perseverance... It's very inspiring."

"Yes, it is." I kiss him. "I'm going to help Iris. Be right back."

"I'll be here."

I walk inside with Kinsley and Naomi, chatting about our two new members and how well they seem to fit in with us. Not that we do a ton of vetting or anything like that, but new people are usually screened by whoever invites them to join. Roni will have taken the time to get to know Angela, and Iris and Gage have befriended Luke as well. It's hard to resist offering our kind of help to people who need it so badly.

Iris assigns me to toss the salad, which has been prepped in advance with containers of chopped vegetables. She's very good at this entertaining thing, probably because she's constantly entertaining all of us. Tom and I should have everyone over to our place sometime to give her a break.

I've no sooner had that thought than a shout comes from outside that has Gage running for the door.

I hear someone yell, "Call 911," and my whole body goes cold with fear. I want to ask what's wrong and who is it, but I'm frozen in place as everything shifts into the kind of high gear that indicates a true emergency.

Iris rushes back inside and comes to me. "It's Tom."

My knees buckle, and I would've fallen to the ground if she hadn't been there to hold me up. Please God. *No. No. No.*

Iris guides me to a chair.

I should be with him, but I can't make my body follow the frantic screams coming from my brain.

"Josie, get the kids and take them upstairs, *now*." Christy's no-nonsense tone is one I've never heard before.

The paramedics come rushing into the house and are led to the patio where Tom, my Tom, is having some sort of crisis.

"I need to be with him."

"No, you shouldn't."

"I need to know…"

"Give them a minute."

She never leaves my side, keeping her arms around me as my mind runs the gamut from worst case to best case.

"Is he dead, Iris? Please just tell me if he is."

"I don't know, honey. Try to stay positive until we know what's going on, okay?"

How do I stay positive just over two weeks since he survived a widow-maker heart attack?

Gage comes rushing into the kitchen. "He's awake and asking for you, Lex."

It takes a few seconds for his words to register, and then I get up and run for him, through the door, down the steps and into the scrum of people surrounding him on the EMS stretcher.

He reaches out when he sees me coming. "I'm okay, baby. I

fainted. That's all it is, but they want to take me in to make sure there's nothing else. I was feeling hungry and a bit light-headed before it happened. It's nothing. I swear."

I fall on him, sobbing.

He runs his hand over my back.

"We'd like to transport him just to rule out any complications after the cardiac incident," one of the EMTs says.

I hear him, but I'm not ready to let Tom go yet.

"It's okay," Tom says again. "I promise, I'm fine. I got light-headed, and the next thing I knew, I was looking up at EMTs."

"We'll get you to the hospital, Lex," Iris says as she helps me up.

"I'll go with her," Joy says to Iris. "You stay and feed the people, Iris. Hopefully, we'll be back soon."

I'm moved along to Joy's car and buckled in. Like before, I feel removed from what's happening around me as we follow the ambulance to Inova. Déjà vu all over again.

"He fainted, baby. He's fine. Probably has nothing to do with the heart attack."

I cling to Joy's reassurances, but I'm unable to form words or thoughts or feel anything other than panic. Right when I started to get comfortable with him, with the idea of a future with him... That it could be ripped away from me in a single second is too overwhelming to process. At least with Jim, I had some warning that he would leave me. I'm not sure how to cope with the possibility of Tom leaving me suddenly.

What if we get to the hospital and he's gone?

I wish I never looked up the meaning of the widow-maker. That was a huge mistake.

My hands are shaking so hard that I tuck them between my knees to control the trembles.

Joy has both hands on the wheel as she tries to keep up with the ambulance. "Talk to me, Lex."

"Don't know what to say."

"He fainted. He's fine. He said so himself."

"Why did he faint, though?"

"Could be anything. People faint all the time. Low blood sugar or overheated. He was sitting close to the fire. That could be it."

"What if it's not nothing?"

"Then they'll deal with it and get him back on the road to recovery."

"We had sex. They told him to wait two to four weeks. We lasted ten days. And there was a lot of sex. What if that's what happened?"

Joy's warm hand lands on my leg, her heat permeating the block of ice I've become. "That's not what happened."

"How do you know?" I sound hysterical, even to myself.

"Baby, that man was glowing tonight. All of us saw it. He's with the love of his life, and nothing in this world will separate him from you if he can prevent it."

"I can't do this again, Joy. I just can't."

"Yes, you can. You've proven to yourself and all of us that there's nothing you can't survive. Look at what Hallie has gotten herself into. Robin will probably die sooner rather than later, but Hallie has decided to spend as much time as she can with Robin, knowing what's in store for her after. She's found the courage to do it anyway, and you can, too."

"I don't know if I can. I'm not strong like Hallie is."

"Oh my God, that's so not true! You're as strong as Hallie, as any of us. If only you could see yourself the way we see you. What you did for Jim, for all those years, my goodness, Lexi! I couldn't have done it."

"Yes, you could have."

"No, I honestly don't think I could. Medical stuff makes me sick. Like, I literally vomit at the sight of anything gross. I couldn't do it the way you did. I'd be useless in that situation."

"I would've thought the same until I had no choice."

"And yet, you stepped up to do what needed to be done, and you will again. No matter what it is. I have complete faith in you, Lex. You're a survivor."

"I'm so tired of being a survivor. I want to be a thriver again."

"You will be. You have been. Look at the strides you've made in the last year, moving out of your parents' basement and forming this deep bond with Tom that's now turned into so much more, and now this new opportunity working for the ALS Association. Your life is on fire, and Jim is so, so proud of the way you've slayed widowhood. I know he is."

A sob erupts from my chest as my composure cracks wide open.

Joy pulls up behind the ambulance.

We can see that Tom is sitting up on the stretcher, probably looking for me.

"Check out your man," Joy says. "Totally fine and wanting to know where his love is. Go to him, Lex. Go to him and stay with him for as long as you possibly can. Enjoy every second knowing it could be the last one for any of us at any given time. Go live your life, baby."

I give her a tight hug. "I love you more than ice cream."

She laughs hard. "I love you more than dogs."

"*Whoa.*"

"Right? Go. Be happy with your man. Live your one wild and precious life."

"I'm going. Thank you for being the best friend anyone could ever have."

"Back atcha."

"Not even close, but I don't have time to argue right now."

"No, you don't."

I get out of the car and run over to where Tom is being greeted by doctors in scrubs as he tells them he's fine, he fainted, and nothing is wrong.

I take the hand he extends to me. "Shut up, Tom, and let them be the judge of that."

"Thank you," one of the doctors says, shooting a smile at me over her shoulder as they roll him inside with none of the urgency that occurred last time.

"Oh no, you've been crying over me. I'm fine, Lex. Completely fine."

"We'll let the doctors decide if that's true."

"I'm so sorry to do this to you—again. I fainted. That's all it was. I was hungry and hot and—"

"Tom, stop. Take a breath."

"I can't lose you, Lex. I think that might actually kill me."

"I'm not going anywhere."

"Really?"

"Really."

"Because I wouldn't blame you—"

"Tom?"

"What?"

"Stop talking."

We've reached the double doors to the treatment area, where I expect them to tell me to have a seat and they'll come find me when they know what's going on.

"Come on back to help us manage him," the doctor says. "I have a feeling it'll go better for all of us if you're there."

Tom smiles. "Everything is better when she's here."

Epilogue

Lexi

Doctors determine that Tom fainted due to slight dehydration and possibly overheating. His EKG was perfect, as was his blood work and the other tests they ran to err on the side of caution due to his recent heart attack.

He's released three hours later.

When it became clear that he would be okay, I sent Joy back to Iris's house to enjoy the rest of the party with my thanks for the ride and her powerful words of wisdom that made all the difference to me in a time of crisis.

We take an Uber back to Tom's and will pick up his truck at Iris's tomorrow.

As we walk into the house together, I'm so thankful to have him here with me that it makes my knees go weak for a second when I realize how differently this evening could've turned out.

He tunes in to my distress and wraps his arms around me. "I'm here. I'm fine. I'm always going to be right here with you because there's nowhere else in this entire world I want to be than wherever you are. We're going to get married and have a family and go to London and do all the things together. Everything is okay, Lexi. I promise."

If I've learned anything on this journey, it's that everything is temporary. Even the best of things. It's all fleeting. All we can do is enjoy every second of the life we're given, the love that comes our way and the joy we find along the road to wherever it is we're going.

Nothing is forever, except love. That outlives us all.

"Let's get you to bed, mister. You need rest and relaxation, and that's what you're getting for the next two weeks."

"Wait... They never said that. They said to stay well hydrated and to be mindful of electrolytes."

"I'm being mindful of your hydration and electrolytes by declaring this a sex-free zone for two full weeks."

"Absolutely not. That's not happening."

"Yes, it is." I pull back from him and lead the way up the stairs, intending to put him to bed and then go sleep in my own room to ensure he gets the rest he needs.

"Lexi."

"Yes, Tom?"

"I want you to step out of crisis mode and get back to normal. I fainted. People faint all the time."

"Right after a major heart attack, after which they started having sex four whole days before it was safe?"

"That had nothing to do with me fainting."

"How do you know that? You were probably dehydrated from having so much sex!"

"Lex." He puts his hands on my shoulders and dips his head to force me to look at him. "Stop. Take a breath. All is well. Despite tonight's evidence to the contrary, everything will continue to be fine. I swear. I had a heart problem. It's been fixed. I feel better than I have in a long time. With hindsight, I can see that the fatigue and shortness of breath I was experiencing for a while was because of the blocked artery. Now that it's fixed, I feel great. What happened tonight had nothing to do with my heart or us having sex too soon or anything other than being slightly dehydrated, hungry and overheated all at the same time. A perfect storm, if you will."

I hate the way my chin quivers uncontrollably and how tears slide down my cheeks, despite my desperate desire to be strong.

"No more tears." He kisses them away. "No more worry or panic or anything other than love, love and more love."

"I'm fine with the love, but there will be no sex."

"Okay, Lexi. If you insist."

"I do."

He guides me toward his bedroom and into the shower, where we wash the stink of hospital off our skin. I hate that smell with a fiery passion.

Since I seem to have the energy of a newborn now that the earlier rush of panic-fueled adrenaline has subsided, he tenderly washes every inch of my skin, which has the usual effect when he touches me in any way.

We kiss passionately under the warm water. My back is pressed against the cool tile, and his hands are full of my breasts.

"I love you more than anything, Lexi. More than anything in this whole world, and I'm going to do everything I can to make sure we get so many decades together, you'll be wishing I'd go away and give you some peace."

I'm laughing and crying at the same time. "That'll never happen."

"I'm making it my goal in life to get to the point where you're begging me to please drop dead so you can have some peace."

I slap his shoulder. "Knock that off right now!"

"I'll never stop loving you or wanting you or needing you. If I have you, I have everything, and I'm smart enough to know that."

"I love you so much. I found out just how much earlier when I thought that I could still lose you."

"You're not going to lose me." He kisses me again and leads me from the shower, drying me as reverently as he washed me.

I'm in such a fog of desire and exhaustion and an overload of emotion that he has me under him in bed before I remember my two-week rule.

"Two weeks, Thomas! I mean it!"

"Hush, Lexi, and let me love you."

I had the best of intentions. I swear I did. But what can I do when he's right there, hard and ready and full of love for me, but go along with a nice, sweet, gentle interlude that ends explosively for both of us.

"I love you forever and ever," he whispers against my neck as we pulse with aftershocks. "I'll never leave you. I promise."

I close my eyes tight against more tears, but these are hard-earned tears of joy. "I love you, too. Forever and always."

Meanwhile, back at Iris's house...

Angela

"That was intense," I say to Luke after the ambulance leaves with Tom, with Lexi and Joy following them out of the yard.

"Seriously." Luke rubs the back of his neck the way people do after a stressful situation. Watching him fly into doctor mode when Tom keeled over was kind of hot. "When Gage said Tom had a heart attack and stent procedure two weeks ago... I feared it wouldn't end well. When he came to and said he was fine, that was a huge relief."

"Poor Lexi. She was frantic."

"This is why I'm never falling in love again. I refuse to take a risk that could lead to the worst kind of heartbreak again. I couldn't bear it."

"I tend to agree," I say. "I'd rather be alone than worry about losing my partner."

"The only thing worse would be something happening to one of my kids."

"Agreed. That'd be unbearable, especially as a single parent totally responsible for their health and safety. I'd feel like it was my fault even if it wasn't."

"Yes, exactly!"

"Jack got hit in the face with a baseball when he was playing catch with a friend in the yard, and all I could think of was if he died, it would be my fault for not keeping him safe."

"Clarissa fell off her bike and broke her arm two months after Bella died, and I felt the same way. Like, what if she'd died? What would I ever do?"

"We should probably recognize that our disaster mentality is a direct result of losing our partners," I say, "and the worst-case-scenario thinking will ease up in time."

"Will it, though? Will we ever stop feeling extra responsible for seeing these kids safely through childhood without our teammates?"

"Maybe not entirely, but I have to believe it won't always be this acute."

"I hope not, because acute anxiety is exhausting."

"We should get together with the kids some time," I suggest. "It's good for them to make new friends who understand what they're going through."

"That'd be great. We'd love it."

We exchange phone numbers and agree to set something up in the next few weeks.

Iris and Gage come out of the house with bottles of water and a plate of dessert for each of us.

"So that was *not* our usual Wild Widows gathering," Iris says.

"That was our first ambulance," Gage adds.

"Hope we didn't scare you guys off of our group," Iris says tentatively.

"Nah," Luke says. "I can't speak for Angela, but I enjoyed it much more than I thought I would, and I'm looking forward to being part of the group—minus the ambulance, of course."

"Same," I say. "No ambulances would be good. I'd like to bring my friend Brad to a meeting sometime. He lost his wife in the same fentanyl nightmare that took my Spencer."

"Please feel free to bring him," Iris says. "Anyone who needs us is welcome."

"Brad has had a rough transition to single parenthood. I think he'd benefit from being with others in the same boat. I'll see if I can get him to come." I check my watch and am astounded to see it's almost nine. "I need to get my kids home to bed, or they'll be up all night."

"Me, too." Luke stands and offers me a hand up.

I take it without thinking, as if it's something I do every day when it's something I haven't done in almost two years. "Thanks." Why do I feel shy all of a sudden? What the hell?

We go inside to collect overtired kids and walk out together, two single parents, six kids and another one at home for me. We're like the ragged survivors of a natural disaster, a dramatic thought that nearly makes me laugh, except there's nothing funny about surviving a disaster—natural or otherwise.

I want my old life back.

I want to be snuggled up to Spence, watching a stupid movie that we'll mostly snooze through while our kids sleep in rooms next to ours.

I want him as much as I ever have.

I can't imagine ever wanting anyone but him.

Some days, I still wake up and wonder where he is.

As I buckle the kids into their seats and listen to their animated chatter about their exciting evening with Josie and Shawn, Luke comes over to me.

"Phoebe says this belongs to your Ella."

He hands me Ella's favorite stuffed dog.

"Oh man, thank you. You just saved me a bedtime nightmare."

"I know all about bedtime nightmares. Call me if you ever need to talk about them."

"I will. You do the same."

"Oh, I'll definitely be calling you, Angela. Drive safely."

He leaves me speechless as he walks away.

What the hell was that?

More to come from the Wild Widows in 2025!

Acknowledgments

Thank you so much for reading Lexi's Wild Widows story! I hope you enjoyed her and Tom and the other Wild Widows as much as I enjoy writing them. This series has become so near and dear to me as I get to know this group better with every new book. It was fun to bring Angela over to the Wild Widows with this story, even if I'm way ahead of First Family timeline with the widows. Juggling timelines is the hardest part of writing series—at least for me—so I hope you'll forgive the time differences between these two series.

If you'd like to know more about Angela's backstory (as well as Roni and Derek's bosses, the first couple), check out the Fatal and First Family Series at *https://marieforce.com/books*.

If you want to talk about Lexi's story with spoilers allowed, you can join the Someone to Watch Over Me Reader Group at *www.facebook.com/groups/someonetowatchoverme/*. Reminder to also join the Wild Widows Series Group at *www.facebook.com/groups/thewildwidowsseries* for updates about upcoming books and the Wild Widows Grief Support Group at *www.facebook.com/groups/thewildwidowsseries*.

A huge thank you to Dr. Sarah Hewitt, family nurse practitioner, for always keeping me straight on the medical details. Any errors in that regard are mine, not hers. Thank you to my editors, Linda Ingmanson and Joyce Lamb, as well as my beta readers Anne Woodall, Kara Conrad and Tracey Suppo. Thanks to the Wild Widow Series beta readers: Marianne, Jennifer, Juliane, Gwen, Gina, Rachel, Amy and Karina.

To the team that supports me every day, I couldn't do this

without you: Julie Cupp, Lisa Cafferty, Jean Mello, Nikki Haley and Ashley Lopez as well as my family, Dan, Emily and Jake.

Thank you most of all to the readers who show up for every new book with so much love and enthusiasm. I appreciate you all more than you'll ever know!

Much love,

Marie

Also by Marie Force

Contemporary Romances Available from Marie Force

The Wild Widows Series—a Fatal Series Spin-Off

Book 1: Someone Like You

Book 2: Someone to Hold

Book 3: Someone to Love

Book 4: Someone to Watch Over Me

The Gansett Island Series

Book 1: Maid for Love *(Mac & Maddie)*

Book 2: Fool for Love *(Joe & Janey)*

Book 3: Ready for Love *(Luke & Sydney)*

Book 4: Falling for Love *(Grant & Stephanie)*

Book 5: Hoping for Love *(Evan & Grace)*

Book 6: Season for Love *(Owen & Laura)*

Book 7: Longing for Love *(Blaine & Tiffany)*

Book 8: Waiting for Love *(Adam & Abby)*

Book 9: Time for Love *(David & Daisy)*

Book 10: Meant for Love *(Jenny & Alex)*

Book 10.5: Chance for Love, *A Gansett Island Novella (Jared & Lizzie)*

Book 11: Gansett After Dark *(Owen & Laura)*

Book 12: Kisses After Dark *(Shane & Katie)*

Book 13: Love After Dark *(Paul & Hope)*

Book 14: Celebration After Dark *(Big Mac & Linda)*

Book 15: Desire After Dark *(Slim & Erin)*

Book 16: Light After Dark *(Mallory & Quinn)*

Book 17: Victoria & Shannon (Episode 1)

Book 18: Kevin & Chelsea (Episode 2)

A Gansett Island Christmas Novella *(Appears in Mine After Dark)*

Book 19: Mine After Dark *(Riley & Nikki)*

Book 20: Yours After Dark *(Finn & Chloe)*

Book 21: Trouble After Dark *(Deacon & Julia)*

Book 22: Rescue After Dark *(Mason & Jordan)*

Book 23: Blackout After Dark *(Full Cast)*

Book 24: Temptation After Dark *(Gigi & Cooper)*

Book 25: Resilience After Dark *(Jace & Cindy)*

Book 26: Hurricane After Dark *(Full Cast)*

Book 27: Renewal After Dark *(Duke & McKenzie)*

Downeast

Dan & Kara: A Downeast Prequel

The Miami Nights Series*

Book 1: How Much I Feel *(Carmen & Jason)*

Book 2: How Much I Care *(Maria & Austin)*

Book 3: How Much I Love *(Dee's story)*

Nochebuena, A Miami Nights Novella

Book 4: How Much I Want *(Nico & Sofia)*

Book 5: How Much I Need *(Milo and Gianna)*

The Green Mountain Series*

Book 1: All You Need Is Love *(Will & Cameron)*

Book 2: I Want to Hold Your Hand *(Nolan & Hannah)*

Book 3: I Saw Her Standing There *(Colton & Lucy)*

Book 4: And I Love Her *(Hunter & Megan)*

Novella: You'll Be Mine *(Will & Cam's Wedding)*

Book 5: It's Only Love *(Gavin & Ella)*

Book 6: Ain't She Sweet *(Tyler & Charlotte)*

The Butler, Vermont Series*

(Continuation of Green Mountain)

Book 1: Every Little Thing *(Grayson & Emma)*

Book 2: Can't Buy Me Love *(Mary & Patrick)*

Book 3: Here Comes the Sun (*Wade & Mia*)

Book 4: Till There Was You *(Lucas & Dani)*

Book 5: All My Loving *(Landon & Amanda)*

Book 6: Let It Be *(Lincoln & Molly)*

Book 7: Come Together *(Noah & Brianna)*

Book 8: Here, There & Everywhere *(Izzy & Cabot)*

Book 9: The Long and Winding Road *(Max & Lexi)*

The Treading Water Series*

Book 1: Treading Water

Book 2: Marking Time

Book 3: Starting Over

Book 4: Coming Home

Book 5: Finding Forever

The Quantum Series*

Book 1: Virtuous *(Flynn & Natalie)*

Book 2: Valorous *(Flynn & Natalie)*

Book 3: Victorious *(Flynn & Natalie)*

Book 4: Rapturous *(Addie & Hayden)*

Book 5: Ravenous *(Jasper & Ellie)*

Book 6: Delirious *(Kristian & Aileen)*

Book 7: Outrageous *(Emmett & Leah)*

Book 8: Famous *(Marlowe & Sebastian)*

Single Titles

In the Air Tonight

Five Years Gone

One Year Home

Sex Machine

Sex God

Georgia on My Mind

True North

The Fall

The Wreck

Love at First Flight

Everyone Loves a Hero

Line of Scrimmage

Romantic Suspense Novels Available from Marie Force

The Fatal Series

One Night With You, *A Fatal Series Prequel Novella*

Book 1: Fatal Affair

Book 2: Fatal Justice

Book 3: Fatal Consequences

Book 3.5: Fatal Destiny, *the Wedding Novella*

Book 4: Fatal Flaw

Book 5: Fatal Deception

Book 6: Fatal Mistake

Book 7: Fatal Jeopardy

Book 8: Fatal Scandal

Book 9: Fatal Frenzy

Book 10: Fatal Identity

Book 11: Fatal Threat

Book 12: Fatal Chaos

Book 13: Fatal Invasion

Book 14: Fatal Reckoning

Book 15: Fatal Accusation

Book 16: Fatal Fraud

Sam and Nick's story continues...

Book 1: State of Affairs

Book 2: State of Grace

Book 3: State of the Union

Book 4: State of Shock

Book 5: State of Denial

Book 6: State of Bliss

Book 7: State of Suspense

Book 8: State of Alert

Historical Romance Available from Marie Force

*The Gilded Series**

Book 1: Duchess by Deception

Book 2: Deceived by Desire

*Completed Series

About the Author

Marie Force is the #1 *Wall Street Journal* bestselling author of more than 100 contemporary romance, romantic suspense and erotic romance novels. Her series include Fatal, First Family, Gansett Island, Butler Vermont, Quantum, Treading Water, Miami Nights and Wild Widows.

Her books have sold more than 14 million copies worldwide, have been translated into more than a dozen languages and have appeared on the *New York Times* bestseller list more than 30 times. She is also a *USA Today* bestseller, as well as a Spiegel bestseller in Germany.

Her goals in life are simple—to spend as much time as she can with her "kids" who are now adults, to keep writing books for as long as she possibly can and to never be on a flight that makes the news.

Join Marie's mailing list on her website at *marieforce.com* for news about new books and upcoming appearances in your area. Follow her on Facebook, at *www.Facebook.com/Marie-ForceAuthor*, Instagram *@marieforceauthor* and TikTok *@marieforceauthor*. Contact Marie at *marie@marieforce.com*.

Made in the USA
Coppell, TX
18 November 2024

40002893R10187